TACKETT

TACKETT 3 TRILOGY

AND THE SALOON KEEPER

OTHER BOOKS BY LYN NOFZIGER

Tackett Trilogy
  Tackett
  Tackett and the Teacher

Nofziger

TACKETT

TACKETT
3
TRILOGY

AND THE SALOON KEEPER

LYN NOFZIGER

TUMBLEWEED PRESS
Washington, D.C.

Library of Congress Cataloging-in-Publication Data

Nofziger, Franklyn C.
Tackett and the saloon keeper / Lyn Nofziger.
  p. cm. — (Tackett trilogy ; 3) Sequel to: Tackett and the teacher.
ISBN 0-89526-480-3 (alk, paper)
I. Title. II . Series: Nofziger, Franklyn C. Tackett trilogy ; 3.
PS3564.O34T33 1994 vol. 3
813'.54—dc20

                                                            94-31996
                                                               CIP

Published in the United States by
Regnery Publishing, Inc.
An Eagle Publishing Company
422 First St., SE, Suite 300
Washington, DC 20003

Distributed to the trade by
National Book Network
4720-A Boston Way
Lanham, MD 20706

Printed on acid-free paper.
Manufactured in the United States of America.

10 9 8 7 6 5 4 3 2 1

Books are available in quantity for promotional or premium use. Write to Director of Special Sales, Regnery Publishing, Inc., 422 First Street, SE, Suite 300, Washington, DC 20003, for information on discounts and terms or call (202) 546-5005.

Dedicated to the memory of my grandfathers,
James Curran and F. U. Nofziger, two of those
who helped build the west.

TACKETT
AND THE SALOON KEEPER

CHAPTER 1

I RECKON IF you took all my poker winnings from the time I left the gold country nearly thirteen years ago until now you could put 'em in my hat and still have room for my head.

It's not that I'm a bad poker player, it's just that I keep running into folks who are better. Neither am I very good at spotting anyone who can deal from the bottom or hold out aces, and you got to mark a card real careless before I notice it.

I've made up for those weaknesses over the years by trying to play mainly with honest folks, and while that hasn't always been possible, it's worked out often enough so I've never really lost my shirt. Of course, the fact is I've never bet it and even if I had of it wouldn't have covered most bets since it's usually so ragged it hardly covers what it's supposed to.

Once in a while over the years, like most folks, I've gotten lucky. Like the time I won my old buckskin horse from a rancher who, even though he knew cows, was a worse poker player than I ever was. His name was Shay, so it seemed only natural for me to name that horse "Old Dobbin," since I kind of unhitched him from the Shay.

But that was a few years back and since then I've won a little and lost a little and broke even a lot. At least that was the case up until that night in the Staghorn Saloon in the little southern Colorado town of Shalak Springs. That night I had one of those runs of luck you only dream about. There was five of us in that game to begin—a rancher, a drummer, a local storekeeper, the man who owned the saloon, and me.

The first three early on saw how my luck was running and got out whilst they still had money in their pockets. But Obediah Shrifft, the saloon keeper, had been a professional gambler and he kind of figured that gave him an edge and ordinarily that would have been the case, but he wasn't counting on my run of luck.

Now I'd known Obie Shrifft off and on over the years here and there around the West. Like me, he'd been a drifter, but a few years back he'd begun putting money aside and a year ago he'd wandered into Shalak Springs and spotted this fancy saloon—the Staghorn—run by an old man who wanted to go back home to Maryland to die, and bought it cheap.

For the first time in his grown life he found a place he really liked and he settled in and became part of the town. When I had rode in a couple of days earlier he'd greeted me like a long-lost brother. I didn't guess at the time that we were going to be more like Cain and Abel than the Smith twins I knew back along the trail—Lorrel and Hardy.

I hung around Shalak Springs for two days just resting up from a long ride down from Denver. I was heading for the R Bar R ranch a little north of the town of Nora down in the Arizona Territory.

There was a girl there that I wanted to see real bad, as well as some other folks and a black dog named Beauty that had saved my life once. But I'd been through some rough times recently and I figured a couple of days' rest in Shalak Springs would do me some good.

Well, it's only natural when you're loafing around town and you got a little money in your pocket that you wind up in a poker game. Leastwise that's the way it usually is with me.

And that's how I happened to be playing five-card stud with Obie Shrifft and how I happened to stomp him half to death and how I happened to wind up owning the Staghorn, neither of which was something I really wanted to do.

Obie Shrifft had always been known as an honest gambler

but his luck was running as bad that night as mine was running good. And by midnight I'd cleaned him out of all his cash money and was ready to fold for the night and go catch some shut-eye before saddling Old Dobbin the next morning and heading south for the R Bar R and a dark-haired girl named Esmeralda Rankin.

But Obie wasn't in no mood to quit. He knew he was a better poker player than me and he was determined to prove it. Besides, as I said, I'd cleaned him out and he was aiming to recoup at least some of his losses before I left town.

"You got a thousand dollars of my money, Tackett," he said, sweat beading his forehead and his voice just a mite shaky. "That's every cent I've got, but I'll tell you what I'll do, I'll put up the Staghorn against what you have got on the table. Five-card stud and deal 'em face up."

"I don't want your dang saloon, Obie," I said. I said "dang" because Ma, who raised me by herself in a High Sierras mining camp where she scrimped by panning for gold, didn't believe in swearing.

He looked at me with a glare that was kind of a cross between mean and desperate.

"Don't go yellow on me now, Tackett," he said, a nasty edge to his voice.

Well, that done it. No man likes to be called yellow and I ain't no exception.

"Any way you want it, Obie," I said.

He called for a piece of paper and scribbled out some words deeding the Staghorn to me. When he was finished I picked up that deck of cards, shuffled them, gave them to him to cut, and dealt them. Face up.

I gave him a nine of hearts and me a two of clubs. Then I gave him a nine of spades and me a jack of clubs. His third card was a five of hearts and mine was a three of clubs. He had a pair showing and all I had was the makings of a club flush. His fourth card was another nine, the nine of diamonds. Mine was the seven of clubs.

"Look, Obie," I said then, "win or lose I don't want this dang saloon. Why don't we just fold now and if you need some money to see you through a while I'll lend you some."

"Damn you, Tackett, deal," he half shouted.

I shrugged and dealt. I dealt him the ace of clubs and me the seven of clubs.

He sat there and looked at the cards a minute, his face as white as the bark on a birch tree. Then he looked up at me.

"You're a damn cheater, Tackett," he whispered and went for the gun I knew he kept in a shoulder holster under his black frock coat.

Well, I give him short shrift. Without thinking I put my hands on the edge of the table and pushed it hard against him. It caught him by surprise in an awkward position and before he could steady himself his chair went over backwards.

Quick as he hit the floor I flipped the table over and it landed on his chest and face. I leaped over his tipped-over chair and landed with both feet on top of the underside of the table. A muffled yell came from underneath it. Which didn't come as no surprise since I'm over six feet tall and weigh somewhere around 200 pounds.

I had me an impulse to jump up and down a couple of times, but instead I stepped off the table, grabbed it by a leg, and pulled it off of him.

He wasn't very pretty to look at. I'd jumped on the table where his face was and his once hawk nose was kind of plastered all over his face. It was bleeding like a stuck pig.

He lay there with his hands over his face, muttering, "Oh God, Oh God."

I leaned over him and taken that hideout gun from its holster and stuck it behind my belt. Then I grabbed him by an arm and hoisted him to his feet. I reached around and grabbed him by the back of his collar and the seat of his pants and ran him to the bat wing doors where without hardly stopping I flung him into the dirt street.

"Obediah Shrifft," I hollered at him, "this here is my saloon and you stay out of it until yer ready to tell me I'm an honest man."

Obie Shrifft lay there for a couple of minutes, then he climbed slowly to his feet and staggered off down the street.

Me, I turned and went back into the saloon. I righted the table and chair and looked around the barroom at the half dozen men still there.

"Drinks on the house," I said.

They all bellied up to the bar and the baldheaded man behind it poured a round for everyone.

I wandered down to the far end of the bar, away from the drinkers, and beckoned the bartender down to me.

"I still got a job?" he asked.

"Yup," I answered. "You and whoever else works here. As long as you don't cheat the customers or steal me blind. By the way, who else does work here?"

"Just me and Chief Two Horse," he said. "Two Horse comes in the mornings and cleans the place up. Sweeps out. Does the dishes. I come in the middle of the afternoon and work 'til closing time. Obie, he used to come down some time in the morning, light up the stove, and make some coffee. Ever' now an' then someone wants somethin' to eat so he keeps a pot o' beans on the stove and usually has some bread and meat around. Either him or Annie'll fix it if they have to."

"Who's Annie?" I asked. "You never said nothing about no Annie."

"Annie Laurie Burns," he said. "She goes by Annie Laurie but Annie's good enough fer me. She come in here right after Obie bought the place. Come in all by herself, drivin' a one-horse rig and leadin' a mule she called Maxwelton. Don't know why. I asked her once and she said something about Maxwelton's brays bein' bonny. I still don't know what she meant.

"She's a good-lookin' woman, too. Mebbe thirty. Lady, too. Real mannerly. Asked Obie fer a job as kind of a manager and a bookkeeper and anything else he needed done so long as it didn't include entertainin' men. Danged if he didn't hire her and he says she's worth every penny he pays her. One thing fer sure, she keeps a close eye on the likker supply. Been down sick the last couple of days which is why she ain't been around."

"Where's she stay?" I asked. "Mebbe I better go see her tomorrow."

"Easy to do. There used to be some rooms upstairs for the girls. Well, Obie he didn't want that kind of a place so he run the girls out and put in a couple of apartments up there. He uses one and she uses the other. They're close but there ain't no hanky-panky goin' on. I'd bet on that."

There was a big old Regulator clock on the wall next to the mirror behind the bar and when I looked at it it said "real late."

"Closin' time. Drink up," I said to the men still at the bar. "Come on back tomorrow."

They downed their drinks and in a minute or two the bar was empty except for me and the bartender.

"You got a name?" I asked.

"Dellah," he said, sticking out his right hand. "Gil Dellah."

I shaken his hand. "Pleased to meetcha," I said. "Name is Del Tackett."

"You say Sackett?" he asked, his eyes widening. "You one of them gunfighters?"

"Tackett," I said. "With a T. And I ain't no gunfighter."

"Wondered," he said. "Batch of 'em live over around Mora, not too far from here. Never come this way, though, not as long as I been around."

I told him to lock up, picked up a lamp, and headed for the stairs. Then I remembered.

"You see Obie Shrifft you tell him he can come in tomorrow and pick up his stuff. Tell him I said for him to walk soft though. I don't wanta have to hurt him again."

At the top of the stairs the hallway ran clear to the back of the building. You could see where there'd been doors on either side opening into the rooms where the girls entertained. I was a mite surprised that Obie had run them out. I hadn't never thought of him as a particularly moral man.

The way the upstairs had been redone there was a door on the left side of the hall and another on the right and it suddenly occurred to me that I hadn't asked which one was the door to Obie's apartment. I shrugged and taken a chance, figuring Annie Laurie would have her door locked.

The one I tried on the right opened easy and quiet. I went on in, holding the lamp high and saw quicklike that I was in the wrong place. It wasn't no man's room. Before I could retreat a sleepy woman's voice called from the next room, "Who's there?"

"Sorry, ma'am," I called back. "I done made a mistake. Don't mean to bother ya."

I was starting to back out when she appeared in the doorway to the bedroom. The light wasn't real good but I could see she wasn't wearing nothing but a nightgown. Even her feet were bare.

"You're not Obie," she said, alarm in her voice. "Where's Obie?"

"Don't rightly know, ma'am. Last time I saw him he was staggerin' down the street."

"Staggering? That's nonsense. He never gets drunk."

"No, ma'am. He wasn't drunk. He was hurtin' bad. Afore he left, though, he sold me this place. I was lookin' for his rooms and got in here by mistake. I was plannin' on talkin' to you in the mornin.'"

"Talk to me now," she said. "Let me get a robe on and I'll be right out."

She turned and went back into her bedroom, returning a

moment later with a robe over her nightgown. She was carrying a lighted lamp and she held it up to look at me. What she saw wasn't much.

Oh, I'm big enough, all right. About six foot two inches tall and, as I said, about 200 pounds, most of it in my arms and shoulders. But I never was no beauty and a couple of scars hadn't added to my looks none. One was on my left cheek where a Mexican who was quick with a knife sliced me before I managed to whittle him down to size. I didn't kill him, just cut him enough to put him out of action. I was glad of that. I've killed some men because I had to but I never liked it and never got used to it.

The other scar was alongside my head where a bushwhacker with a rifle didn't quite miss me. You couldn't see the scar because of my hair but you could tell where it was because the hair there had come in white. Speaking of hair, I hadn't had mine cut since I don't know when so I was pretty shaggy looking. The fact that I needed a shave didn't help none, either.

What she saw didn't seem to faze her. "So who are you?" she said.

"Name is Tackett, ma'am. Del Tackett."

"Not Sackett?"

"No, ma'am. I ain't one of them. But sometimes I wish I was."

She eyed me up and down, then put her lamp on a small table and sat down in one of them spindly little chairs women dote on but would break under a good-sized man.

Like Gil Dellah said, Annie Laurie Burns was a good-looking woman. She had black hair which made her pale skin look even whiter. Her eyes were dark, and later, when I saw her in the daylight I saw they were a blue, so dark as to be almost black. Her face was small and oval-shaped. Her nose wasn't anything special but it fit the rest of her face. Her mouth was small but her lips were full.

She was slim and moved gracefully. She was small-boned and not very tall, even though her white neck was longer than most.

10

She caught me looking at her. "Don't get any ideas," she said and lifted her right hand to show me she was holding one of them little two-barrel derringers.

I felt myself flush and was glad she couldn't see well enough in the dim light to notice.

"Sorry, ma'am. I surely didn't mean to stare."

"Apology accepted," she said. "Now tell me what's happened? Where is Obie?"

CHAPTER 2

I CAME DOWNSTAIRS about nine o'clock the next morning aiming to head for the town restaurant and have about a gallon of coffee and something to eat.

Usually I'm an early riser but Obie Shrifft's bed was a comfortable one and besides, me and Annie Laurie Burns had stayed up talking for a long while after I went upstairs. I'd explained to her how I happened to wind up owning the Staghorn and how I didn't really want the place, seeing as how I wasn't cut out to be no saloon keeper.

"I can see that," she said drily.

Then she made me a proposition. She'd run the place in return for half the profits. At the end of two years I'd give her a chance to buy me out at a price we both agreed on.

"I ain't no businessman," I said. "You can't expect me to know what its gonna be worth."

"I will keep the books," she said. "And you're going to have to trust me to keep them honestly and then at the end of two years you can bring in anyone you want to go over them and to advise you on a fair price for the Staghorn."

"What if I decide I don't want to sell?"

"We'll put it in writing tomorrow," she said. "I don't intend to stay here and work for wages or even a share of the profits. I'd already made that plain to Obie and we were trying to work out a deal for me to be a part owner. Then he had to go and pull that stupid trick tonight. Damn him anyway."

She caught me looking at her funny when she swore. "Haven't you ever heard a lady swear before?"

"Oh, yes, ma'am," I said. "Only thing is, my ma didn't believe in swearing. Didn't matter if you was a man or a woman. I swear a mite, but I try not to. And I just ain't never got used to hearin' a woman cuss."

"I'll try not to," she said, but I thought I caught just a bit of sarcasm in her voice.

"Don't matter none to me, ma'am," I said. "You cuss if you want. I'll get used to it."

After that she asked me about myself and for some reason I couldn't figure I told her how I'd grown up in this little mining camp in the Sierras where Ma scraped out a living panning for gold.

I told her how Ma had sent me out on my own when I was sixteen and how I'd been wandering ever since, but now I was thinking of settling down. I told her Ma had died about a year back, but I stopped there.

I decided I didn't want to tell her how we'd come to be in that mining camp and I decided I didn't want to tell her about Esmeralda Rankin either, the girl who owned the R Bar R down near Nora and who I hoped someday to marry. It wasn't none of her business, I figured.

But when it come her turn she clammed up pretty good. About all she said was she'd come down from Denver where she'd worked as a bookkeeper, but that was all I got out of her. It didn't matter none, I thought. There was no reason for her to tell her life history to a stranger.

I started to go, but of a sudden I remembered something. "Ma'am," I said, "that mule. Why'd you name him Maxwelton?"

"You heard about him," she said, amused. "Well, I'll tell you but it probably won't mean anything to you. I named him Maxwelton because his brays are bonny."

She waited expectantly and finally I said, "Yer right, ma'am. It don't mean a thing to me."

"You'd have to be Scottish," she said, laughing a little.

I waited for her to tell me more, but she just sat there, so finally I said, "Obie Shrifft. What about you and him? What if he offers to buy back the Staghorn? What kind of deal we got here?"

She smiled but I noticed that this time there wasn't no warmth in her eyes when she smiled. Underneath that soft and pretty female outside there was, I began to figure, one tough lady.

"What about him and me, Mr. Tackett?" she said. "We were business associates, that's all, just like that's all there will ever be between you and me. Since he sold you the Staghorn he and I are no longer business associates; you and I are. He doesn't have first call to buy the Staghorn. I do. And I will draw up a paper tomorrow stating that I have the first call and we will deposit it with Mr. Nathan Hale, the banker, and he will keep it in his safe until we need it. Now, is there anything else?"

"Yup," I said. "You can call me Del."

As I got up to go I began having second thoughts. That woman wasn't about to do me no favors. "What you said sounds all right to me, ma'am, but I got to sleep on it. I'll see you in the mornin'."

"Fine," she said, "and Del, you may call me Annie Laurie."

I picked up my hat which I had set on a chair, took up the lamp, and walked out, kind of feeling her eyes on my back as I left. I walked across the hall to the door to what had been Obie Shrifft's quarters. Wasn't much in the front room, a huge old oaken rolltop desk with a swivel chair to match and a couple of other chairs, leather covered and stained with use. In the back room there was a big old-fashioned bed and a dresser with a china pitcher and basin on it. There was a batch of men's clothes hanging on hooks along a wall.

I figured Obie Shrifft would come around in the next few days and pick up his clothes and any other personal belongings he had. Maybe by then he'd have cooled off, as I already had, and if he had maybe we could figure a way for him to get his saloon back, unless

15

by then I'd signed the deal with Annie Laurie Burns. She was going to push me to do that, I knew, and when I came right down to it, I knew that was the smart thing for me to do. For sure I didn't owe nothing to Obie Shrifft, not after him going for his gun that way.

The smell of fresh coffee greeted me as I walked toward the kitchen. It surprised me some because I hadn't thought Annie Laurie would be up that early. But she was.

She was dressed in a shirtwaist, a kind of a cross between a blouse and a man's shirt that had been popular among working women for the last few years, and a tailored skirt. Her dark hair had been brushed until it shone. Her eyes which I'd thought were black showed a tinge of dark blue in the daylight. The daylight also showed that she was older than she'd appeared last night in the dim lamp light, over thirty, to be sure. But she was still a mighty attractive woman.

She was not alone.

There was a man sitting at the kitchen table drinking coffee. He wasn't very big, kind of slight. He was dark complected and had straight black hair. He looked to me like an Indian.

"Mornin' ma'am," I said to Annie Laurie. "Can ya spare a cup o' that coffee?"

She smiled and it seemed to me that this morning it was a warm smile, one that was reflected in her eyes and her voice.

"Of course, Del," she said. "I made it knowing you'd be down soon and I'd have been very surprised if you hadn't wanted a cup of coffee."

She picked up the big tin pot and poured me a mugful. I taken it from her and went over and sat down at the table across from the Indian. I taken a big sip. It was black and scalding hot and it tasted good.

"This is Chief Two Horse, Del," Annie Laurie said. "He helps keep the saloon clean and neat. I don't know what we'd do without him. I've been telling him that you're the new owner of the Staghorn."

"Howdy, Chief," I said. "Glad to meet you."

"The pleasure is mine, Mr. Tackett," he said in English that was as good as that Annie Laurie spoke.

He noticed my surprise and smiled. "I'm not a Western Indian, Mr. Tackett. I'm half-Indian, actually. My father who was white died when I was young. My mother was a Mohican Indian, a tribe which is almost extinct. In fact, I may well be the last of the tribe. I'm originally from the state of New York. I was reared in a white community and went to the white man's schools, which is why I speak the white man's language so well.

"My white man's name is Fenimore Hyde. I came to Shalak Springs two years ago with two horses. I was riding Old Paint and leading Old Dan. When I came West I had thought at first to go to Montana because I'd heard of some magnificent scenery there, but winter was coming on so I headed south instead. I reached Shalak Springs just ahead of a big early winter snow storm, so I stayed.

"The white people here noticed I had two horses so they took to calling me Chief Two Horse, which out here in the West is probably better than Fenimore. Although I must admit that Two Horse Hyde is a bit of an unusual name."

"I don't know what brung ya here, Chief," I said. "But yer sure welcome to stay as long as I own the Staghorn. You got a place to stay?"

"Oh, yes. I have a little cabin out a ways from town."

"The people here treat ya all right?"

"For the most part. Some people looked at me at first as if they thought I should be wearing moccasins and a breech clout but as soon as they find out I'm from the East and fairly well educated they tend to accept me. Of course there are always those few who think the only good Injun is a dead Injun. And that goes for half-breeds, too."

"I got nothin' against Injuns," I said. "But out here in the West they're different from the white man. Got their own ways and customs. I fit 'em a time or two a few years back down along the Arizona-Mexico border but they've been pretty quiet for a while."

Chief Two Horse swallowed the last of his coffee and got to his feet. He was taller than I thought when he was sitting down, though not as tall as me, and he was lean and wiry. It was hard to tell how old he was; he could of been thirty or fifty. He fetched out the makings and rolled himself a cigarette and offered the sack of Bull Durham to me.

I shook my head. "Ma didn't approve," I said.

He kind of chuckled. "Your ma heap smart squaw," he said and walked out.

"Your ma heap smart squaw," Annie Laurie mimicked with a laugh.

"Miss Burns," I said with dignity, "I'd consider it a favor if you could put some water on to heat. I'm goin' down to the stable and get my gear and I'll be wantin' to shave."

"You may call me Annie Laurie since we're to be working together, Del," she reminded. "You go along and I'll have hot water for you when you come back. Maybe even enough for you to have a bath."

I figured she was trying to tell me something so I finished up my coffee and went back through the barroom where Chief Two Horse was busy sweeping out the place. Out on the street I waited a moment for my eyes to adjust to the bright morning light.

Then I started for the stable but I hadn't gone but a few steps when a figure stepped out from the shadow of a building and in a loud voice said, "Tackett!"

I stopped in my tracks and peered at the man who was still partly in shadow. It taken me a minute to recognize him because his face and nose were all swollen.

"Oh, it's you, Obie," I said. "Whyn't you back off and let me by?"

"You cheated me out of my saloon," he almost shouted, "and I'm gonna kill ya for it."

He went into a crouch, his right hand poised over a colt .45 six-gun that he had shoved into his waistband.

"Back off, Obie," I said again. "I don't wanta have to hurt you again."

"Do what the man says, Obie, and back off," a voice behind me said. "If you don't he'll kill ya. And if he don't, I'll see ya hang."

"That you, Sheriff?" I said without taking my eyes off of Obie Shrifft.

"I'm the town marshal," the voice said.

"Kind of thought you was a lawman from the way you talk," I said.

The marshal didn't reply, but walked on by me toward Obie Shrifft. He was a big man and walked with a swagger. When he got up to Obie he reached out and taken the gun from his waistband.

"I'm gonna keep this 'til you cool off, Obie," he said. "You'll thank me for it when you get yer sense back. Now go along."

He watched as Obie walked off then turned to me. "I won't have no gunfightin' in my town, Sackett," he said.

"I ain't no Sackett, Marshal," I said. "Name is Tackett. Del Tackett. I ain't no Sackett and I ain't no gunfighter."

"Somebody give me a piece of bad information," he said. "But now that I look at ya I can see you ain't one. Most of them are gettin' a little long in the tooth anyway. You're younger'n them. And uglier, too."

Well, I couldn't get mad at him for saying that because I'm sure not no raving beauty, so I just laughed. "Thank's for runnin' Obie off. I sure didn't want to have to fight him. He used to be a friend."

"Heard about that fight last night," he said, running a hand through his long, blond hair. "Too bad. That saloon was Obie's life. Stay away from him, huh? If yuh think he's gonna give yuh trouble send for me. Name is Johns, Wayne Johns."

"I usually round up my own cows, Marshal," I said. "But I sure ain't huntin' trouble with him or anyone."

I made my way on down to the livery stable, checked on Old Dobbin, and gave the boy working there a quarter to curry him. Then I gathered up my gear and went on back to the Staghorn.

Annie Laurie had three big kettles of water boiling on the stove and from somewhere had dragged out a big old beatup tin washtub which she'd placed in the middle of the kitchen floor and partly filled with cold water.

"There's enough water for a bath and a shave both," she said. "If you like I'll stay and wash your back."

I knew she was teasing me but I felt myself getting red anyway. "I can manage," I said shortly.

She laughed and left the kitchen.

I poured enough hot water in the tub to warm the water already there. Then I stripped off my clothes and stepped in. I was too big to sit down so I stood there and dowsed myself with water and scrubbed myself with a big bar of homemade lye soap that Annie Laurie had left along with a good-sized piece of heavy toweling.

After I washed and dried off I dragged out my other pair of long johns which I'd been saving for when I took a bath. I put them on along with a clean pair of worn black jeans. I was just buckling my belt when there was a knock on the door and Annie Laurie called, "May I come in?" and came in. She walked up close to me.

"You certainly smell better," she said. "Don't forget to shave."

"Thinkin' about growin' a beard," I grumbled, feeling myself going red again.

I hadn't given much thought to how I smelled but I reckoned from here on I would, as long as I was running the Staghorn. Out on the range the cows don't care if you smell, but it's different in town. I fetched out my razor and began to strop it on my belt, not looking at her. She slipped out whilst I was soaping up my face but was back a moment later with a small hand mirror in a carved wooden frame. She propped it up on the sink so I could see what I was shaving.

"Would you like me to shave you?" she asked.

"I can manage," I said stiffly.

She laughed again and walked out again.

After I finished shaving I put on my clean shirt and went looking for her. I finally found her in the front room of Obie's, now my, apartment. She was sitting at the big rolltop desk working on some ledgers that she'd spread out in front of her.

When she looked up I asked, "There a barber in this town?"

She smiled. "Would you like me..."

"Dang it, no!" I interrupted. "I don't want you washin' my back or shavin' me or cuttin' my hair, neither. I want a barber."

She laughed merrily and it seemed to me that this was an entirely different person from the hard-nosed woman I'd talked to last night.

"There's one down by the hotel," she said.

Then suddenly she was all business. "But before you go I want to go over the books with you. Oh yes, I've drawn up the papers you and I discussed last night."

She turned toward me and I could see that cold look in her blue-black eyes. No doubt about it, she was two different women: soft and feminine most of the time but hard as nails when it came to business.

"After I left yuh last night I began havin' second thoughts about doin' business with yuh, Annie Laurie," I said. "Mainly because I didn't want to be stampeded into anything. I still don't. That's a mighty fair offer yuh made me, but I want to sit on it for a day or two."

Her face softened and she was again the Annie Laurie who'd offered to wash my back a little bit ago.

"I understand, Del," she said. "And I guess I was a bit impetuous. But I could see my deal with Obie falling through and it concerned me.

"Remember, I'm a woman in a man's world and I have to do whatever I can to protect myself. I have no husband and if I don't take care of myself no one else will."

"Purty woman like you oughtn't to have no trouble snaggin' a man."

She frowned. "I'm not interested in snagging a man. And, Del, don't wait too long because I don't intend to. If you and I can't strike a deal in the next few days I will have to look elsewhere."

CHAPTER 3

Annie Laurie took the next half hour showing me the books and trying to make me understand what the columns of figures meant. Finally I gave up.

"Only thing I understand is that we're makin' money," I said.

"Yes," she said. "And we will continue to make money as long as someone who understands the saloon business runs this place."

"I hope you'll stay until I figure out what I want to do."

"I'll give you a little time," she said, closing the ledger and putting it in one of the drawers. "But not too much."

Rising, she commanded, "Come with me. I need to get some things at the general store and I'll show you where the barbershop is."

We went outside, her holding onto my arm, me feeling a mite uncomfortable. She was a beautiful woman and she walked close beside me, but the thought of Esme Rankin and the crew at the R Bar R kept me from enjoying her closeness the way I might have. As we started down the boardwalk she gently but firmly moved me to the side next to the street.

"A gentleman always walks on the outside," she said. "That way the lady is protected from mud that could be splashed up or anything that might happen in the street, such as a runaway horse."

Dang, that Annie Laurie woman had a way of making me feel like what I was, an ignorant clod. Nobody had ever told me before that I was supposed to walk on the outside. Of course I hadn't walked many women down city sidewalks and them I had for the most part were country girls who wouldn't care where I walked, as long as I walked with them.

Four doors down from the Staghorn, past the Colorado & Arizona stage station, the restaurant and the building that passed as a hotel was the barber shop. Across the street from it was the Shalak Springs general store. Next to it was the Shalak Springs Bank, then a vacant space, and then a building with a sign on it that said JAIL.

Then the town just sort of faded away into the livery stable, the blacksmith shop, and one or two other nondescript places. Off to one side were three or four other shacks occupied by some of the girls Obie Shrifft had thrown out of the Staghorn.

Down at the other end of the street, sitting by itself, was a one-room building with something that was supposed to be a steeple perched on it. It was meant to double as a school on weekdays and a church on Sundays. Only trouble was, as I found out later, it lacked a couple of necessities, a preacher and a teacher. What kids there was in town either learned at home or didn't learn. About once a month a hellfire-and-brimstone circuit preacher came by and usually drew a pretty good crowd since there wasn't much else to amuse folks.

At Annie Laurie's request I walked her across the street to the store, waiting at first for three riders to pass by. They'd come in from the church end of town and looked like cowboys from one of the nearby ranches. I didn't pay much mind to them.

"See," Annie Laurie teased. "If one of those horses were to run away you'd be here to protect me."

"Ma'am," I said, "somehow I don't think you need much protectin'."

I deposited her inside the door of the store, then walked back across the street to the barbershop with just a casual look at the three riders who were tying their horses in front of the jail.

A bluff, red-faced man about fifty was lounging in the barber chair. "What'll it be?" he asked, standing up. "You want your hair cut or a tooth pulled or a tonic to pep you up?"

"Haircut," I said, sitting down.

"You might be more comfortable if you take off your gunbelt," he suggested.

"I might live longer if I leave it on," I said.

I settled back into the chair and he threw one of those big cloths over the front of me to keep the hair off my clothes and fastened it tight around my neck.

Before he could pick up any of his barber tools the back door of the shop opened up and a man wearing a bandana over most of his face said, "All right, you two. Neither of you move."

He was a tall, thin galoot with squinty eyes. His black, flat-topped hat pretty much hid the color of his hair. His voice was kind of on the high side but the six-gun holding steady in his hand showed he meant business.

The barber backed away from me, at the same time raising his hands to shoulder height.

"Don't shoot," he said, a quaver in his voice. "I don't have any money."

"Take it easy, Pop," the masked man said. "You two behave and yuh won't git hurt."

He eased over to the front door and peered out, looking across the street to where the bank was, at the same time keeping his gun pointed in our general direction.

Well, I sat quiet. Wasn't nobody paying me to be a hero. But almost in spite of myself I felt my right hand under the barber cloth moving slowly and carefully toward the gun on my hip.

He must have sensed some movement because he turned and looked at me, but too late. I was sitting there like a statue.

He turned back to look outside but glanced back frequently at me and the barber who stood there with his hands up and his knees shaking, for which I couldn't blame him. No telling what damn fool thing a man with a mask on his face and a gun in his hand might do.

Well, we had sat there for two or three minutes, maybe more, when someone across the street fired a gun. Immediately the masked man turned all his attention to what was going on outside. There was another few seconds of silence, then the sound of another gun firing four times in rapid succession. At the same time the masked man let off with three or four shots as fast as he could pull the trigger. Then, hearing a noise behind him, he started to turn away from the front door, but he was too late.

The instant he'd begun firing I'd launched myself out of that barber chair like somebody had stuck me on the seat with a hot branding iron.

I hit him in the shortribs just as he was trying to pull his gun down on me and the two of us went careening out of the door, skidded across the boardwalk, and rolled into the dust and dirt of the street, with me on top.

I staggered to my feet and saw him still down on all fours groping around for his gun that he'd lost when he hit the ground.

"No yuh don't," I said as I saw his hand closing on the butt of the gun and I kicked him in the jaw. He sprawled out, face down in dirt, and didn't move.

I yanked off the barber cloth that was still around my neck, picked up his gun, and stuck it behind my belt.

Across the street I saw a stout, white-haired man holding a gun in one hand, staring after the two men racing out of town at a gallop.

I watched as he lowered his gun arm, then dropped his gun in the street and slowly crumpled beside it.

A small crowd quickly began to gather. The first person to reach the old man was Annie Laurie who had just been leaving the general store when the shooting began. She knelt down in the dirt beside him and cradled his head in one arm.

About that time someone yelled, "Where's the marshal?"

But Wayne Johns wasn't nowhere to be seen. In a second a man dashed into the jail and dashed right out again.

"Marshal's been hurt," he shouted.

A man brushed by me in a hurry, carrying a small black bag. It was the barber who I now gathered was also the town doctor-of-sorts.

I brushed the most of the dust and dirt off of me and reached down and flipped the skinny gunman over on his back. I pulled down the bandanna that still covered his face, taken a good look, and decided I hadn't never seen him before. His jaw was at a crooked angle and I figured I must have broken it when I kicked him.

I reached down and taken him by the collar and began dragging him across the street toward the jail. I was almost there when Marshal Johns came to the jail house door on wobbly legs. He held onto the door jamb with one hand and onto his head with the other.

"Got a prisoner for ya, Marshal," I said. "He was in the barber shop coverin' the escape of his pals but he got a mite careless."

Johns shook his head, trying to clear out the cobwebs. "Take him inside and throw him in the cell," he said. "Key's in the desk drawer."

He stepped slowly and carefully down the stairs and tottered off toward the crowd by the bank, still holding his head.

I dragged my would-be bandit into the jail and into the single cell where I left him sprawled out on the floor. I found the cell key in a desk drawer, locked the cell, and put the key back where I found it. Then I went and joined the crowd at the bank.

By this time two of the townsmen were carrying the banker, for that's who the fat man was, into the hotel.

Annie Laurie had run ahead of them and had gotten a blanket and had it laid out on a cot that the hotel clerk had quickly brought in and the men deposited the banker on it.

He was conscious and cursing a blue streak.

"Hush up, Nate, there's a lady present," the barber told him as he prepared to cut the clothes from around a wound in the banker's shoulder.

"Damn you, Ed. Don't you cut into my suit," Nate said unhappily. "You take it off of me. I can have that bullet hole patched."

At that moment Annie Laurie came from somewhere carrying a kettle of hot water. Setting it down, she took the scissors from Ed and began cutting the banker's clothes away from the wound.

"You hush," she admonished when he began to protest. "You're the richest man in town and you can afford to go to Denver and have a new suit made as soon as you can travel."

"They got all my money," the banker whined.

"I know better, Nate," she said. "We'll talk about it when you're well, unless you want to talk about it now in front of all these people."

Nathan glared at her but quit talking.

It turned out that the banker, whose name was Nathan Hale, had been shot twice, once in the left shoulder where the bullet had gone all the way through and once in the right upper arm where the bullet had skidded off the bone and lodged in the muscle.

Ed, the barber-doctor, suggested leaving it there, but Nathan whose fat exterior hid a rawhide toughness, told him to dig it out, which Ed did while Hale bit down hard on a wadded-up towel and sweat great drops, but never made a sound.

The robbers had shot him in the shoulder when he moved too quick as they were leaving. He was ducking under the counter, reaching for his pistol when that happened and all but one of their shots missed. He was so mad that he paid no mind to his shoulder wound. He grabbed his gun, ran out the door, and blazed away at them as they galloped off.

He was hit in the arm with a lucky shot from the skinny robber firing from the barber shop and that had caused him to drop his gun. He was stooping to pick it up when shock and the loss of blood caused him to lose consciousness and fall in the street.

No, he told Johns, he hadn't recognized any of them. "How the hell could I?" he asked irritably. "They had their faces covered."

"How much they get?" Johns asked.

"Can't be sure. But it had to be more'n a thousand dollars," the banker said. "Now let me rest. I'm tired and I'm hurting. I'll talk to you tomorrow."

The hotel clerk taken the front end of the cot and I picked up the rear and we carried it, with the banker on it, to the nearest hotel room where we gently set him down.

The clerk left, but as I started to follow him out the door, Hale called, "You. Sackett or Tackett or whatever your name is, stay a minute. I need to talk to you."

I turned back. "Name is Tackett," I said. "Del Tackett. I ain't no Sackett and I ain't no gunfighter. What can I do for yuh?"

"Heard you won the Staghorn Saloon off of Obie Shrifft in a poker game."

"Yup."

"You going to sell it to Annie Laurie?"

"She been talking to you?"

"I'm no mind reader. Of course she's been talking to me. We talk all the time. Next to me she's the smartest, toughest person in this town. You ought to sell to her."

"Thinkin' on it."

"Don't think on it. Do it. Without her you'll go broke in a month's time. Big, dumb, ignorant cowhand like you has no business trying to run a business."

Now I should have gotten sore at that, but I didn't, because he was right and I knew it. But still I kind of got my back up. He was pushing on me and I don't like to be pushed.

"Like I said, I'll think on it," I said and walked out.

Annie Laurie was waiting for me in the lobby of the hotel. She was pale and her clothes were rumpled and there was a spot of blood on the front of her shirtwaist, but she smiled when she saw me.

"Ed told me how you captured the robber in the barbershop," she said.

"He wasn't very smart," I said. "He should have tied us up or made us lie down on the floor."

"Ed said you kicked him in the face. Was that necessary?"

"Better'n shootin' him. He's got a busted jaw but he's alive."

"Of course," she said. "You're right. Take me to the cafe, will you, please? I could use a cup of tea."

"Yes, ma'am," I said. And I walked her to the cafe, her holding my arm and me walking on the outside, next the road, with one eye cocked for signs of a runaway horse.

CHAPTER 4

WE WERE SITTING there, Annie Laurie and me, in this little restaurant, her drinking tea and me having a mug of coffee, when Wayne Johns came strolling in. He spotted us first thing and came over.

"Mind if I sit?" he asked, pulling out a chair and sitting down. The plump young waitress came over and he ordered a mug of coffee.

"Take more'n that to get rid of this headache," he complained. "I don't know why that feller had to hit me so hard."

He touched his head gingerly. "Knew what they were doin', all right. Put me out of commission and then robbed the bank. Sent that feller to the barber shop to cover 'em. Not his fault you were damn fool enough to take on a man with a loaded gun.

"Just come from talkin' to Nate Hale—he's the banker. The mayor, too. Says he thinks they got at least a thousand dollars. That's two years' pay for me. More, if you're punchin' cows for a livin'."

"You recognize any of 'em?" I asked.

He shook his head. "Never saw 'em before. For that matter, I never saw the galoot you dragged into the jail. Asked him his name but he can't talk on account of you busted his jaw. Gave him a piece of paper and told him to write it down. He wrote back that he couldn't read or write. Thought he had me fooled but I'm smarter'n that. Asked him how come if he couldn't read or write he could write that he couldn't read or write. But he couldn't answer me because of that damn busted jaw.

"Got Ed Alliso lookin' at it now, but he ain't much of a doctor and even if he was I don't know how you'd put a splint on a jaw. Anyway, old Ed claims he set out once to be a doctor but wound up settlin' for hair-cuttin'. Says it pays better."

"He claims to pull teeth, too," I said.

"I'd have to be hurtin' real bad afore I let him pull one of mine," he said. "All he uses is a old pair of pliers."

"Marshal Johns," Annie Laurie broke in, "what are you doing about catching those men?"

"Not much I can do, ma'am," he said. "I got no jurisdiction outside the town limits. Besides, by the time I get a posse organized them fellers'll be long gone. Probably got fresh horses stashed not too far from here. Far as I can see old Nate's just gonna have to grin and bear it. Thousand dollars won't hurt him much. He's rich.

"Stage comes in tomorrow and I'll send a letter to the sheriff tellin' him what happened. Soon as the feller in the jail can travel I'll take him over to the county seat for trial. Means Tackett here'll have to go testify against him. Him and Ed both."

"I aim to be headin' for Arizona in a day or two," I said, "as soon as I figure out what to do with the Staghorn."

"Gonna have to ask yuh to stick around," Johns said. "Won't be too long. The way I see it I can take that feller over to the county seat next week and they can have a trial a couple of days after that. You and Ed testify, he'll go to prison, sure."

"Sorry, Marshal," I said, "but I'm leavin' in the next day or two."

"You try to leave and I'll throw you in jail with that feller you hurt," he said.

Annie Laurie all of a sudden started laughing. "You might as well stay, Del. You can loaf here for the next two weeks as easily as you could in Arizona."

"I got business down in Nora," I said irritably. "Oh hell, it can wait, I guess."

"Your ma wouldn't like you saying 'hell,'" Annie Laurie said, laughing again.

I stood up and flung a 50 cent piece on the table. "Take you back to the Staghorn," I offered grumpily.

"No, thanks," she said. "I have some errands to run. Thank you for the tea."

"See you later," I said and stomped out, taking my hat off the rack by the door as I left.

I didn't want to go back to the Staghorn, even though I owned it, so I kind of wandered down to the livery stable to see how Old Dobbin was doing. That big old bay gelding was standing easy in his stall just loafing away the day and he nickered when he saw me, he was that glad.

On impulse I saddled him up, led him out of the stable, and swung into the saddle. The road through Shalak Springs ran pretty much north and south but outside of town a ways there was a trail heading west toward the high country. All the country around here was about a mile high but there were mountains over to the west that stood even higher.

I turned Old Dobbin west on that trail and gave him his head. He cantered for bit then stretched out at a gallop. About a mile down the road I saw a shack off to the right, built next to a big granite outcropping. A narrow trail branched off toward it and there was a sign staked in the ground with an arrow pointing toward the shack. It said Hyde and Seek Ranch.

Now I'm not much at reading and writing but I knew that hide is spelled h-i-d-e so I figure that when hyde is spelled with a Y it has to be someone's name and the only man I knew named Hyde was Chief Two Horse Hyde. I slowed Old Dobbin back down to a canter and swung him onto the trail to the shack.

When I got up to it I hollered, "Hello, the house" a couple of times and after a minute or two Chief Two Horse came around the side of the shack wiping his hands on his pants.

He held up his right hand shoulder height, palm out, and said, "How."

"Danged if I know," I said.

"We Injuns always say 'How,'" he chuckled. "Get off your horse and come on in back. I'm just finishing up."

I swung down from Old Dobbin, tied him to the hitching post, and followed Two Horse around to the back of the shack.

He had a kind of a three-legged stand set up under the shade of an old cottonwood tree and he had a piece of canvas stretched tight on a frame sitting on the stand. And I could see he'd been paint- ing on it. As I walked up closer I saw it was a picture of his shack with the mountains in the background. It was almost like one of those camera pictures I saw once in Kansas City, only in color.

"Like it?" he asked.

"Sure looks real," I said. "Where'd you learn paintin', anyway?"

"All us Injun warriors know how to paint," he said. "We go on warpath we paint um our faces. After that painting pictures easy."

"You got to quit joshin' me, Chief," I said. "I know I ain't noth- in' more than a dumb cowboy, but I ain't that dumb."

"I know you're not," he said. "But Marshal Johns came out here one day and I told him what I told you and he believed me. So you can't really blame me for seeing if it would work on you.

"Actually I studied painting at the Albany Institute of Art in New York and I made my living as a painter, both landscapes and por- traits. I even have a few hanging in galleries. I came West hoping to paint real Indians, not us tame Eastern types, but there aren't any around this area, although I understand we're not too far from Ute country.

"As I think I told you, when I came West I planned to go to Mon- tana where a man named Houlihan had promised to guide me into Sioux country. But an early winter storm stranded me here. After a while I ran out of money and I got the job cleaning out the Staghorn, which is about the only kind of work an Indian can get around here. If I were a cowboy I could have hired on at a ranch but we don't have cattle ranches in upper New York. As it was I was about at the end of my rope when Obie hired me. It's not the best job in the world, but it feeds me.

"Besides this way I have time to paint."

While he talked he was cleaning his brushes and putting away his paints. He leaned his painting against the cottonwood and began folding up his three-legged stand which he told me was called an easel. Now I don't know nothing about art; I don't even know what I like, but I was curious. Where would a picture painter get his paints?

"Well," he said, "I brought a lot with me. I've been able to send to Denver for some, and some I've made by powdering colored plants or colored rock. I've made myself a crude mortar and pestle just like the Indians south of here use to make corn flour."

Picking everything up but the easel, which I carried, he nodded toward the shack. "You come," he said. "We have um drink of fire-water."

"No thanks, Chief," I said. "I wanna see some more of this country before dark. You wanta saddle Old Paint and ride along?"

He shook his head. "Had to sell Old Paint to get enough money to see me through that winter. And Old Dan's been off his feed. I've walked back and forth to town for the last week. It doesn't take long."

"I don't reckon you saw any sign of them bank robbers when you was walkin' home today," I said.

Chief Two Horse frowned. "Come to think of it," he said, "I crossed the tracks of three horses headed west on my way from town. No riders, though, just the tracks.

"They were south of the trail and riding parallel to it. I was taking a shortcut as usual, cutting across country when I saw them. I didn't think anything of it until just now."

"You any kind of a tracker?" I asked.

"Mohican hunt deer and bear, paddle canoe, take scalp, no track."

"Well," I said, "I guess I'll see if I can foller 'em a ways."

"Stop by any time," he said as I mounted Old Dobbin. "My tepee your tepee."

I mounted Old Dobbin and headed back to the main trail and then rode south of it until I came across the tracks of three horses headed west at what appeared to be a canter. Lucky for me they were easy to follow in the soft soil. After maybe half a mile they began angling north until they joined up with the trail. The trail was not well traveled and theirs were the only fresh hoofprints.

A mile farther the trail crossed a small stream burbling gently down from the base of a mesa some distance to the north. I crossed the stream and stopped. There were no more tracks. The shallow stream was only about three feet wide which meant any riders trying to hide their tracks would have to ride single file.

I rode south a ways, the way the stream was flowing, looking for signs of horses leaving it. Nothing. I turned around and went back to the trail and on beyond it for a quarter of a mile and suddenly I spotted them. Tracks coming out of the stream on the same side they'd gone in on.

I followed along for another hour until I came to the base of the low mesa which stretched out from the mountains to the west. The stream flowed out of a crevice in the rock at the mesa's base, but the riders, instead of heading for the mountains had turned back east as if planning to go around it. The mesa was less than a hundred feet high at its highest point but it stretched a good mile into the plain. It taken me nigh on to half an hour to follow the tracks to the east end of the mesa and by the time I got there it was in deep shadow.

On the way I had scanned the cliff carefully looking for any kind of a trail to the top but found nothing. The riders turned back north at the east end of the mesa and I followed. I hadn't gone but another hundred yards or so when I lost the tracks in the deep shadows. They had cut abruptly in close to the base of the mesa, climbing a slope of sand and gravel that had washed down over the years and that filled in the hoof indentations nearly as quick as a horse lifted his hoof.

I cut back and forth a few times but there wasn't nothing but sand and gravel and a scattering of rocks. A good tracker might have found something in the bright of day but not me and especially not in the deep shadows.

I thought about heading back to Shalak Springs but decided instead to go back to the stream and camp for the night. In the morning I would look for tracks again. Then, if I didn't find any I'd go back to town.

I made camp at the base of the mesa where the stream came out from between the rocks. I hadn't brought any food but there was beef jerky in my saddlebags and a packet of coffee. Up against the side of the mesa I built a small, nearly smokeless fire out of bits of dried sticks that lined the stream bank and filled my beat up old coffeepot with water from the stream. While it was getting hot I staked Old Dobbin so he could graze on some of the sparse grass that was native to the area.

The sun was just going down when I went back to the stream to wash off some of the accumulated dirt and trail dust. I was about ready to dunk my face into the water when a piece of branch wood about a foot long came drifting by. Idly I reached out and grabbed it and was about to throw it to one side when I noticed that one end was charred, like it had been in a fire, and not too long back.

Now that stumped me. It's easy for twigs and branches to wash into a stream during a heavy rain but there hadn't been any rain since I'd been in the area nor had there been any forest or brush fires. Strange.

Only thing I could figure was that someone had tossed a piece of wood from a campfire into the water farther upstream, but how far up was anyone's guess. The stream came out of the crevice in the rock, but did it originate in the rocks of the mesa or did it come from beyond the mesa? If that last was the case it meant the crevice ran the width of the mesa.

I shrugged. There wasn't anything for me to do about it in the dark. In the morning I'd take a careful look.

CHAPTER 5

When I awoke the moon was still high in the sky but there was the first light of dawn in the east. I crawled out of my blankets and stomped my feet into my boots after first shaking them out to make sure no crawly critters had crept into them during the night.

I found a couple of live embers in the ashes of my fire of the night before, fed a few pieces of dry bark on them, blowed on them a bit, and before long had a fire going.

Whilst the dregs of last night's coffee were heating I chewed on my last piece of jerky. Breakfast over, I saddled Old Dobbin, throwed a cupful of water on the ashes of the fire, tied my bedroll behind my saddle, and checked my Winchester rifle and my Colt .45 to make sure all was in working order.

Then I walked over to the stream and stared long and hard at the place where it came out of the rock. The crevasse at its base was no wider than the stream which was still only about three feet wide.

Looking upward the crevasse seemed to widen out to about ten feet wide at the top. About fifteen feet up there appeared to be a narrow ledge that led back about twenty feet where the crevasse seemed to end. It was dark back there but it looked like the stream poured out of the base of the rock.

On a hunch I went back to my saddlebags and got out a pair of moccasins I carried with me in case I had some walking to do. I tied them together and slung them around my neck. Then I taken off my boots and waded into the stream, following it into the crevasse.

The water was icy cold. I walked carefully back to where it seemed be coming from the rock and got a surprise. The crevasse took a hard left turn back toward the mountains. I followed for another few feet, then it took a right turn so it was paralleling the crevasse where it came out of the mesa. Here the crack got narrower as it went up and closed entirely before it reached the top of the mesa.

I began to feel like the walls of the crevasse were closing in on me. Damp and slimy, they were just inches from my shoulders and it was almost pitch dark. I turned and headed back to the opening and daylight. I didn't like that closed-in feeling one little bit.

I had almost reached the turn when I heard voices. I froze.

"Where do you suppose he went?" a deep voice asked.

Another said, "He cain't of went far. He wouldn't of walked off and left his horse."

A third voice said, "Looky here, fellers. His boots. He must of went wading. You don't s'pose he went into the mountain, do ya?"

The second voice said, "If he did I ain't follerin' him. Anybody'd be a sittin' duck goin' in there with the daylight at his back."

"Ifn he went in he's gotta come out. He's left his horse and his gear here," the third voice said.

The second voice said, "Look fellers, we don't have ta worry about him. We take his horse and his gear, he cain't keep follerin' us, that's for sure.

"Dang fool ain't very smart leaving his horse and gear like this. Rocky, whyn't you get his horse and we'll bring his rifle and boots and we'll see how far he follers us walkin' barefoot. Come to think about it, Slim. I got a job fer you. I want you to stay here a while and see if he comes out of there or from wherever he went."

"And if he does?" the deep voice, who apparently was Slim, asked.

"Shoot him," the man who owned the second voice and who was evidently their leader said. "He sure cain't follow us if he's dead. We'll meet ya at the..." His voice faded as he moved off and I didn't catch the last part of what he was saying. Then there was silence.

I stood there in that icy cold water, cursing myself silently, not even worrying about whether Ma would approve. It just hadn't occurred to me that the bank robbers would double back. Sometime late yesterday they must have caught a glimpse of me and waited to waylay me. When I didn't come along they came back to see why. And there I was in that crevasse, standing barefoot in that icy stream, when they came across my camp.

I stood there, beginning to shiver and my feet beginning to feel numb from the cold, wondering what to do. I couldn't stay where I was and if I tried to walk out Slim couldn't miss.

Soon as I figured I didn't have a choice I turned and started to follow the stream back into the mesa. Maybe there would be a place somewhere where I could get out of the water before my feet froze.

The bed of the stream was smooth and sandy. Any sharp rocks had long since been worn down. One good thing, I thought as I inched my way along, there was no way I could get lost.

I came to the place where I had stopped a few minutes earlier, taken a deep breath, and kept on going.

With every step I told myself, "Don't panic, Tackett. Don't panic."

Suddenly I realized I was saying it out loud and I clamped my lips together. No telling how far sound would carry in that tunnel-like crack and there didn't seem to be much sense in letting anyone, if there was still anyone around to hear, know where I was. Or that I was scared half out of my wits.

After another hundred feet I rounded one more curve and stepped into a large, dimly lit room. Actually it wasn't a room and it wasn't all that big. It was a cave the stream had washed out over the centuries and it was maybe ten feet wide and twice that long. At the far end there was a shaft of daylight where the stream entered.

I stepped out of the stream and on to the floor of the cave, and then quick-stepped back into the stream. The cave floor was strewn with small pebbles, probably washed in when heavy rains cause the stream to flood its banks. The way they got there wasn't all that important. What was important was that they were there and making it difficult on the soles of my feet.

Bushes on both sides of the stream hid the entrance to the cave. I pushed them aside, stepped out on a grassy bank, and looked around. I was in a small park, not more than a few acres in size and surrounded on all sides by cliffs in some places close to a hundred feet high. It was long, I estimated somewhere between a quarter and half a mile, and narrow, like a wide split in the mesa, with the little stream running through it. There were a few trees scattered around and brush growing alongside the stream.

I slipped on my moccasins and looked around carefully. There didn't seem to be any sign of life except for a few birds and some insect life. There was a cicada chirping somewhere and a bee buzzed by me as I stood there.

Figuring I could explore the area later if I wanted to, I followed the stream up to the point where it entered the little valley, hoping that there would be an opening that would lead to the outside. There wasn't. At least not so far as I could see. It came out of the base of the cliff with maybe a foot between the surface of the water and the top of the natural tunnel through which it ran.

I sat down in the grass and pondered a while. I couldn't stay here and I knew it. First thing to do was explore around the edges and see if there was a way to the top. If there wasn't I'd wait until dark and go back the way I came. By that time the man called Slim might have given up on me and gone to join his companions. And even if he hadn't, I might be able to sneak by him and hoof it back to Chief Two Horse's shack.

I started making my way slowly around the edge of the valley, looking for any kind of a trail or a break in the valley wall that might take me to the top. Nothing. I was working my way along the base of the cliff on the west side of the valley when something caught my eye among the rocks and brush.

It was the remains of a horse, its dried hide covering nothing but bones. But the thing that caught my eye was that it was still wearing a saddle, or what was left of one. I went over and with a stick poked around in the debris that time had piled around it. As I scattered the dead leaves and twigs and small stones the sun suddenly glistened off of something in the dirt. I leaned down and picked it up.

It was a gold coin, minted since the War Between the States. I tossed the stick aside and went down on my knees, and began carefully brushing away the accumulations of years. I spent half an hour looking but there wasn't nothing more, just that single gold coin.

Suddenly it occurred to me. Where was the rider? I started looking and it wasn't long before I found him, or rather his bones, about ten feet farther out from the cliff than the horse. He was almost buried in leaves and dust that had settled on him and around him. Only a piece of his cowhide vest was visible and I looked twice before I saw what it was. I carefully scraped the dirt and leaves away from the bones and remains of his clothes. I looked carefully but found nothing to identify him. If there had been something it had long since rotted away.

It seemed plain how horse and rider had gotten here. They'd taken the direct route from the top of the cliff and from the looks of it the horse had been running all out when it happened. I wondered, was he running from a posse or from Indians? For sure he wasn't out for a moonlight ride.

I continued my circuit around the valley, looking for a way out. Nothing. Or almost nothing. There was a sort of a break in the cliff on the east side that a desperate man might try scrambling up. But the more I looked at it the more I decided that the only way out that made sense was the way I'd come in.

I'd almost finished working my way around the valley when I saw something that brought me to a halt in a hurry. It was the remains of a campfire, or rather, campfires. Somebody or several somebodies had made camp here, not recently but certainly within the last

43

few years. Was the mysterious horseman one of those? Come to think of it, it wasn't likely, unless his horse had wings.

On a hunch I cut across the valley to where the skeletons lay. I checked the man first and it taken but a minute for me to find the bullet hole in his skull. After that I knew what I was looking for when I went to look at the horse and it was there, too—the bullet hole in the skull. I'd been wrong on my first guess, then. They hadn't ridden off the cliff. They'd come in here somehow, probably the same way I'd come in, and they'd either been trailed in here or run into someone in here. Or, and it struck me all of a sudden, they'd been bushwacked by someone sitting on the cliff with a rifle.

Without thinking I dived to the ground and rolled behind a handy boulder hardly breathing. Cautiously I lifted my head and began scanning the cliffs foot by foot. There wasn't nothing there. I'd been scared by my own imagination. This time, anyway, but regardless, I determined to keep an eye out. I had no desire to be the second dead man in the valley.

I went back to the remains of the campfires and continued working my way back to the stream. There was nothing else to indicate anyone had been here. By the time I'd finished it was midafternoon and already the valley was in shadow. I was hungry but the trouble was there wasn't nothing to eat. I'd never been much on finding out which plants it was the Indians ate and medicated with.

But now I was wishing I'd paid more attention to those sorts of things, especially since by now I knew for certain that there wasn't no game in the valley, not even a rabbit or a squirrel. There weren't no fish in the stream, either.

It had been oppressively hot when the sun was overhead, with no breeze to stir the air, but now with the sun no longer hitting the floor of the valley it was cooling off. I found a flat place under a big cottonwood and lay down and took a nap. I slept the sleep of the innocent for nearly two hours, if where the sun was hitting high on the eastern cliff after I woke up meant anything.

It was, I figured, about another two hours until dark, when it would be time to go. I didn't like the idea of the walk back in that icy cold water with the crevasse walls closing in on either side, but there wasn't no other way as far as I had been able to tell.

When the eastern cliff was all in shadow I went to where the stream flowed into the cave, slang my moccasins around my neck, taken a deep breath, and stepped into the water.

Dang, it was cold.

The walk back didn't seem as long as the walk into the valley, likely because I knew there would be light at the end. One thing I noticed, you could lead a horse through here into the valley if he was willing to come. In ten minutes I came to the final turn of the stream and looking up I could see the stars overhead and the last faint trace of daylight in front of me.

I eased carefully up to the mouth of the crevasse and looked around. There was no sign of life. No campfire. No horses. Nothing. I waited a few more minutes then moved a step beyond the crevasse and, like a fool, out of the shadow of the cliff. I was just starting to step out onto the stream bank when something buzzed by my head and ricocheted with an angry whine off the rock cliff at my back. At the same time there was the sound of a rifle shot magnified by the bounce of the sound waves off the cliff.

Without thinking I threw myself on the ground beside the stream and rolled without stopping back into the deep shadow at the base of the cliff and squirmed silently along it for about ten feet. As soon as I came to a stop I hauled out my Colt .45, figuring that, with any luck, I might get a chance to use it.

Any noise I made was hidden by the deep voice of Slim shouting, "Gotcha, you sonofabitch. You won't be follerin' us around no more."

I lay there without moving, almost without breathing.

"But just ta make sure," Slim said conversationally, and began methodically pumping rifle bullets into the area where he'd seen me fall. I could see the flash from the barrel of his rifle each time he fired but he was too far away for me to take a chance at shooting back with my six-gun. Besides there wasn't no cover where I was lying. To all intents and purposes I was naked as a jaybird.

Finally he quit shooting and I heard him say, "All right. Let's see who we got here."

He ducked out from behind a scrub oak and began walking carefully toward where he thought I was, holding his rifle at the ready.

I let him get almost up to the cliff. "You're a dead man, Slim," I said.

Oh, he was fast and good. He'd been facing the cliff and as soon as I began speaking he turned and fired his rifle from the hip in one motion. But he was too fast and not quite good enough. His bullet was high and I never gave him a second chance. I was firing even as he was firing and I caught him dead center. He took a step backwards, dropped his rifle, and stumbled backward into the stream. He was lying there in the stream, staring at the sky with empty eyes when I came up. I didn't need a second shot and neither did he.

The ground there was rough and rocky and I suddenly realized I was barefoot and walking on that rocky ground wasn't doing my feet any good. I unslung my moccasins and put them on. Then I reached down and grabbed the dead man by the shirt collar and pulled him out of the stream. He was rightly named Slim; he was all skin and bones and it wasn't much of a job.

I had no idea how far away his two pardners were or whether they could hear the gun fire and I wasn't anxious to find out. I left him lying beside the stream, picked up his rifle, and went looking for his horse.

When I reached that scrub oak where Slim had been shooting from, I heard him nicker. He was another fifty feet away. He was a strawberry roan gelding and he was saddled and ready to go. I untied him and climbed aboard. Him and me were going to be a long ways from there in a hurry, just in case Slim's amigos had heard the shooting. In the morning maybe I'd come back and bury him. Then again, maybe not.

CHAPTER 6

I<small>T WAS DARK</small> by now with just the sliver of an old moon above the mountains to the west. I headed the roan downstream a ways and then cut in toward the mountains while I was still north of the east-west trail I had followed from Chief Two Horse's shack. When I came to an outcropping of rock I stopped. There were a few trees growing around it, watered by a small spring that sank back into the ground almost as soon as it trickled out of the pool.

I unsaddled the roan, let him take a drink, rubbed him down with a couple of handsful of dried grass, then tied him back close to the rocks. Digging around in the outlaw's saddlebags I came across some stale bread and a little bit of beef jerky. There was a small side of bacon, too, but I didn't want to risk a fire so I made do with the bread and jerky and water from the spring, which was sweet and tasted good.

I unrolled the bedroll that had been tied behind the saddle, sat down and taken off my boots, and using the saddle as a pillow, drifted off to sleep, after first murmuring a prayer that it didn't have no lice.

When it was still dark I was awakened by a rooster's crow.

A rooster's crow?

He crowed again and I sat up with a start. What was a rooster doing out here in the middle of nowhere? He crowed a third time and I was glad I hadn't told any lies in the last day or two. I'm not much of a reader, but I've been to church enough times to know the story about Peter and the cock.

The sound indicated this cock was roosting somewhere on the other side of the rocks, which was a long ways from Jerusalem. As soon as it was light I would see what was over there. Until now I'd figured I was alone in the middle of nowhere. Certainly I'd had no reason to think any different.

In the meantime I pulled on my boots, rolled up my blankets, and splashed some spring water on my face. Breakfast was more bread and jerky.

Then I led the roan over to the spring and after he had a drink I saddled him up and walked him slowly and quietly around the outcropping.

By now it was beginning to lighten up in the east and the trees were throwing long shadows toward the west. I rode south and swung wide of the trees looking for some kind of a trail. I found it a few yards west of the trees and rocks. It had branched off from the trail to Chief Two Horse's place but I couldn't see any sign that it had been used recently.

I turned the roan onto it and we went up it at a walk, me keeping my eyes peeled as best I could. The trail skirted the trees and swung around the rocks and there on the backside of the outcropping and tight up against it was a small house built of rock but with a log addition that I took to be a stable because there was no door on its wide entry.

There was no sign of life except that suddenly the cock crowed again. Looking around I spotted him sitting on the low branch of a spreading sycamore tree. He was a big, red rooster who somehow had managed to escape marauding coyotes or wolves or bobcats or even Indians, although I hadn't seen any sign of Indians in the area.

There was no telling how long he'd been here, but when I rode closer I could see by the droppings under the branch that he wasn't no newcomer to the place.

I turned and rode up to the door of the stone house. It was shut and was fit snugly into the doorjamb. Whoever had built it knew what he was doing. There was one window but it was covered with what appeared to be a heavy oaken shutter that was pulled tight and had to be locked from the inside. A glance showed me the roof of the cabin was thick wooden planks covered with sod. That would keep the heat in in the winter and out in the summer. And it would also make it almost impossible for unfriendly Indians or anyone else to burn out whoever lived there.

I dismounted and tied the roan to a log hitching post that had been sunk into the ground a few feet from the cabin door. There was a weathered rawhide latchstring poking through a small hole in the door. I pulled on it gently, not knowing how rotten it was and not wanting it to break before I got inside. Well, that bar that locked the door raised up easy as pie and I pushed the door open and went inside.

First thing I noticed was a damp smell. As I looked around the light coming in the open door showed me a dirt floor, a table and two benches that obviously had been made on the place, and a handmade bed big enough for two, with a straw mattress but no blankets on it.

The room was bigger than I thought it would be because it extended back under the rock. And way back under the overhang was a pool of clear water, which accounted for both the damp smell and the site of the cabin. Off to one side a small, solid-looking wooden door looked like it opened into the log addition. On the same side, closer to the front, was a fireplace that had also been used for cooking. There was a small stack of wood piled neatly against the wall next to it. Over against the wall by the bed was a handmade wooden clothestree with some pieces of a man's clothing hanging on it.

The furniture was covered with dust so it taken me a minute to notice the piece of paper under the dust that covered the top of the table. I picked it up and blew off the dust. Someone had written in pencil in a flowing handwriting that somehow looked vaguely familiar:

Welcome stranger. The place is yours. My husband disappeared six months ago and there's nothing here for me. I'm
going back to civilization.

It was unsigned and undated.

There was no way to tell how long she, whoever she was, had
been gone but I figured anywhere from one to two years, what with
that rooster still looking in his prime and the fact that the cabin was
still in good shape. The thought crossed my mind that I might have
me a chicken dinner that night, but I quickly thought better of it.

I had a lot of respect for that old bird, hanging in there the way
he was, what with coyotes and wolves and weasels and who knows
what else prowling the nearby prairie. He might be dinner for one
of those wild critters one day but no bullet of mine was going to do
him in.

I stood there a minute looking at that note and knowing almost
for sure that I knew what had happened to her husband, even if she
didn't. His bones were in that sunken valley along with those of his
horse. I didn't know if he'd managed to stash the money I thought
he'd been carrying or if whoever had shot him had found a way into
the valley and had gotten it. Life is full of mysteries and that for the
moment was one, for sure.

I shrugged. Wasn't anything I could do about it even if I knew
for certain who the widow was or where she was.

"Civilization" was Denver and that was close to 300 miles to the
northeast and I didn't think a lone woman would head that way on
her own. There was, however, a town called Durango near the
southwest corner of Colorado and that might be her first stopping
point, or, if she knew where it was, she could head for the isolated
town of Shalak Springs which wasn't all that far away on the New
Mexico side of the border.

I stood there a minute, trying to figure out what she might have
done. No reason for it. Just idle curiosity and the fact that that

handwriting had a familiar look to it.

Then, suddenly, I began to get a funny feeling, like I was an intruder in that cabin, like I just didn't belong there. I folded the note carefully and tucked it in my shirt pocket, and wasted no time going back outside, pulling the door shut behind me and making sure the bar on the inside fell into place.

Even though I'd chewed a piece of jerky and eaten a chunk of bread when I first got up I was hungry and the thought of the bacon I was carrying roiled my insides. So I built me a small fire back under the trees and taking the hide-out knife I always carried in a sheath strapped to my right calf I shaved some of the bacon into a frying pan the robber had stashed in one of his saddlebags.

After I had it fried and eaten I taken the rest of that stale bread he'd been carrying and soaked it in the bacon grease and was about to take a bite when I saw that old rooster scratching in the dirt a few feet away. He felt me looking at him and he looked up and stared right back.

Without thinking I said, "Here you go, boy. Here's your breakfast," and I tossed the bread at him. As soon as it hit the ground he went after it, pecking away like mad. When he'd finished he stood up on his tiptoes, throwed his head back, and let loose with his loudest cock-a-doodle-do of the day.

"Yer welcome," I said.

I stood up and put the fire out, made sure every ember was dead, wiped the frying pan out with a handful of grass, taken it over to the roan, and stowed it in the saddlebag.

I had gathered up the reins and had one foot in the stirrup when, suddenly, in the not too far distance I heard a horse whinny. I stopped in midmount, took my foot out of the stirrup, and clamped a hand over the roan's nose to prevent him from answering. As soon as I knew he was settled down I led him back into the trees where there was deep shadow, but where there also was a clear view of the cabin.

It wasn't long before I heard the clop, clop of hoofs and a man riding a nondescript gray came into view. To my surprise, a second look told me it was Fenimore Hyde better known to me as Chief Two Horse, half-breed Mohican, artist, and swamper at the Staghorn Saloon. Now what in the hell was he doing here? I started to call out, then thought better of it.

Instead I quickly tethered the roan to a small sapling and eased back toward the yard, being careful not to make any noise. There was something about Chief Two Horse that was different today. He didn't look much like the tame Indian who was the swamper at the Staghorn or even like the artist-painter I'd visited, was it just the day before yesterday?

All at once I knew what it was. He was wearing a Stetson hat and he had a six-shooter swinging from his hip and there was a Winchester rifle tucked in a boot in front of his right leg.

This wasn't no tame half-breed Eastern Mohican Injun; this was a full-fledged fighting man who looked as much at home in the saddle as I did.

He rode up to the door of the cabin and called, "Hello, the house. Anybody home?"

When no one answered he dismounted and still holding onto the reins began a careful study of the ground around him. In a minute he looked toward the woods and said in a conversational voice, "Come on out, Tackett. It's me. Chief Two Horse."

"I know it's you, Chief," I said, without moving. "What I want to know is what yer doin' here."

"I was hunting you," he said. "Got worried about you when you never came back by my place. So I followed you and when I heard the rooster crow I thought you might have found someone living out here. But I guess not."

I moved warily out from the trees, ready to react to any funny move he might make.

"Thought you said you couldn't read sign," I said.

"You were easy to follow. There weren't any other tracks."

Now that there was a lie. There were the tracks of the robbers' horses beginning where the stream came out of the rock. And there were Old Dobbin's tracks going off with the robbers. And I was riding the roan that belonged to the dead robber. Oh, he could read sign, all right. He just didn't want me to know.

"You been here before?" I asked.

"No," he said, "I never had reason to come this way."

"I thought you said Old Dan was feelin' poorly?"

"He's better."

"So I see."

"Now that I know you're all right I'll be going," he said.

"Hold up. I'll go with ya," I said, figuring I didn't want him out there somewhere without me knowing where he was.

I backed into the trees, ignoring the funny look he gave me. I wasn't going to turn my back on that breed until I found out the truth about him and why he'd followed me. Once in the shadows I hurried to the roan, mounted, and rode out in the open, being careful to ride so I could draw and shoot without having to twist around.

Chief Two Horse noticed it.

"You're a mighty suspicious man, Mr. Tackett," he said.

"I'm alive, too," I said shortly. "Lead on. I'll follow."

He shrugged, tickled Old Dan with his spurs, and taken off at a fast trot, with me right behind.

It was after noon before we rode up to his place. We'd gone maybe three hours without a word between us. I dismounted first, watching him carefully and making sure to keep the roan between him and me.

"Like I said, you're a mighty suspicious man, Mr. Tackett," he said.

"Like I said, I'm alive," I said. "Besides there's some things botherin' me. Like, how come you didn't clean up the saloon today?"

"That's easy. I told Miss Burns last night that if you didn't show up by morning I was going to look for you. She and I were both worried."

"That warms the cockles of my heart," I said sarcastically, wishing in the back of my mind that I knew what a cockle was.

"And what's somebody who says he's an Eastern half-breed Injun doin' actin' like a gun slinger? And how come Old Dan got well so quick? And how come you knowed where to look for me?"

He sighed and took off his hat and wiped his forehead with his shirtsleeve. Then he dismounted and tied Old Dan to the hitching post.

"Come on in," he said over his shoulder. "I'll make some coffee and we can talk."

I tied up the roan and followed him into the shack. He taken his gunbelt off and hung it on a peg on the wall and hung his hat on top of it. Then he stirred up the fire in the stove, throwed on a couple of small logs, and set about making coffee.

I looked around the shack. It was a two-room affair but the door to the other room was closed. But he'd fixed up this room pretty nice. He had pictures he'd painted hanging on the walls and more leaning against them. The shack actually had a pine wood floor and there was a table and a couple of chairs along with a bench and a small cook stove. The homemade chairs were built sturdy and I slouched down in one, hitched my gun around so it was in easy reach, and waited for him to begin talking.

When the coffee was done he taken down a couple of mugs, filled them and handed one to me. The coffee was black and strong and tasted good.

He looked at me levelly with his beady, black eyes from across the table.

"I am what I said I was," he said. "I'm a half-breed Mohican Indian. My mother was Mohican. My father was a Scotsman. He was a cooper by trade. You know, made barrels when there was a need for them. When there wasn't he did whatever he had to do to stave off the poor house. I grew up in upper New York and attended Albany Art Institute. Worked nights to pay for it. Now I'm a painter—an artist—and a pretty damn good one.

"But like a lot of other Easterners and even people from other continents I was attracted by the West and I came out here back in the late seventies, not to hunt or to settle but to paint. Like a lot of other men who came here I learned out of necessity to ride and to rope and to use guns. I'm not a gunfighter like you, Tackett; I've only killed one man and that was in a fight he started, but I won't back up to any man."

He looked me square in the eye when he said that and I knew he meant it.

He went on, "But the other thing I told you is true. It's hard for an Indian, even a part-Indian, even an educated Indian, to get a decent job out here. Especially one that in my case would give me time to paint. That's why I'm a swamper in your saloon. One day I will crate up my paintings and I will either go back East or west to San Francisco and I will sell them and that will give me enough money to paint what I wish to paint and where I wish to paint and live in style while I'm doing it.

"Satisfied?"

"I got no reason not to believe ya," I said. "Except ya lied to me about Old Dan." And I think you lied to me about why yer here, I thought.

He shrugged. "I didn't want to go with you so I used the first excuse I could think of."

"You can read sign, too," I accused.

"Of course I can," he said. "All us Injuns can track a snake across a bare rock."

I had no answer for that so we sat and sipped our coffee in silence for a bit and after a while he poured us each a second cup.

Then he said casually—too casually, I thought, "How'd you find that cabin back there?"

"Like you, I heard the rooster crow," I said.

"Didn't look like anyone had lived there for a while."

"That's kind of how it looked."

"You go inside?"

"Yep. Wasn't nothin' there, though. Just a few men's clothes hangin' on a hook."

"No indication of who lived there?"

I thought about the note in my pocket. "Nope," I said.

I drained the last of my coffee and stood up. "You make mighty good coffee, Chief," I said. "But I'll be going. Got to check up on my saloon and maybe get a bite to eat. All I had since I left town is jerky, a couple of slices of bacon, and some stale bread."

"I have some beans I could heat up."

I shook my head. "Thanks, but I'll be goin'. See you in the mornin' if yer still workin' for me."

I put on my hat and went out the door.

"See you in the morning," he called, as I pointed the roan toward Shalak Springs.

CHAPTER 7

THERE WAS A lot of loose ends running around in my head as I rode back into Shalack Springs. It seemed like I'd been gone a long time but this was only the third day. Still, a lot had happened even though none of it seemed to add up.

First there was the bank robbers. I'd killed one of them. In self-defense, I told myself, and only after he'd taken a shot at me. I didn't see where I'd had much choice but I hadn't never liked the idea of having to kill someone and it always weighed on my conscience, for a while, at least.

And dang, I hadn't even had time to bury him, seeing as how I wanted out of there before his friends came back. And what about his friends? Had they come back or had they just taken off? Did they come from around here or were they a gang of professionals?

Funny, I thought, that Chief Two Horse hadn't mentioned the body of the man I'd shot, because he must have seen it when he tracked me up the stream to the base of the mesa. Maybe his friends had come back and taken him away or buried him before Two Horse got there. Or maybe there was a reason for Two Horse not to mention him.

It still seemed mighty strange him getting there so soon and then following my trail to the cabin even before it got cold. He'd have had to be tracking me in the dark and he didn't look to me to be equipped with cat eyes. What was more likely was that he'd been spying on the robber who was waiting for me to come out from the mesa. And after he saw me shoot him and light out he followed along.

Next, I got to thinking that maybe I should have gone back and tried to pick up the trail of the remaining two robbers. But it didn't take me long to recognize that that would have been a dumb thing for even me to do. At best I'd have lost it and at worst they'd have laid in the weeds for me and I might right now be lying alongside the trail with a bullet in my chest. Only thing bothering me was not the money they got away with but the fact that they'd taken Old Dobbin, and I loved that horse. Him and me had been together for over four years, which was longer than I'd ever spent with any human, man or woman, except for Ma, of course. Dang, but I was going to miss that pony.

Then there was the mystery of that skeleton in the sunken valley, and the gold coin he was carrying. Was that the only one or was there more? And if there was, had he stashed it somewhere or had it been taken by whoever shot him? And who was he, anyway, and why was he carrying a lot of money, if he was?

I thought it likely that he'd come from the stone cabin but there was no way I could be sure. Somebody or some group must have been chasing him, though, because otherwise he wouldn't have been trapped in that sunken valley.

And then there was the riddle of the stone cabin itself. Who built it? Where'd the folks go who'd lived there? And had Chief Two Horse known it was there? And, if so, why had he lied to me?

Finally there was the biggest riddle of all—Chief Two Horse, also known as Fenimore Hyde, the last of the Mohicans, or so he claimed. What he'd said might well be true, but there was a lot he hadn't said. It didn't make much sense to me that an educated man like him would be earning money cleaning a saloon, especially if he was as good a painter as he claimed to be. In fact, nothing about him made much sense.

Maybe Annie Laurie would have some thoughts about him. But

there was another riddle. All I knowed about her was what she'd told me and that sure wasn't much.

Maybe the smart thing for me to do would be to quit worrying about all this stuff, since none of it was really my business, and make a deal with Annie Laurie for her to buy the saloon now. Then I could pack up and head for Nora and the folks at the R Bar R ranch.

Well, I'd sleep on it.

By the time I finished running all that stuff around in my head it was late afternoon and that roan, that I was beginning to take a shine to, was trotting into the outskirts of Shalak Springs. Come to think of it by the time you got into the outskirts you were almost out of town on the other side, Shalak Springs was that small.

I headed for the Staghorn, dismounted, and tied the roan—by now I was calling him Boy—at the hitching rail and went on in. Gil Dellah, the bald and skinny bartender, was behind the bar wiping it off with a damp and dirty towel. There was only one customer at the bar and he was kind of sagging against it and pouring himself a drink from a bottle Dellah had set in front of him.

He was a big, shaggy man and something about him looked familiar, even from the back. I walked up to take a closer look, and stopped short.

"Well I'll be danged," I said in surprise. "Jack Sears. What in tarnation are you doin' here?"

He turned to look at me and almost fell, not from surprise but from liquor. I could see he wasn't real sober. Matter of fact, he was real drunk. He steadied himself and with an effort focused his eyes on me.

"Tackett!" he said in a whiskey-thickened voice. "You mean you ain't dead?"

"No, and I ain't drunk, neither," I said.

"Heard you was dead. Heard you was killed in a shoot-out up north. Guess I'm gonna hafta kill ya myself."

He started to go into a crouch and fell face forward on the floor.

He tried to struggle to his feet, but finally gave up and flopped down again with his face in the sawdust. He lifted his head and looked in my general direction.

"Tomorrow," he slurred. "I'll kill ya tomorrow."

His face dropped back into the sawdust.

"Seems like he knows ya," Gil Dellah said from behind the bar.

"Help me get him upstairs and we'll put him to bed," I said. "He's so drunk he don't know he don't wanta kill me no more."

Between the two of us we half-dragged, half-carried him upstairs and flopped him onto my bed. I pulled his boots off and threw a buffalo robe over him. He was snoring loudly when I left.

"He rode in right after you left and has been drinkin' pretty steady ever since," Dellah said when I went back downstairs.

"Say what he was doin' here?"

"Said somethin' about bein' on the trail of some bank robbers. He called 'em the Fierman gang. Said they held up a bank down at some town over in the Arizona territory called Nora, I think he said. I told him he likely come to the right place on account of our bank bein' held up, too."

"Fierman?" I said. "I heard of them. Used to operate over in Nevada and parts of Idaho. Feller name of Cy Fierman runs 'em. Hear he's kill six men."

I changed the subject. "Seen Annie Laurie?"

He nodded. "She's over takin' care of Nate Hale. They're pretty close."

I went on over to the hotel and ran into Annie Laurie as she was coming out of the banker's room.

"How's he doin'?" I asked.

"Fine, just fine. He says he'll be up and around in a day or two, but I think it'll be nearer a week. Where have you been?"

"Funny thing," I said. "I set out to take a ride, see if I could clear my mind, do some thinkin', and I wound up runnin' across them bank robbers. Join me for supper and I'll tell you about it."

We walked down to the little cafe, me being careful to walk on the side nearest the road. She didn't say anything but I knew she noticed.

Whilst we ate I told her how I'd gone riding and stopped by Chief Two Horsc's place and then had followed the tracks of the bank robbers up to the mesa. Then I lied a bit and told her one of the robbers had come back and I'd killed him in a gunfight, then had lit out of there before his friends could come back and find me.

I watched her close when I told her about hearing the rooster crow and finding the stone cabin but she never said anything or changed expression. And I thought that was kind of funny in itself since it isn't often you run into roosters living around deserted stone cabins.

"I shot him," I said.

She blanched. "Oh, no," she gasped.

"Just kiddin'," I said. "Just wanted to see what you'd say."

She recovered quick. "What a terrible thing to do. That poor rooster!"

"He'd of made a good meal," I grinned. "But I left him for the coyotes."

She looked down at her plate and didn't say anything.

"What d'ya suppose Chief Two Horse was doin' out there?" I asked, changing the subject.

"Looking for you, just as he said," she replied.

"I wonder," I said. "Seems strange to me he'd refuse to ride out with me but then foller me. He was carryin' a rifle and a six-shooter, too. If he wasn't lookin' fer trouble he sure wasn't tryin' to avoid it."

"He's a strange man," she mused. "He came here shortly after I did. Obie hired him when he said he needed a job. But he never seems to need money. I asked him about it once and he said he sells a painting every now and then but I don't know anyone who's bought one. Except me."

She noticed my raised eyebrows. "It's just a landscape but it's really very good."

"Feller named Jack Sears come to town whilst I was gone," I said. "Spent the last two days gettin' drunk in the Staghorn. You seen him?"

She nodded. "I knew there was a stranger in town. But I didn't know his name. He wasn't making any trouble so we didn't make any for him, just let him drink."

"Didn't say what he's doin' here?"

"Not to me."

"He said somethin' to Dellah about chasin' bank robbers," I said. "But he's passed out drunk right now so I guess I'll have to wait 'til he sobers up to find out anything more."

"Have you thought any more about my offer?" she asked.

"I think I'd like to sell out and get out," I said. "Maybe we can talk about it tomorrow. I know it's early but I'm thinkin' about turnin' in. Been a long couple of days."

We went along the street, such as it was, and walked on to the Staghorn which was doing a pretty good business. The bar was crowded and there was another half a dozen men sitting at the tables. Since I'd only come to town a week ago I didn't see anyone I knew except one person sitting alone at a table by the wall. He was nursing a drink and a swollen nose and when he saw me he beckoned me over.

I went over and pulled out a chair and sat down. "How's it goin', Obie?" I asked.

He touched the bandage across the bridge of his nose gently. "Not so good," he said. "I'm broke. Ya cleaned me out."

I reached for my pocket. "I can help ya out 'til yer back on yer feet."

"That ain't why I come here," he said. "I come to tell ya I acted the damn fool the other night. You won fair and square and I had no call to try and pull a gun on ya. I'm just glad ya didn't kill me.

Ya could of, ya know. Stomped me to death, if nothin' else, and I'd a had it comin'."

"No hard feelin's, Obie," I said. "Can I do anything fer ya?"

He looked embarrassed. But after sitting quiet for a minute he said, "Ya might lend me a few bucks. I got a pal runs a saloon down in the Arizona Territory, little town called Nora, and he'll let me run a table there. Stake me, too."

"Nora," I said. "I been there."

I fished into my pocket and found a double-eagle and handed it to him. "Don't worry about payin' me back. If I ever need it I'll holler."

He swallowed the rest of his drink and got to his feet. "I won't forget," he said and headed for the door.

Annie Laurie, who'd been standing by the bar talking to Dellah when he wasn't pouring drinks, came over.

"What was that all about?"

"Obie's leavin' town. Wanted to mend his fences first."

"It looked as if you were the one paying for the mending," she said drily.

"It wasn't much and it was a loan. I'll get it back."

She laughed skeptically. "You go on to bed," she said. "You're too tired to think straight. I'll keep an eye on things."

"Thanks," I said. "I got to check on Jack Sears. He's conked out on my bed."

She looked at me funny-like, but I paid her no heed and went on up the stairs. Jack Sears hadn't moved since we'd put him on the bed and he was snoring loud enough so I heard him when I reached the top of the stairs. I shook him a couple of times but it was plain it would be morning at least before he came to his senses.

I went out the door and met Annie Laurie at the top of the steps.

"What is that terrible noise?" she asked.

"That's Jack Sears snorin'," I said. "I'm headin' for the hotel to get some shuteye."

"You could sleep in my bed," she said. "And I could take the couch."

"That's mighty thoughty of you, Annie Laurie," I said. "Mighty thoughty, but I think mebbe I better try the hotel."

"Suit yourself," she said shortly.

We went down the stairs together and I went on out the bat wing doors and headed for the hotel. That was one place I was sure I'd get a good night's sleep.

CHAPTER 8

THE ROOM CLERK gave me a room on the first floor and as I walked down the hall I had to pass a room where the lamp was lit and the door was open. Without thinking I glanced in and caught the eye of the round-faced, white-haired man lying propped up in the bed there. It was the banker, Nate Hale.

"Come on in a minute, son," he called in a voice that was surprisingly strong for a man who'd been shot in the shoulder and arm less than a week ago.

"You're Sackett, aren't—"

"Tackett," I said irritably. "I told ya before it's Tackett with a T."

Immediately I was sorry I'd been rude, but he paid me no heed.

"Tackett, Sackett, whatever," he said. "Just wanted to thank you for doing your best to stop that robbery. Annie Laurie told me you captured one of them. That's a tough bunch if they are who I think they are. Looking back I think I recognized one of them, even though they were all wearing bandannas over their faces. Fellow named Cy Fierman. I knew him over in Nevada before he went bad.

"I looked different then, but he hasn't changed hardly at all. Back then my hair was black, I had a mustache, and I weighed 50 pounds less. A good thing, too. If he'd recognized me he'd probably have shot me. I was working in a bank in Carson City and we foreclosed on his ranch. After that he took to robbing banks, as much to get even with bankers as anything, I suppose."

He quit talking for a moment and chuckled. "So your name is

Tackett. I guess I forgot you told me that the other day. I was hoping you were one of those gun-fighting Sacketts from over around Mora. I'd have tried to hire you to run down the Fierman gang. Law around here isn't much.

"Say, you wouldn't be interested in taking on the job, would you? You seem to be a pretty tough hombre, even if your name isn't Sackett."

"I ain't no manhunter," I said. "Anyways, I'll be headin' out in the next day or two."

"It was just a thought," he sighed. He closed his eyes and I could see he was tired and drifting off to sleep.

I went out, closing the door behind me, and went on to my room. I was up early the next morning and strolled on over to the Staghorn. Early as I was Annie Laurie was already stirring around the big kitchen and I could smell the coffee as I walked in. She looked bright and chipper as a speckled pup.

"Don't you never sleep?" I asked.

"I work nights because I have to," she said, "but I like mornings best."

"You and me, both," I said, sipping at the mug of coffee she'd set in front of me. It was hot and black and it tasted good.

"Hear anything from Jack Sears?"

"He was still snoring when I came downstairs," she said.

"I'll go roust him out," I said, setting my coffee down. "Time he was up, anyways. I just hope he didn't get sick all over the bed."

I headed for the door and almost ran into Chief Two Horse coming in. He was dressed in his beat-up work clothes that looked like he'd stolen 'em off someone about five sizes bigger and he didn't look at all like either the painter or the fighting man I'd been dealing with in the last few days.

"Howdy, Chief," I said. "Glad to see you decided to stay on the job."

"Injun need um heap wampum. Need um coffee, too. Real bad," he said and brushed on by me.

I went on up the stairs and to my room. Jack Sears was sitting on the edge of the bed, running his fingers through his shaggy hair and yawning.

"Thought I remembered seein' ya," he said. "What in the hell are you doin' here?"

"I own this place. That's my bed yer sleepin' in. What are you doin' here?"

"You runnin' a saloon. That's a laugh."

"I won it in a poker game," I said defensively. "I'm gettin' ready to sell it. There's coffee down in the kitchen. Come on down. You got some talkin' to do."

I turned and went back to the kitchen where Annie Laurie and Chief Two Horse were drinking coffee. Whatever they were talking about they quit when I came into the room.

"Sears'll be down in a minute," I said. "He'll be needin' a gallon or two of coffee."

"There's plenty," Annie Laurie said.

She poured a mug and set it at an empty place. A moment later Jack Sears shuffled into the room looking like a bum down on his luck. His black hair was shaggy. He had a three-day's growth of black beard. His eyes were bloodshot and when he picked up the mug of coffee in both hands they were shaking so much he had trouble getting it to his lips without spilling. He sat at the table without talking and drank it down as fast as the heat would let him.

When he'd emptied the mug he sighed and looked at Annie Laurie. "Good coffee, ma'am. Ya got any more?"

"There's more, Mr. Sears," Annie Laurie said. "There's also a pan of water, a bar of soap, and a towel just outside the back door. As soon as you've cleaned up I'll be glad to pour you another."

Sears heard one of us giggle and looked around belligerently at Two Horse and me but we were both looking elsewhere.

"You got a razor I can borrow, Tackett?" he asked.

"I'll get it for ya," I said and headed back upstairs. When I came

67

down he was already outside washing up. When he came back in a few minutes later he looked almost human. He'd shaved and combed his hair with his fingers and his eyes seemed to have cleared up a bit. Only his breath was sour.

He sat down at the table and Annie Laurie set another mug of coffee in front of him.

"You gentleman will want to talk," she said. "Chief, you and I need to get to work."

The two went out the door leaving me and Sears alone.

We sat across the table from each other not saying anything. A lot of thoughts and memories were racing through my mind.

Jack Sears had been my enemy and had sworn to kill me. Instead he had saved my life and become my good friend. He'd settled down on a ranch outside the town of Nora down in the Arizona Territory and adjacent to the R Bar R ranch which was owned by a lady named Esmeralda Rankin. I'd worked on the R Bar R and I was headed back that way when I'd stopped off in Shalak Springs.

About the time I'd left the R Bar R nearly a year before Sears was getting ready to marry a young woman named Mary Lou Schmidt and now here he was a long way from Nora looking like a down-and-out cowboy.

"What's goin' on, Jack?" I asked.

He looked at me and I saw his eyes begin to water. "Mary Lou's dead," he said hoarsely.

"Ya wanna talk about it?" I asked, not knowing what else to say.

"The Fierman gang killed her. I'll find 'em if I have to track 'em to hell and back."

That big, tough man started to cry silently. He clamped his lips together trying to control himself but his shoulders heaved and tears ran down his cheeks. I reached across the table and squeezed his calloused hand.

"I'm sorry, Jack. I'm sorry," was all I could think to say.

After a minute he got control of himself.

"I loved that girl," he said. "I know what she'd been but I loved her. Wasn't a nicer, sweeter woman in the world."

"What happened?" I asked.

"The Fierman gang," he said. "They'd robbed the bank and were racin' out of town. Me and Mary Lou was walking along the boardwalk with our backs to 'em. We didn't know they'd robbed the bank and we sure didn't see 'em comin'. Mary Lou was walkin' on the outside next to the road and one of their horses come too close. Knocked her flyin' and she hit her head against a hitching post. Never did regain consciousness. She died a week later.

"I been follerin' 'em ever since. They been hittin' banks all over this part of the country and I been right behind 'em. God help 'em when I catch 'em."

He looked at me steadily. "We heerd you was dead, Del. Word come you was killed in a gunfight at some town up north of here. Banana, Bonanza, somethin' like that. Miss Rankin was all broke up. Took off for the East. Left Blackie Harrington in charge of the ranch until she can sell it. Said she hates the West. Said there's too much violence and killin'."

He gave a short, sarcastic laugh. "She don't even know about Mary Lou."

I barely heard him say that. My heart had dropped clean down into my boots when he said Esme had gone East. The only woman I had ever loved had gone out of my life. For a second I had a wild impulse to mount up and follow her East but as soon as I had the thought I discarded it. She hated the West and sure as cats have kittens I'd feel like a hog on ice in the East.

I wouldn't fit in there and I sure wouldn't fit in with her fancy, educated friends, talking politics and literature and sticking their little fingers out when they drank their tea.

I got ahold of myself.

"What about Beauty?" I asked. "I love that dog. Hadn't been for you and her I'd be long dead now."

"Miss Rankin took her along. But you remember her horse, Baby. She give her to Mary Lou."

"Damn, damn, damn," I swore softly under my breath, forgetting all about how Ma felt about cursing. "Everything's really gone to hell, ain't it? I should never of left."

"Been better if you hadn't," Sears said.

We sat silently, sipping our coffee and my mind went back to the day old one-armed Billy Bob Doyle had found me and taken me out to R Bar R, which was owned by a girl named Esmeralda Rankin. With the help of Sears and a couple of cowboys named Blackie Harrington and Lew Haight we had saved her ranch from a gang of rustlers headed by a man who, unbeknownst to her until later, was her half-brother.

We'd fallen in love, but because I could barely read or write I was too proud to ask her to marry me. Instead I went off to Texas to find Billy Bob Doyle's daughter. From there her and me went to Colorado to find a mine she'd inherited. Along the way, before she taken up with a lawyer named Kooby Rarbil, she taught me reading and writing, which is why I was heading back for the R Bar R.

I had some money in my pocket and some more in Chase Hattan's bank in Bonanza and now I could read and write. And I had the fancy notion that because I could I could ask Esme to marry me. But now she was gone, and I was back where I'd been before I met her—just a drifter. It looked like I'd be punching cows, riding shotgun, doing whatever was handy until I was too old to ride.

Finally I said, "Things have sure gone to hell in a handbasket."

"Yeah," Sears said. "They sure have. And I'm gonna send Cy Fierman there, too."

I sighed. "I'll help ya," I said. "Fact is, I already have. We got one of them in the jail over across the street and I killed another one of 'em over by the mountains a couple of days ago. That leaves two."

"No it don't. Not unless you got Fierman hisself. From what I been hearin' he's got a hideout somewhere back in the mountains with maybe a dozen men there. He takes a different bunch on every job he pulls."

I had a sudden thought.

"Jack," I said, "if we come out of this alive I'm gonna try and buy the R Bar R if Esme hasn't already sold it. Then you and me can get back in the cow business and quit all this runnin' around the country and gettin' shot at.

"Let's you and me go get some breakfast and figure out what we're gonna do."

"I know what I'm gonna do," Sears growled. "I'm gonna go over to the jail and get ahold of that feller you got there and I'm gonna beat him half to death if he don't tell me where Fierman's hideout is. Soon as I get somethin' to eat, that is."

"Yer gonna have to wait, Jack," I said. "He can't talk. I busted his jaw."

There was a stout, middle-aged woman running the only restaurant in Shalak Springs. She was red-faced and white-haired and perpetually cheerful. She was the cook. Her daughter who was also stout and red-faced was the waitress and she seemed as happy as her mother. She remembered me from when I'd been in before and said a cheery hello.

Jack and me went in and sat at a table along the side of the room. There were a couple of tough-looking cowboys eating at one of the other tables and the town's barber/doctor/dentist, Ed Alliso, was at another table. He looked up when we came in and waved at me.

"Howdy, Sackett," he called. "Haven't seen you since the robbery. Where've you been?"

"It's Tackett," I said, sitting down.

"Nosy feller, ain't he?" Sears said.

"Oh, he's all right," I said. "He was about to cut my hair when the bank was robbed. Come to think about it, I never did get it cut."

The waitress came over and smiled at us. "We have eggs today,"

71

she said. "And flapjacks. And ham and bacon. And beans. And venison. And beefsteak."

"Eggs and flapjacks and ham," Sears said.

I said, "Make it two. And coffee for both of us."

She took the order and then went over and handed one of the cowboys a check. He looked at it, threw down a couple of coins, and the two of them sauntered out.

Half an hour later I wiped up the last of the egg yolk with the last bite of ham, put it in my mouth, swallowed the last of my coffee, and pushed back my chair. Sears was already standing.

"Let's get over to the jail and see if we can light a fire under Fierman's boy," he said.

I tossed a couple of coins on the table, thanked the waitress, and we headed out for the jail.

When we got there I opened the door and went in with Sears right behind me. Wayne Johns, the town marshall, was sitting behind the desk. He didn't get up when we came in and he didn't say anything. He couldn't. He was tied tight to his chair and a gag was stuffed in his mouth.

CHAPTER 9

JOHNS HAD A wild look in his eyes and he made grunting noises through his gag. Behind me I heard Sears say, "Damnation!"

I taken a quick look at the cell and sure enough the robber whose jaw I had busted had left without even closing the cell door behind him.

I took my Barlow folding knife from my pocket, opened it, and went over and cut the ropes binding Johns to his chair and undid the bandanna that held the gag in place.

After listening to his language for the next few minutes I almost wished I'd left it in. Ma, I knew, would not have put up with it for a second. But when you came right down to it he had a kind of a right to cuss. This was the second time in less than a week that Fierman or some of his boys had walked right into his jail in broad daylight and done him wrong.

When he'd quit cussing and sputtering he said, "You two. You're deputized. You help me round up a posse and we'll go after 'em. They ain't been gone more'n half an hour."

"Thought you said yer jurisdiction stops at the town limits," I said.

"I don't give a damn," he hollered. "We're goin' after 'em. Ain't nobody comin' into my town and stealin' my prisoners."

"They've already did it," Sears pointed out mildly.

"Well, damn it. What are we goin' to do?" Johns shouted.

"I don't know about you, Marshal, but me and Tackett are going back to the Staghorn and maybe have a drink. You want to join us?"

Johns glared at us a moment, then stomped out of the building.

"I guess I'll go see if I can pick up their trail," Sears said, as we headed for the Staghorn.

"We don't even know which way they went," I said.

"There's only two roads out of town," he said.

"There's also a dozen trails and a lot of open country to cut across," I said. "I think I got a better idea. Let's see if there's any coffee left in the kitchen and we'll talk about it."

Over mugs of coffee I told him about following the Fierman gang, if that's who it was who had robbed the bank, to the base of the mesa. I told him about following the stream into the sunken valley after I spotted the piece of charred wood in the stream.

"It didn't come from the valley," I said. "It come from the other side of the mesa which I think means his hideout is back there somewhere.

"I ain't even sure he knows about the sunken valley. If he does he's too smart to camp there 'cause there's only one way in and out and he could be trapped there awful easy."

I went on and told him about killing the gunman who was lying in wait for me as I came out of the valley and I told him about hearing the rooster crow and finding the stone cabin and everything I knew about Chief Two Horse.

I told him about the skeletons I'd found of the horse and rider and how I thought they'd been shot from the rim of the valley. But I didn't tell him about the note the woman had left on the table in the cabin. There was something about that note that bothered me and I figured to keep it to myself until I figured out why.

"Even if their hideout ain't around back of the mesa that's still the best place to start trackin' 'em from," I said. "It's gotta be better'n tryin' to pick up their tracks from here."

"Yer right," he said. "I'll get my gear together and we'll take off."

"Hold on," I said. "Before I go gallivantin' all over the country with ya I got some business I got to tend to first. I oughta be able to take care of it today and then tomorrow we can get an early start."

"You backin' out on me, Tackett?"

"Any more cracks like that and I'm likely to."

"Hey, I'm sorry," he said. "I'm in a hurry to get after 'em. Tomorrow mornin'll be fine. See ya then."

After Sears had left I wandered into the barroom where Chief Two Horse was just finishing cleaning up the place. "Me go now," he said. "Injun gottum many things to do before sun go down."

"Annie Laurie pay ya?"

"Yes," he said. "And I appreciate the extra money she said you told her to pay me. It brings the day a little closer when I can leave this God-forsaken part of the country. As soon as I can I'm going back to civilization and begin painting scenes and people from the white man's civilization."

"Chief," I said, "out there the other day ya looked like you was born to this part of the country. Too bad ya don't stay."

He shrugged. "There's no demand for original paintings out here, no matter how good. Most people have better things to do with their money. In the East or in San Francisco or maybe even in Denver there are people with money who appreciate talent and good art. I intend to take advantage of that situation.

"Chief Two Horse, him go now."

I nodded, and after he walked out I went looking for Annie Laurie. I found her in my apartment working on ledgers at the big roll-top desk Obie Shrifft had had shipped in. She looked up when I entered.

"I've drawn up an agreement along the lines that I talked about," she said.

"The bank robbers come back," I said. "Pulled guns on Johns and tied him up, then turned loose the feller he was holdin'."

"I think the town needs a new marshal," she said. "Why don't you take the job? That's more in your line than running a saloon.

"Besides," she smiled, "you couldn't do any worse than he's done."

"Jack Sears is goin' after them bank robbers tomorrow and I'm going with him," I said.

She eyed me speculatively. "Sign this agreement before you go. Then in case you don't come back you won't leave me empty-handed."

"And here I thought you didn't love me," I said.

"Mr. Tackett," she replied, continuing to look me in the eye, "I am a woman alone in a man's world. If I don't look after myself no one else will. I'm not about to marry some unwashed, sour-smelling cowboy or miner or join the girls on the line or take a job as a waitress or as a clerk in the general store. I am smart and educated and I know how to run a business and I can make enough running this saloon so I don't wind up as an old woman living off the largess of friends or in a county poorhouse somewhere."

I looked at her sheepishly. "You know, I never thought of them things. I guess I been purty selfish, Annie Laurie. Gimme that paper and I'll sign her."

"I've made two copies," she said. "We'll both sign them both and you keep one and I'll keep the other. That way if there's ever any problem or one of us dies we'll both be protected.

"You ought to read it before you sign it, however."

"Annie," I said. "If ya cheat me we'll both be the poorer for it. And if I can't trust ya I don't want to be in business with ya."

She looked away from me, dabbed a finger at the corner of one eye, and said in a small voice, "That's one of the nicest things anyone's ever said to me. And, Del, I won't cheat you and you can trust me."

She stood up and came over to where I was sitting and leaned over and kissed me square on the lips. "You're a very special man, Del," she whispered.

Under my five-day's growth of beard I felt my face grow red and after a minute I finally mumbled, "It ain't nuthin'. Gimme somethin' to write with and I'll sign 'em now."

We went back to the desk and she handed me a pen, which was the wrong thing to do. I hadn't never been to school or had any formal education and I'd never in my life written with an ink pen. She saw my embarrassment and took it from me.

"It's nothing to be ashamed of, Del. Many people out here can't read or write."

"I can do both," I snapped indignantly, and this time it was her turn to be embarrassed.

"I-I-I'm sorry," she said, turning red and looking away.

"But I just learnt in the last year," I confessed, seeing she felt bad about what she'd said. "Thing is, though, I've always writ with a pencil. Never done any pen writin'. Mebbe you could show me how."

Well, after I'd torn a hole a couple of times in the piece of paper she gave me to practice on I finally got the hang of it and signed both the pieces of paper she had prepared.

"I think we had better get these witnessed," she said. "We should have done it when we signed, but it's all right, we can do it now. Ed Alliso and Nate Hale will do it for us."

"Sure thing," Ed Alliso said when we went to his barber shop, and he signed both papers without even looking at them.

"Johns was by. Said a couple of fellers busted his prisoner out of the jail."

"Yep," I said. "Me and Jack Sears are goin' after 'em soon as I take care of some things here."

From Alliso's shop we went to the hotel.

"Is Mr. Hale awake?" Annie Laurie asked the clerk.

"Was earlier but I ain't heard nothing from his room for the last couple of hours," he said. "Why don't ya go knock?"

We went down the hall to the banker's room. His door was slightly ajar and I pushed it open. At first I thought the old man was asleep and then I saw the haft of a knife blade sticking straight up from his chest.

I let out a string of cuss words and behind me Annie Laurie said, "What is it, Del?"

"Somebody's kilt him," I said. "Go get the marshal."

Instead she pushed by me and ran over to the bed, with me right behind her.

He'd been dead for a while, you could see that. What blood there was, and there wasn't much what with the knife still in him, had already congealed and there was a few flies beginning to buzz around. A closer look showed a bump and an abrasion on the side of his head and I quick decided he'd been slugged before he could holler for help and then stabbed.

By now Annie Laurie, who was white as a ghost, had picked up a piece of paper that was lying on Hale's chest, next to the knife. She read aloud what was printed on it in large, block letters:

He stole my ranch. He won't steal nobody elses.
(signed) Cy Fierman.

"He recognized him after all," I said.

"What do you mean?" she asked.

"I visited him last night and he told me he knew Fierman over in Nevada and had foreclosed on a ranch he owned. Said it was a good thing Fierman hadn't recognized him or he'd be a dead man."

I heard a step behind us and turned. It was the room clerk. "Go get the marshal," I ordered. "Hale's been murdered."

His face turned pale but he didn't say anything. He just turned and hustled out.

Annie Laurie turned to me and buried her face in my chest for just a moment but as I started to put my arms around her she backed off and looked up at me with tears trickling down her cheeks.

"Poor Nathan," she said in a tremulous voice. "He was a truly good man. And he was very good to me. I don't know why Fierman had to kill him. It wasn't his fault the bank in Carson City fore-closed on him. He told me the whole story once when we got word Fierman robbed a bank down in Rollinsville. He was president of the bank but his board of directors ordered him to foreclose on Fierman. It wasn't his fault. Fierman should have known that."

"It don't look like he did," I said.

I started nosing around the room looking for something, I didn't know what, and I hadn't found it when Johns came stomping into the room with the clerk right behind him.

"What in the hell goes on here?" he demanded loudly.

"See for yerself, Marshal," I said. "Somebody done killed Nate Hale."

"Got any idea who done it?"

"Well," I said. "That there note might mean somethin'."

He picked it up and read it laboriously.

"Damn," he swore. "Them fellers who busted old Broken Jaw— I never did learn his name—out of jail must of come by here first and stabbed old Nate."

"They didn't come in the front way. I been out there all morning and the only folks to come in was Miss Burns here and Mr. Tackett," the clerk said.

"You got a back door, ain't you?" Johns said.

"Oh, yes, sir," the clerk said, "And we always leave it unlocked. In case of fire, you know."

"Well, let's go take a look," Johns said, and we followed him out of the room and down the hall to the back door. It was wide open, which it hadn't been when I'd left the hotel earlier.

We went outside.

"See here," Johns said, looking around. "Three horses was tied to the hitchrail this morning. You can tell because their droppings are still fresh.

"To hell with the town limits. I'm gonna get a posse together and go after 'em."

"You do that," I said. "And if you get too close them fellers will lie in the weeds and pick off half your men afore you know what's hit you, Best thing fer you to do is take care of things here—you and Annie—and let me and Jack Sears see if we can track 'em to their hideout. If we can then you can put together a posse."

"That makes sense," he said. "You a purty good tracker?"

"I can track a snake across a bare rock," I lied. "I don't think Fierman'll be any trouble."

"In the meantime you need to get yer townspeople together and try to figure out what to do about the bank. Ranchers and townfolk who do business with it are gonna be askin' questions. And I guess yer gonna have to elect a new mayor now that Nate's dead."

"He's right, Wayne," Annie Laurie said. "There's a lot to be done. We need to tell Twain Sawyer down at the bank that Nate's dead and he's going to have to hold the fort until we find out just what the situation is. Then we're going to have to arrange for Nate's burial and, finally, we're down to three councilmen what with him dead and Obie Shrifft gone."

"Old Obie a councilman?" I said wonderingly. "Dang! Now I am sorry I took his saloon away from him."

"It wasn't your fault," Annie Laurie said. "Obie should have known better. But that's behind us now. We're going to have to call a town meeting and see about electing two more councilmen.

"Wayne, why don't you round up Mr. Smith and Mr. Jones and Mr. Wislon. Ask them to come to the Staghorn. Let's see"—she pulled out a gold locket that hung from a chain and had been hidden in her bosom and opened it and lo, it was a tiny watch—"it's almost noon. Ask them to come at one o'clock."

She dropped the locket back in its hiding place.

"Huckleberry," she said to the clerk, "you go find Ed Alliso and tell him we need to make arrangements to bury Nate. Del, you and I need to get over to the bank. Twain Sawyer, who's the cashier and who's been running the bank since Nate was shot, needs to know."

She tugged at my sleeve and I followed her out the door, marveling at the way she had taken charge. Too bad she's a woman, I thought. If she was mayor she could make something of this two-bit town.

CHAPTER 10

"**Y**ER QUITE A woman, Annie Laurie Burns," I said as we headed for the bank, me walking where I was supposed to, next to the street.

She knew what I meant and laughed self-consciously. "Not really," she said. "There just wasn't anyone else to say what needed to be done. I'm sure you've noticed, Wayne Johns is a well-meaning man and he tries hard but he's a couple of cards short of a full deck.

"And, Del, as I said a little while ago, you're a very special man, but you're pretty much a stranger in town. So, since there was no one else I did what had to be done. We couldn't count on Wayne Johns or young Huckleberry Faine to do anything. This way the good old boys on the town council won't be sure who called the meeting so they will meet somewhere, if not at the Staghorn, early this afternoon, and they'll probably set a date for a town election to pick two more councilmen. In the meantime they can appoint two to serve until the election and then the five of them will elect a mayor from among them.

"We're really going to miss Nate Hale. He was working to build this town and I'm not sure there's anyone else capable of it."

I didn't say anything to that but I thought, yes, there is, if the town fathers are only smart enough to know it.

Almost as an afterthought she continued, "And I especially will miss him. He'd become almost like a father to me."

By then we'd reached the bank and I pushed open the door and followed Annie Laurie inside. A man who I took to be Twain Sawyer was in the teller's cage taking care of two of the local matrons. Like so many Western women their faces were weathered and lined from the sun. Both wore bonnets and were dressed plainly but neatly. They were, I figured, the wives of two of the town's businessmen.

We waited patiently until the ladies finished their business and left, then Annie Laurie said, "Twain, I think you should close for the day."

He started to argue but then clamped his thin lips shut and went over and locked the big oaken door after hanging a sign on the outer door knob that said CLOSED.

He taken a look at our faces and said, "It's Nate, isn't it? Something's happened to him."

Annie Laurie nodded. "He's dead. Cy Fierman killed him— stabbed him—and broke his man out of jail. We came to tell you and to find out if you knew what arrangements Nate had made in case of his death."

Twain Sawyer pursed his thin lips and spoke with a nasal twang that sounded like it was right out of the boot heel of Missouri.

"Miss Burns, I just don't know. Nate was mighty close-mouthed about that. He's got a small safe in his office and I imagine that's where he keeps—kept—his personal papers. Only trouble is, I don't know the combination. There's another, bigger safe in his office where he keeps his business papers and the money that we need on a daily basis. We were lucky, we only had about a thousand dollars on hand when they robbed us."

I looked at him. He was a scrawny man, about fifty, I guessed, with thin, gray hair, a thin face with small, watery eyes surrounded by wire-rimmed spectacles, and a pinched mouth. He was wearing a worn brown suit and a tie that had seen cleaner days.

"Where were you during the robbery, Mr. Sawyer?" I asked.

"Down on the floor on my face, just like they said to do."

Well, I couldn't argue with that. I looked at Annie Laurie.

"See if you can find the combination to that safe," I said. "He's got to have it around somewhere, less'n he keeps it at his house. Afore we're done we may have to go through it, too. We need to find out who his kin are, if he has any."

She looked thoughtfully at the two of us, then spoke suddenly as if she'd made a decision.

"Twain," she said, "I don't think you should look for that combination yet. Mr. Tackett and I have a lot to do in the next few hours and if you should find the combination when nobody is here some folks might think you opened the safe and took something. You don't need that. None of us do. Why don't you come with us and then later several of us can look for the combination and be here when you open the safe."

Pretty smart, I thought. I wouldn't have thought of that. You're pretty dumb, Tackett.

Sawyer looked at her indignantly. "Miss Burns, I am an honest man. Nobody has ever questioned my integrity."

She smiled sweetly at him. "And we wouldn't want them to start now, would we?"

Twain Sawyer shrugged his thin shoulders. "Maybe you're right. I'll go with you."

The three of us walked back to the hotel. By this time Ed Alliso was in the room with Nate Hale's body and two other men were standing outside the door. Annie Laurie introduced them as Anthony Jones and Smedley Smith, two of the three remaining councilmen. "Mr. Jones," she said, "is the owner of our general store."

Smith, she said, was, appropriately, the town blacksmith, but I had already figured that out from the work clothes he wore.

Whilst we were talking about how terrible it was that Cy Fierman had murdered Nate Hale whilst he lay helpless in his bed, a skinny dark-haired man about forty hurried up. He was wearing bib overalls and smelled of horses.

"My God, what's going on in this town?" he burst out before

anyone could say anything. "First Obie Shrifft has his saloon stolen from him, then the bank is robbed, and now Nate Hale is murdered. What'll happen next?"

He found out real soon. I reached out and taken him by the front of his overalls. "Mister," I said, "nobody stole Obie Shrifft's saloon from him. Now, did they?"

I had pulled him up real close to me and was staring him in the eyes from about six inches away. He could see he had riled me a bit.

"Oh, no sir! No sir! I apologize. You won it fair and square, Mr. Sackett."

I shoved him away. "Apology accepted," I said. "And one more thing, the same is Tackett with a T. Don't make that mistake again."

"Yes sir," he said. "Yes sir."

"Del," Annie Laurie said, looking like she was trying to keep from laughing. "This is Ferd Wislon, the other councilman. Mr. Wislon owns the livery stable. I'm sure he meant no offense."

I stuck my hand out. "Glad to meet you, Mr. Wislon. Sorry I lost my temper there for a minute."

He shook my hand perfunctorily, then turned away to talk to the other two councilmen.

Just then Alliso came out of the room and began talking to no one in particular.

"This kind of weather, we probably ought to bury him tomorrow. I always keep a coffin in the back of the shop for this kind of emergency so that won't be no problem. Gonna need a suit to bury him in, though. I had to cut the other one off when he got shot. Made him madder'n hell. Remember, Annie?"

"I remember," she said unsmilingly. "Del, if you will ride out with me to Nate's place I'm sure we can find an appropriate suit. Mr. Wislon, could I ask you to hitch Mouse to my trap?"

"Sure thing, Miss Burns," Wislon said, hurrying off.

"Mouse?" I said. "Hitch Mouse to your trap?"

She laughed. "She's small and gray. So I named her Mouse."

"She eat cheese?"

She shook her head and turned to Twain Sawyer who had been standing silently to one side. "It might be helpful if you would come along, Twain," she said.

He shook his head. "This has been a rather difficult day for me, Miss Burns. Besides I have a number of things to take care of with Nate gone, so if you don't mind I will stay here."

She opened her mouth as if to argue but changed her mind. "Suit yourself," she said. "Del, we had best be going."

Nathan Hale's house was about two miles south of town. It was a one-story, rambling building and at one time had been headquarters for a large ranch. But Hale, Annie told me, had sold off most of his land and all but a few of his cattle. He had a hired couple on the place to keep house and do the cooking as well as look out for the horses and a few chickens and farm animals that he kept mainly for food.

Their names were Billy Jeff and Hallie Hope Linton and, Annie told me, Nate Hale had told her that they were first cousins. They'd had two children during the time they worked for Hale but both were stillborn.

Annie Laurie shook her head as she told me. "Folks that closely related shouldn't get married," she said sadly. "It's just not right. They're probably lucky the children didn't live. They could have been idiots."

"Seem to me they'd of had idiots fer parents," I said.

We picked up the trap and Mouse at the stable and I drove us on out to Hale's place.

Hallie Hope Linton came to the door as we trotted up to the front of the house. I climbed down and tied Mouse to the hitching rail and we went up the steps to the big front porch. Hallie Hope was a pretty, plump young woman with a placid face and big dull doe eyes.

"Howdy, Miz Burns," she said to Annie Laurie. "You bringin'

word from Mr. Hale? When you go back you tell him to come home. We all air lonesome here 'thout him."

"He's not coming home, Hallie Hope," Annie Laurie said softly. "Someone killed him in his bed."

Hallie Hope's round face crumpled and she burst into tears. "Oh, Lordy," she said between sobs. "Lordy, Lordy. Who would ever do a thang like that. Oh, Lordy, what we ever gone do now?"

Annie Laurie reached out and took her hand It was a different-looking hand and it took me a minute to figure out why. She had an extra little finger. I looked at the other hand. Same thing. Annie Laurie didn't seem to notice.

"Don't cry, Hallie Hope," she said gently. "Everything will work out all right. You'll see.

"Now, we need to go in and find one of Mr. Hale's suits. The one he was wearing when he was shot was ruined. And we need something nice to bury him in."

"Bury him. Oh, Lordy, Lordy. Po' Mr. Hale," Hallie Hope wailed.

"Now you hush, Hallie Hope," Annie Laurie admonished sternly. "You take me inside and together we'll pick out a fine suit for Mr. Hale."

"He love his suits, Miz Burns. He be happy ifn he was buried in one of his good uns," Hallie Hope said.

A long-geared man with sandy hair, buck teeth, and his left eye cocked to the outside came up at a trot.

"You all right, Hallie Hope? I heered you a-hollerin."

Hallie Hope puddled up again. "It's Mr. Hale, Billy Jeff. Someone done kilt him."

"What's that, you say? Someone done kilt Mr. Hale?"

Hallie Hope nodded silently.

Tears formed at the corners of Billy Jeff's eyes. He brushed them away with fists he made of his big, horny hands.

"Lordy, Lordy," he moaned. "Mr. Hale's been kilt. What we ever gone do now, Hallie Hope?"

Annie Laurie had had it. "Now you two settle down," she snapped. "We'll work things out. In the meantime, Billy Jeff, the two of you have to keep on taking care of this place. If you need anything you go see Mr. Jones at the general store. He'll give you what you need, I'll see to that. All you'll have to do is sign for it.

"Can either of you read or write?"

They both shook their heads glumly. Annie Laurie sighed. "All right, then, if you need something come see me at the Staghorn and I'll talk to Mr. Jones for you."

She took Hallie Hope by the arm and led her into the house.

I found a bench next to the wall of the house and sat down. Billy Jeff leaned against a porch post and sucked on a straw. "We gone miss Mr. Hale," he said after a moment. "Gone miss seein' Miss Burns, too."

"She come 'round here a lot?" I asked idly.

"Yessir. Her and Mister Burns was good friends."

"Good friends," he said, but I couldn't read anything into the way he said it. "Good friends" seemed to be all he meant, or at least all he knew.

"Mr. Hale got any kinfolk?" I asked.

He shrugged. "Ain't been none around."

Annie Laurie came out just then, carrying a black broadcloth suit and a white shirt. "We'd best be getting back," she said.

"I could fix you-uns some vittles," Hallie Hope offered.

"Not this time, Hallie Hope," Annie Laurie said.

I helped her into the trap, unhitched Mouse, said "giddyap," and we taken off for Shalak Springs.

"Billy Jeff says you spent a lot of time out there," I said as Mouse trotted down the road.

"It's not what you might be thinking," she replied resentfully. "Nate Hale was a fine old man and when I came to town he kind of took me under his wing. I used to go out there on Sundays and we'd talk, that's all. He taught me a lot about banking and business. Even though he was an important man in town he never had any close friends that I know of. Except for me, of course. And I think that toward the end he might have thought of me as the daughter he never had."

"He never had no family?"

"He was married a long time ago but his wife couldn't stand the West so she picked up her two children and went back East. He never heard from her or the children again. He didn't like to talk about it. He said it made him want to cry."

"That old man didn't look like the cryin' kind to me."

"He wasn't. But sometimes when a man gets in a woman's company he'll relax a little. I guess that's what happened when he and I were together."

"You didn't take a look for the combination to his safe whilst you were gettin' his clothes, did ya?" I asked.

She looked at me kind of peculiarlike. "I didn't have to," she said. "I have it. And Ferd Wislon has it. Ferd doesn't look like much but Nate said he is a shrewd businessman—has the first dollar he ever made, Nate said—and is absolutely honest."

"Well I'll be danged," I said. "How come you never said nothin' before?"

"I didn't want to say anything in front of Twain Sawyer. He's a sneaky little man and I don't trust him. Then, after we left him I just forgot."

She reached over and put her hand on top of mine. "I would have told you."

"It don't matter none," I said. "He ain't got nothing that I'd be interested in."

"I don't think Ferd knows I have the combination and if that's true I think it would be better if he's the one who opens the safe."

"It don't matter none to me," I repeated. "Jack Sears and me'll be headin' out tomorrow, anyway. See if we can locate Fierman's hideout. We do and we'll come back and Johns can put together his posse."

Out of the corner of my eye I saw her fetch that little locket watch from its snug resting place. "It's nearly one o'clock," she said. "We need to hurry to get back. The councilmen will be meeting at the Staghorn if they do what I suggested."

"That's a cute little watch." I said. "Your mother's?"

"I never knew my mother," she said. "My hus—a friend gave it to me."

I flicked the whip lightly at Mouse's flank. "Giddyap, horse," I said, as a bee whizzed by my head.

But it wasn't no bee. A fraction of a second later the sound of a shot echoed from a clump of rocks ahead and to the right. A quick glance showed me Annie Laurie was all right. I swung Mouse hard to the left, lashed her with the whip and hollered, "Hi! Giddyup there!"

The trap bounced off the road and across the range land with Mouse running all out. The right wheel hit a rock and the trap bounced high in the air. When it came down Annie Laurie landed sideways and flipped backward off the trap. All I seen was skirt and petticoat and legs as she tumbled off. I hauled on the reins, swung the trap around, leaped to the ground and went running back to where she lay.

She didn't seem bad hurt because already she was starting to sit up. "Down!" I hollered. "Get down!"

Just then another shot kicked up dirt in front of me and I hit the ground in a long dive that brought me almost on top of Annie Laurie who lay sprawled behind the wide, low rock the trap had hit when it threw her off.

A third bullet whined off the rock as the two of us flattened ourselves out behind it.

"You all right?" I gasped.

"I think so," she replied. "Nothing seems to be broken."

Lifting my head I looked around. Aside from our little rock there wasn't any cover at all.

"Looks like he's got us pinned down," I said. "Lucky for us

there ain't no way he can get closer without showin' hisself."

"But we've got to get to that meeting," she said. "There must be a way."

"You go," I said drily. "I'll stay here."

CHAPTER 11

WE HADN'T LAIN behind that low rock for but a few minutes when my ground side ear caught the vibrations of a fast-moving horse coming from the direction of Nate Hale's place. In another moment I could hear it plain. I squirmed to where I could look around the rock and saw it was Billy Jeff Linton, who I'd heard of, riding a big red gelding.

When he saw Mouse and the trap he reined the big horse over toward them and as he drew near he spotted me and Annie Laurie.

"You-uns all right?" he called as he changed directions again and came riding toward us.

Since nobody was shooting at him I sat up and Annie Laurie did the same and introduced us.

"We're fine, Billy Jeff," I said, getting up and brushing the dust from my shirt and jeans.

"Hccrd some shootin'," Billy Jeff said, "and thought ya might be in trouble so I come a-runnin."

"That was mighty good thinkin', Billy Jeff," I said. "Somebody took a couple of shots at us, but I think you scared off whoever it was."

"You want I should go after him, Mr. Tackett?"

"He's long gone, Billy Jeff."

"Yes suh, Mr. Tackett," Billy Jeff said. Dismounting he walked over to Mouse and led her over to us. Annie Laurie, pale and dirty with her hair mussed and blowing in the slight breeze, went over to the trap and Billy Jeff assisted her aboard. I went around to the other side and taken up the reins.

Annie Laurie turned to him and said, "That was mighty brave of you to come to our rescue that way, Billy Jeff."

"Twarn't nuthin', Miz Burns," he replied obviously pleased and somehow managing to focus both eyes on hers.

He stood there straight and slim and I noticed then that he had a gun slung low on his right thigh and tied down. Another look showed me a Winchester rifle in a boot on his saddle and suddenly, just like what had happened with Chief Two Horse a few days back, he didn't look like a country bumpkin any more, but instead looked like a first-class fighting man.

"You ever use that pistol, Billy Jeff?" I asked.

He ducked his head and kind of scuffled his boots. "Time or two down in Arkansas," he said. "Me and Hallie Hope come up here to get away from all that feudin' and fightin', though. I ain't never used it up here."

"I might need to call on ya, sometime," I said.

"You or Miz Burns call and I'll come a-runnin', you kin be sure of that." He swung aboard the big red horse, gave us a wave of his hand, and headed off at a gallop toward the Hale place.

I headed Mouse back to the road and in a minute she was trotting at her usual pace back toward Shalak Springs. I had a notion to swing around the rocks where the shots had come from but decided there wasn't anything there that couldn't wait.

Back in town I dropped Annie Laurie at the Staghorn, saw her safe inside, and headed off to the livery stable. I gave the red-haired boy on duty a quarter to unhitch Mouse and rub her down and put the trap under cover in a leanto built out from the stable.

On a hunch I walked into the stable and down its length, touching every horse. None appeared to have been ridden recently. I went out and asked the boy, "Anyone taken a horse out of here today?"

He shook his head. "Just you-uns."

On a hunch I got my saddle and put it on the roan that had belonged to the outlaw I had shot back at the base of the mesa and headed north out of town away from Hale's place. At the edge of town I spotted a horse pulling a light buckboard trotting toward me. To my surprise the driver was Twain Sawyer, still dressed in his suit and tie and wearing a narrow brimmed hat like you see Easterners wear from time to time. On the seat next to him was a Winchester repeating rifle.

I pulled up and waited for him. "Howdy, Twain," I said. "What brings you out here?"

"Don't know as how that's any of your affair, Mr. Tackett," he replied testily. "I had business out here and I came to take care of it."

"Shootin' business?" I asked casual-like.

"I don't know what you're talking about. Now let me by," he snapped nastily.

I pulled the roan to one side and Sawyer flicked his whip at his horse's flank and trotted off to town.

You don't suppose, I mused as I watched him go. Nah, not that little pipsqueak. Besides, wouldn't be no reason for him to take a shot at me. Or maybe he was shootin' at Annie Laurie. No, that didn't make sense either. Probably, just like he said, he was out seeing someone on business. Maybe to tell one of the big ranchers who did business with the bank that Hale was dead.

I went on a little farther but didn't see any hoofprints except those of Sawyer's horse. It didn't look after all like what I'd thought might be the case, that the person who'd shot at us had circled around and come in from the other end of town. Of course he could still be out there, waiting until later to come in, but I doubted it.

As long as I was out this way I debated about going on farther and dropping in on Chief Two Horse but before I made up my mind I spotted a horseman coming in from the direction of Two

Horse's place. It was the chief hisself, riding Old Dan. When he drew close he held up his right hand and said, "How."

Here we go again, I thought.

"Wisht I knew," I said. "How what?"

"Injun always say 'How'," he said.

But he didn't look much like an Indian again today. He was dressed much the way he had been that day at the stone cabin, with a gun slung low on his right thigh and a rifle jammed in a boot up toward his horse's neck.

"You on the warpath, Chief?" I asked.

He shook his head. "Not really. But there's some funny things going on. Nate Hale being killed and all. Things just don't feel right and I figured it could be that you and Miss Burns might need some help."

"Never can tell," I said noncommittally.

Despite what he said it seemed strange to me that Two Horse would be coming back to town so soon after finishing his clean-up work at the Staghorn. Could he have been the gunman who shot at me and Annie Laurie and then circled around to pretend he was coming from his place? I couldn't say. However, this was the second time he had showed up at an odd time in an odd place. Coincidence, maybe. Anyway it didn't seem to make sense to say anything about my suspicions, so I didn't. I taken a look at the sun and saw that it was well past noon.

"There's a meetin' at the Staghorn," I said. "Annie Laurie and some of the town fathers. Me bein' the owner of the Staghorn I oughta be there, too. You could help me ifn you could find Jack Sears and the two of ya meet me there."

We touched spurs to our horses and galloped back into town. We pulled up at the Staghorn and I dismounted, tied the roan to the hitching post, and went inside. Instead of dismounting the chief reined Old Dan around and headed for the hotel.

The Staghorn was cool and dark and I stopped for a moment to let my eyes adjust. There was a scattering of customers standing at the bar but no sign of Annie Laurie or the remaining councilmen. Gil Dellah spotted me and jerked a thumb toward the stairs. I took them two at a time and at the top I heard the sound of voices coming from my apartment.

I went in and there were half a dozen people sitting around the room or leaning against the wall. Annie Laurie was sitting in my desk chair which she had swiveled around to face the room. I recognized the three councilmen I had met earlier in the day, Wislon, Jones, and Smith as well as Ed Alliso, the town barber/doctor/dentist/undertaker.

The sixth person kind of looked like pictures I'd seen of old Abe Lincoln afore he growed his beard. Annie Laurie introduced him to me quickly as Gus Simpson, the owner of the hotel, a hay and feed store, and a combination cattle ranch and farm west of Shalak Springs. His real name, I learned later, was Grant Ulysses Simpson and even though he was dressed like a working rancher he was the richest man in town and the most important, especially now that Nate Hale was dead.

He grew most of the hay and feed he sold. He had a big smokehouse on his place where he made hams, sausage, and bacon, and beef and venison jerky. He also supplied eggs to the Shalak Springs restaurant and to Jones' general store. He'd recently planted an apple orchard and on top of all this he was running about five thousand head of cattle up against the mountains.

Between the farm operation and the ranch he hired about forty men, and most of them spent a lot of their free time in the Staghorn. Shalak Springs wouldn't have been much of a town without Gus Simpson. Fact is, it wasn't much of a town with him.

He'd been speaking when I came in and after he'd said he was glad to meet me he continued where he'd left off. It didn't take me long to figure that Shalak Springs was pretty much his town, which I hadn't known before because he'd just returned from a month-long trip to St. Louis.

95

"Gentlemen and lady," he orated. "As I was saying, we're here to pick two new councilmen, but, frankly, we have something to do that is even more important. We have to catch the men who robbed the bank and murdered poor Nathan Hale. Clearly, Marshal Johns is not the man for the job. Therefore as soon as we select our new councilmen I propose that the council take action to hire a man to run down Cy Fierman and bring him back dead or alive. As an incentive I will put up a $500 reward for his capture and I urge the council to put up a like amount."

He turned to me. "Mr. Sackett, it seems to me you might be the ideal man to track down and kill Cy Fierman. Are you available?"

I felt my face growing red but before I could answer Annie Laurie spoke up. "Mr. Simpson, this is Del Tackett, not Sackett. He is the new owner of the Staghorn. We are meeting in his quarters. He was with me when we found Nate's body."

"Well, welcome to Shalak Springs, Mr. Tackett," Simpson said. "Sorry about confusing you with the Sacketts. You're big enough and look tough enough to be one."

"Well, I ain't," I said shortly.

He didn't back off an inch. "Well, then, are you here because you're interested in a seat on the town council?"

"I ain't at all interested, Mr. Simpson," I said. "But I will tell you this, if the people of this town want a can-do councilman you all ought to ask Annie Laurie here to take the job."

I looked around the room and all I saw was shaking heads and stony faces, except for Annie Laurie who looked both pleased and embarrassed.

"Councilman is no job for a woman," Simpson grunted.

"Seems to me a councilman's a job fer anyone what can do it," I said. "It don't take muscle, it takes brains and when it comes to brains Annie'll run rings around most of the men in this room."

"Mr. Tackett," Councilman Jones spoke up, "we appreciate your interest but you are new in Shalak Springs. Otherwise you would know that the job of picking successors to Nate Hale and Obie Shrifft belongs to the remaining members of the council. We welcome advice from all citizens but Mr. Smith, Mr. Wislon, and I will make the final decision."

And Gus Simpson, I said to myself, who'll tell all three of you how to vote.

Aloud I said, "Well I got my two cents' worth in and it was worth about that. Annie, I'll be downstairs. When yer through here I need to talk to ya."

I walked into the barroom just as Chief Two Horse and Jack Sears pushed their way through the batwing doors. I motioned them over to a corner table and called to Gil Dellah to bring over three beers.

"There's a meetin' goin' on upstairs to pick a couple of new town councilmen," I said. "I told 'em they oughta pick Annie Laurie but—."

"Ain't no job fer a woman," Sears interrupted.

"That's what some feller named Gus Simpson said," I said. "But I'll tell ya somethin', Jack. I'd want you on my side in a fight but I'd pick Annie over you any day if I needed someone with good sense and brains."

"You and me are gonna have that fight I been promisin' you yet," Sears said, only half kidding.

"White men fight, red man referee," Two Horse said.

"We ain't gonna fight, Chief," I said. "Jack and me are goin' out and see if we can track down Cy Fierman. Matter of fact that feller Simpson is a big gun around here and he's put a $500 bounty on Fierman's head, dead or alive, and asked the council to match him."

"I ain't no bounty hunter," Sears said, "but since we're goin' after him anyway it wouldn't do no harm to take the money."

"That's kinda the way I feel," I said. "But, Jack, there's somethin' fishy's goin' on in this town. It don't make sense to me that Fierman would've snuck in and kilt Hale that way. He's a lot of things but nobody ever said he was a sneak killer.

"Besides, how would he know Hale was at the hotel instead of at home? Like I say, it don't make sense.

"And then me and Annie gettin' shot at that way. That don't make sense neither. You can bet Fierman wasn't waitin' around to try to knock one of us off. If it'd been him he wouldn't of missed. And, besides, who around here would wanta kill either one of us? If Obie Shrifft was still around it could of been him, but he's long gone."

None of us said anything for a minute and then I heard boots clumping down the stairs. The meeting in my apartment had broken up. They all headed for the door except Simpson who spotted me and came over to where we were sitting.

"Tackett," he said, "or whatever your name is, from what Alliso said upstairs you're a real ring-tailed terror. That bein' the case, I want to hire you to go after Fierman. I'll pay you $1,000 if you bring him back dead. That's on top of the reward I've already put up."

"Really hate him, don't ya?" I said.

"Nate Hale was my friend and Cy Fierman killed him in cold blood. I want him dead."

I jerked a thumb at Jack Sears. "This here is Jack Sears. He wants him dead, too. Mebbe you ought to talk to him."

Jack shook his head. "I'm a lot o' things but I ain't a cold-blooded killer, not fer any of ycr money. I aim to go after him fer what he done to me and if I kill him then so be it. But I won't do it fer yer money."

"I don't care how or why you do it, just bring me his body and I'll pay you," Simpson said and strode off.

"Injun go too. Bring um back Fierman scalp," Chief Two Horse said to Simpson's retreating back.

"You been around this country fer a while, Chief," I said. "You got any idea where Fierman might of gone?"

"That's rugged country in the mountains on the other side of the mesa. A lot of canyons, a lot of forest. Some of those mountains back there are over 14,000 feet high. They could be anywhere up there. All you can do is go up that way and see if you can cut their trail."

"That Simpson feller sure was eager to have him dead," Sears said. "You gonna be ready to go tomorrow, Del?"

"I think so," I said. "But I got to talk to Annie Laurie first. And Chief, I'd appreciate it if you'd stay in town whilst we're gone and kind of keep a eye out fer her. Things just don't feel right around here."

"You no-um worry. Noble red man take good care of pale face squaw," Two Horse said.

"What kind of a crazy Injun are you, anyway?" Sears said, looking at him funny-like.

"Me Mohican Indian," Two Horse said. "Me last of Mohicans."

"Thanks, Chief," I said. "That's a load off my mind. I won't ferget."

CHAPTER 12

I WENT BACK upstairs looking for Annie Laurie. She was still sitting in the big swivel chair and I could see she'd been crying. She looked up when she heard me.

"Oh," she said. "I wasn't expecting anyone. And I certainly didn't mean for you to see me crying."

"I didn't think you was the cryin' type," I said.

"I'm not. It's just that I'm so angry. Those backwoods hicks who run this town saying I shouldn't be a town councilman just because I'm a woman.

"You were right, Del. I can run rings around those men either as a councilman or a businessman or businesswoman or whatever. I could give them aces and spades and still beat them. And I may just take it in my mind to prove it."

"Give 'em hell, Annie Laurie," I said. "I like where yer comin' from. In fact, I mebbe'll hang around and help ya. That is, if ya want my help."

"I thought you were leaving," she said. "Isn't there a girl down in Nora waiting for you?"

"Jack Sears told me she got tired of waitin'. She's gone East and he don't know if she's ever comin' back."

"I'd have thought if she really loved you she'd have waited."

I shrugged. "Jack says there was a rumor I'd been kilt. I guess she figured that was the gospel."

"I want your help if you stay," she said. "But if you stay that doesn't change our deal. I run the Staghorn for the next two years and then it's mine."

I laughed. "I gave ya my word and besides that I signed yer paper. That oughta be good enough fer ya."

"It is. I'm sorry I said anything. It's just that, like I said, a woman alone in a man's world can't afford to take chances."

"You ain't takin' none with me, Annie Laurie," I said. "And I don't think I'm takin' any with you."

She looked me square in the eye. "Believe me, Del, you're not."

She changed the subject abruptly. "Are you and Mr. Sears really going after Cy Fierman?"

"Jack blames him fer the death of his wife. He swears he's gonna run him down if it takes the rest of his life. And, well, Jack's my friend. He saved my life a couple of times and I got to stick with him."

"Yes, of course," she said with just a tinge of sarcasm in her voice. "And how do you intend to go about finding Mr. Fierman?"

"Well, we got a startin' point," I said. "Remember, I told ya I stumbled across their tracks after they robbed the bank and trailed 'em to a mesa that juts out from the mountains over beyond Chief Two Horse's shack a few miles. Well, we'll start from there. I think their hideout is in the mountains on the other side of the mesa. If it is we'll find 'em."

"Or they'll find you. Del, please be careful. That's a ruthless man you're chasing. And you and Jack will be outnumbered. Please, I don't want you to be killed."

The look she gave me made me squirm inside. Like I've said, she was quite a woman, but she wasn't the woman for me. Not even if Esme Rankin was gone for good.

I changed the subject. "Remember that stone cabin I told you I stumbled across. Well, I found this note inside on the table. It was all covered with dust. Must of been sitting there for a year or two."

I fished the note out of my shirt pocket and handed it to her.

She read it and handed it back to me without saying anything.

"I wonder what happened to her husband?" I said. "Don't seem right he'd just go off and leave her."

"No, it doesn't," she said.

"Seems like she waited for him a long time."

"Maybe she didn't know what else to do."

"That's probably it," I said. "But how do ya suppose she got by?"

She shrugged. "She could do it if she had a store of staples like flour and sugar and coffee. Butcher a steer once in a while. The ranchers wouldn't know the difference. Shoot a deer. Plant a garden. There's some little towns and trading posts scattered through the mountains. She could get things she needed there if she had any money. She could have come here, as far as that goes."

"I don't think she did," I said. "At least not for a while."

"It doesn't matter," she said. "A person alone could make it out there for a year or so, as long as Indians or outlaws didn't bother her."

"Come to think of it I saw signs of an old kitchen garden," I said. "But I didn't get a chance to look around real good before Chief Two Horse showed up and we come back to town. Tomorrow when Jack and me go back to the mesa maybe we'll swing by the cabin again, see if there's somethin' there I missed. Whilst we're gone I've asked Two Horse to stay in town and kind of keep an eye on things for ya. Help ya if ya need any help."

"That's thoughtful of you, Del," she said. "But I'll be all right. The people in this town know me. Nobody's going to bother me or give me any trouble."

"I hope not," I said. "I hope not." But still, while I didn't say anything more, I worried about Gus Simpson now that Nate Hale was gone and I didn't trust that sneaky little Twain Sawyer.

103

"Well, anyway, the chief'll be here if ya need him," I said again, getting up. "I got a few things to do now, afore I go."

"There's one thing you could do for me first," she said. "I'm supposed to meet Mr. Wislon and Twain Sawyer at the bank in a few minutes to go over Nate's papers and see if we can find the combination to his safe. I don't want anyone to know I have it unless I have to. Would you come with me, please? I'd feel better if you would."

"Be my pleasure, ma'am," I said.

When we got there the door to the bank was unlocked and we went on in and back to Nate Hale's office. That door was open and we could seen Ferd Wislon and Twain Sawyer standing inside looking at something. As we entered I could see what it was. It was Nate Hale's private safe and the door to it was wide open. There were a few papers scattered around the floor but if there had been any money in it there wasn't now.

"Looks like somebody knowed the combination," I said. "How about it Sawyer? Was it you?"

He drew himself up to his full five feet seven and puffed out his scrawny chest. "Mr. Sackett, I told you and Miss Burns I did not— do not—know the combination. In fact, Miss Burns, you were very close to him. I'm surprised you did not know the combination."

He emphasized the "very close" and there was kind of a nasty tone to his voice when he said it.

Annie Laurie's face flushed red. I saw it and took a step toward Sawyer who kind of shrank back. "You tryin' to say somethin', Sawyer?" I asked softly, trying hard not to put my hands on him.

"No," he squeaked. "Nothing at all."

"Gentlemen! Gentlemen!" Ferd Wislon interrupted. "Enough bickering. Mr. Tackett, if you're going to stay in this town you're going to have to learn to keep your hands off of people. But we'll talk about that later. In the meantime we have a problem here. Someone has robbed the safe. Clearly somebody in this town knows the combination. Right now it's important that we look at what wasn't taken, since we don't know what was."

"You folks look," I said. "I'll get the marshal. Not that he can do anything, but he's the law so I guess we oughta notify him."

I spent the next half hour looking for Wayne Johns and finally found him down at the livery stable. When I asked the boy if he'd seen him he jerked a thumb inside and when I went looking I found him napping on a saddle blanket tossed across a bed of hay. He stopped snoring when I nudged him with a boot and he sat up, shaking his head groggily.

"Sorry to disturb you, Marshal," I said. "But someone busted into Nate Hale's safe and the folks there think you oughta take a look."

Johns let out a string of curses. Finally he said, "Damn it to hell, Tackett. This was a peaceful town until you got here. Since then there's been nothin' but trouble. You must be a damn Jonah."

"There's somethin' fishy goin' on here all right, but don't go blamin' it on to me, Johns," I said. "It weren't me robbed the bank or kilt Nate Hale or slugged you on the head."

"I know it," he said as we tromped toward the bank. "I didn't mean nothin' but this job is gettin' me down. I was hired to keep order, not to figure out murders or chase bank robbers."

"Find out anything?" I asked Wislon when we walked into Hale's office.

He shook his head. "Either there wasn't much there or the thief took everything of importance. Only thing he left was a few receipts and some stock certificates that may or may not be worth anything.

"There was nothin' to tell us who his heirs are, if any. Or anything about kinfolk. In fact there was nothing personal at all. If there was anything, either the thief got it or it's out at his place."

"If it's out there it's safe," I said. "If I was the thief I wouldn't want to go up against Billy Jeff Linton. That there is a real fightin' man, even if he is cockeyed."

"It's a little late to be going out there tonight. Perhaps we could all go out tomorrow," Wislon suggested.

"Not me," I said. "Tomorrow me and Jack Sears are goin' Fierman huntin'."

"Well, the rest of us then," Wislon said. "You, Miss Burns and Mr. Sawyer and you, too, Johns. It would be good to have an officer of the law along. Suppose we meet at the Staghorn at nine in the morning."

"Me and Jack'll be long gone by then," I said to Annie Laurie as we left the office.

"Who do you suppose broke into the safe?" she asked as we walked to the Staghorn.

"Somebody who knew Nate well enough to have the combination but not well enough to know what was in it."

"Del," she said as we pushed through the bat wing doors into the saloon, "come upstairs. I need to talk to you."

She led the way into my apartment and I slouched into the big old leather easy chair and she took the swivel chair.

She didn't beat around the bush. "I know what was in that safe, Del. Nothing."

"What d'ya mean nothin'?"

"Oh, there may have been a few dollars in there. And maybe some papers where he loaned money personally instead of through the bank. But that's all. Anything else is out at his house in a wall safe. He showed it to me one day and made me memorize the combination."

"How come you didn't say nothin' at the bank?"

"Because I don't know who to trust—except for you. I think I can trust Ferd Wislon; Nate did. But I don't know how far. And I don't trust Twain Sawyer, even though he's probably an honest man.

"I wish you could stay at least another day. I'd feel better if you were there when we open the safe."

"What's in it, Annie Laurie, that's so danged important?"

"A will, for one thing. And I think it leaves everything to his children if they can be located. If they can't be then I don't know what the next step is.

"But it's not just that. We're burying Nate tomorrow and I just think you ought to be here."

"I don't know," I said. "I'll talk to Jack. If he'll agree to wait a day I'll stay."

I found Sears down in the saloon, gossiping with Gil Dellah.

Dellah was saying, "...ain't a bad man. Sure ain't the kind to kill that old man in his bed."

"He killed my wife, sweetest woman what ever lived. And that's good enough fer me."

"That were a accident, Jack. You got to know that. He didn't try to run her down. She kind of stepped out in front of his horse."

"How would you know that?" Sears growled. "You wasn't there."

I jumped in. "Yeah, Gil. Just how do you know?"

"Story's around," Dellah mumbled, busily wiping off the bar and not looking up. "Yeah. That's it. Feller driftin' through here t'other night, heerd you was in town and talked about it."

"How do ya happen to know Fierman, anyway, Gil?" I asked.

"He comes from Carson City an' that's where I was afore I come to Shalak Springs. He was a rancher 'til the bank foreclosed on him. That was about five years back.

"Funny thing, when I come here a while back I found Nate Hale here, too. I knowed he'd left Carson but didn't know he was here."

"You tell yer old friend, Cy Fierman, Nate was here?"

"No, I—I didn't hardly know Fierman. Just served him a drink once in a while. Ain't seen him since I been here."

He rubbed the bar vigorously with his bar towel and still didn't look at me. I asked him for a beer and headed for the corner table, motioning Jack to follow me.

"I wanna hold off one more day, Jack."

"Dammit, Del. You duckin' out on me? If you ain't comin' just say so."

"Don't get on yer high horse. I'm comin'. But one more day won't make any difference. They're buryin' Nate tomorrow and Annie Laurie thinks it's important that I stay. Thinks I oughta go out to Hale's place with her and Wislon in the mornin' and so do I. 'Sides, I wanna keep an eye on Gil Dellah this evenin'. See who he talks to. Maybe you could spell me from time to time."

"All right, Del," Sears said. "But that's all. After that I'm goin', with ya or without ya."

"Thanks, Jack," I said. "We leave fer sure day after tomorrow."

I went back to where Dellah was continuing to wipe on the bar. "Seen the chief?"

"Said if you was lookin' for him he'd be around sometime this afternoon."

I went back and slouched down at the corner table, still nursing my bottle of beer. Sears had drunk his and left. The place was quiet; a couple of cowboys were sitting at a table on the other side of the room and every now and then one or two men would drift in, have a drink, and leave. It was getting on toward dinner before the chief walked in. He didn't see me and went over to where Dellah was standing. The two of them talked a minute, then he looked around, saw me, and strolled over.

"I ran into Sears and he says you're not leaving right away. That being the case I'm going back to my tepee. Me see-um you in the morning."

He went out without looking at Dellah. I followed him to the door and watched as he mounted Old Dan and headed out of town.

I went upstairs and knocked on Annie Laurie's door.

"I gotta be gone awhile," I told her when she answered.

"Here's what I want ya to do. Just keep an eye on Dellah. See who he talks to or if he does anything unusual."

I left her and walked on down to the livery stable, saddled the roan, and took the road outta town at an easy walk. I was headed for Chief Two Horse's place, but I wasn't in no hurry to get there.

CHAPTER 13

IT WAS BARELY dark and the moon still wasn't up when I drew near to Chief Two Horse's shack. I found a small tree well off the trail, in the shadow of the big rock outcropping that was close to the shack, and tethered the roan to it.

He was a large gelding, and of late he and me had gotten used to each other except I still figured on getting Old Dobbin back from Cy Fierman and his gang. The roan was a good horse but me and Old Dobbin were family; we'd rode a lot of range together.

I took my moccasins out of a saddlebag and slipped them on, then tied my boots together with a pigging string and hung them around the saddlehorn. Checking my gun to make sure it was loose in its holster I started off for the shack.

There was a light glowing through the one window in the front and I injunned up to it, being careful not to step on anything that might make a noise. Standing to one side I taken a quick look inside. Chief Two Horse was alone. He was sitting at a table and crushing something with a mortar and pestle. He never looked up.

Well, it was early yet. I backed away from the shack, turned, and walked back to the roan. Pulling my boots on I sat down with my back against the side of the rock and began my wait. If my hunch was right someone was going to come see the chief or in a little while he would saddle Old Dan and go to meet someone. In either case I was pretty sure I knew who it would be.

I had been waiting maybe half an hour when I heard the sound of hoofs coming from the direction of the mesa. It was plain from the sound that there were several horsemen.

I went over and put a hand over the roan's muzzle to keep him from nickering and the two of us waited there as the horsemen drew near. It wasn't long before I spotted their silhouettes—there was five of them—and I watched as they rode up to the front door of the shack.

Only one of them dismounted. He handed his reins to one of the other riders, then went up to the door and knocked loud enough for me to hear, and I heard him call out, "It's me, Fierman. Open up!"

The door swung open and Chief Two Horse stood there with a shotgun in his hands. Fierman pushed it to one side and stepped inside, closing the door behind him. In the dark I hadn't been able to see much of him except to make out that he was a tall, lanky galoot wearing a wide-brimmed, peaked hat that looked familiar. After a moment's thought I remembered that one of the men who had robbed the bank had worn a hat just like it.

He was inside no more than ten minutes. When he came out he took his horse's reins from the rider, mounted, and without so much as a backward look headed down the trail toward Shalak Springs with the others trailing along.

I was surprised. Last thing I'd figured was that they would head for town; I'd hope to follow them back to the mesa or at least to where they would make camp. Then I was going to hightail it back to town, get Jack Sears, and, funeral or no funeral, see if we could track them to their hideout.

But maybe this was better. Maybe if we handled things right we could isolate Fierman from his gang and capture him. I started to chuckle; sometimes I dream big dreams that don't have much to do with reality and this was one of those times. There was no way me and Jack were going to take on that bunch and there was no way that I was going to be able to put together a posse of townspeople who would take out after them. They wouldn't go. And rightly so. There were five tough customers there and they would lie in the weeds and pick off the members of the posse one by one. The only possible way to get them would be to ambush them instead. That would mean driving them or leading them into a trap.

Well, now, there was a thought. An ambush. It was worth thinking about.

But I had something else to think about, too. Why were they headed for town? What was there for them? They'd robbed the bank. They'd killed Nate Hale. There wasn't enough of them to try to take over the town. Why were they still hanging around?

Puzzled, I mounted the roan and eased him onto the trail that led back to Shalak Springs, being careful to stay back out of hearing distance.

We weren't much more than a mile from town when all of a sudden I realized I was no longer smelling their dust. I drew up and listened. There was silence; not even a coyote howling in the distance, no sound of night birds. I turned the roan around and scanned my back trail. Nothing. They had disappeared.

I began a systematic search, starting with my eyes on the horizon and slowing bringing my gaze down to the nearest objects. Facing away from town I started on the far left and gradually worked a semicircle all the way to the far right. Nothing. I started over. They had to be somewhere. I made the complete semicircle again and again nothing. I was about to give up when out of the corner of my eye I caught a flicker of light. It was a campfire, maybe half a mile away.

I found a scrub oak a little ways off the trail and tied the roan to it. Then for the second time that night I taken out my moccasins and switched my boots for them. Instead of tieing them to the saddlehorn I looped them over a small branch of the tree. Then I headed for the campfire.

Now I ain't no Indian but I can move pretty quiet if I have to. Walking carefully and kind of feeling my way I got to within about fifty feet of the campfire, close enough to hear voices but not near enough to make out what they were saying. I counted four of them sitting around the fire but couldn't locate the fifth man.

Which wasn't strange because he was right behind me, poking something in my back that felt mighty like a gun barrel.

Damn! I wondered, and not for the first time, how I had lived so long.

Whilst I was wondering a voice said in a lazy, kind of conversational tone, "Move, stranger, and yer a dead man."

In theory he was right. If someone has stuck a gun in your back the smart thing to do is exactly what you're told. But my mother never raised no genius.

I never even thought. I pivoted hard to my right, at the same time raising my right elbow high and swinging it backward as hard as I could. It caught him in the side of the neck and knocked him sideways just as he instinctively pulled the trigger on his six-gun. I heard the sound at the same time that I felt a burning sensation along the left side of my back and the back of my left arm It was like someone had run a hot branding iron across me.

But it didn't take any brains at all to know that it wasn't a branding iron but instead was a bullet that had dug into my back above my kidney and skidded on through to crease my arm. I didn't know how bad I was hurt and I didn't have time to care. I knew that shot was going to bring the rest of the gang on the double.

Ignoring the man who had shot me I dived into a low clump of brush, rolled through it, and came to my feet running.

Behind me I heard the man cursing and then four shots fired in quick succession. But he was just guessing and none came close. As I ran I heard him shout, "Go after him. Get the sonofabitch. He went thataway."

Thataway turned out to be the wrong way for me. In the confusion and in the dark I had panicked and lost my bearings and was running directly away from my horse, my boots, and even my saddle. But I didn't realize this until I stopped and tried to get my bearings after I'd been running for what seemed like an hour but was more like five minutes. I was gasping for breath by this time so I sat down on a convenient rock and listened for sounds of pursuit. There were none. There were no sounds at all except for my breathing.

I looked around and decided that I had no idea where I was or how far I'd come. All I knew was that my feet hurt and the soles of my moccasins felt just about worn through. And now I began to feel the stinging, burning pain where the bullet had torn furrows in my back and arm and where sweat was now dripping into the open wounds. But I didn't feel any blood running and I decided that the wounds weren't too deep and that the bullet had missed any arteries or big veins.

They were in awkward spots though and I couldn't see them, no matter how hard I twisted and turned. It didn't make any difference though because I had nothing to bandage them with anyway. All in all, I figured the best thing for me to do was find the roan and get back into town where maybe Ed Alliso could bandage me up.

I looked around for the North Star and after I found it decided that the trail and the roan lay south of me. I headed that way, moving slow because my back was stiffening up from the wound and my legs were stiffening up because this was the first time for as far back as I could remember that I'd done any serious running. I've heard stories about white trappers escaping from Indians by outrunning them on foot. Maybe so, but I was glad there wasn't no Indians out there looking for me, only white outlaws who, like most cowboys, never walked or ran when they could ride.

I'd been walking about fifteen minutes when I spotted the light from Fierman's campfire. I started to walk wide around it but then on impulse decided to see if I could get close enough to hear what they were talking about, maybe find out what they were doing out here so near to town. I figured they wouldn't think I was dumb enough to come back and I kind of wondered myself about how dumb I was being.

But a man's gotta do what a man's gotta do, or so I'd been hearing most of my life, and I figured what I had to do now was find out what was going on with the Fierman gang.

Moving as careful and as quiet as I could and taking advantage of every shadow and every bush I injunned up to maybe within thirty feet of the fire and settled down in the shadow of a large sage bush, on which I couldn't see no silver.

Lying flat on my belly with only my head raised I counted them. Dang! There was only four of them again. Where was the fifth? I felt a chill go up my spine and back down it again as I imagined number five sneaking up on me again. Trying to put the thought out of my mind I strained to hear what was being said.

"...that feller was?" one of them said.

"...kept lookin' for him," another remarked.

Finally one who I couldn't make out because he was sitting off to the side of the fire said, "It don't matter. When he goes to get his horse Charlie'll nail him. And this time he'll shoot first and talk later."

They all sort of chuckled and the last one who'd spoken spoke again. I guessed it was Fierman because he said, "I guess we better turn in. Bailey you take the first watch. Check on the horses and take a walk around the camp. We wouldn't want that feller walkin' in on us."

"He ain't comin' back," Bailey said.

"Just do it," Fierman ordered and Bailey, muttering low, climbed to his feet and headed out for the horses which were across the camp from me.

I'd thought briefly about trying to turn them loose and leave the gang afoot but they were too close in to the fire to risk it. Now all I thought about was getting out of there without getting caught. I began inching backward on my belly and then on my hands and knees. I was a hundred feet from the fire when I spotted the silhouette of Bailey walking carelessly around the perimeter of the camp and coming within a few feet of where I'd been lying. After he'd gone on by I stood up and began walking toward where I'd left the roan.

A hundred yards from the spot I went back down on my stomach and began squirming toward the roan, stopping every few yards to see if I could see or hear the man named Charlie, the man who had surprised me and, unbeknownst to him, had shot me and now was waiting to kill me.

I thought about walking wide around Charlie and hoofing it into town but the thought of leaving the horse, leaving my boots, and leaving Charlie off scot-free made me mad. I was danged if I would leave without the roan. They had Old Dobbin but they wasn't going to get the roan.

As I inched closer I spotted the scrub oak where I had tied the roan and saw a darker blob that had to be the horse, but I couldn't see anything that might give me a clue to Charlie's location. I knew he had to be close to the roan, though, close enough to get an easy shot at me when I went to untie him. Half-hidden by a small bush I settled down to wait for Charlie to make a noise, move, or in some way tell me where he was at.

Whilst I waited I reached down to my right calf, pulled up my pant leg, and carefully removed my hideout knife from the sheath strapped to my leg. The knife had a six-inch blade that held a razor edge better than any steel I'd ever come in contact with. I'd bought if off a down-on-his-luck sailor in a bar at the port of San Pedro near Los Angeles. He'd picked it up in New Orleans from a gypsy whose side he took in a barroom brawl. That was after I'd quit punching cows out at San Bernardino because the blossoms on the orange trees they were planting there give me a bad case of hay fever.

That knife had saved my hide on more than one occasion. I was counting on it to do so again, if need be. Now I didn't want to kill Charlie because I don't hold much with killing, but I sure wanted to get my horse back and Charlie wasn't going to stand in my way. At the same time I didn't want to make any noise that would bring his friends on the run.

I lay there quiet, just waiting, for maybe minutes. Then someone who I took to be Charlie sneezed. It was loud and sudden and it startled the roan who moved nervously.

I heard Charlie say, "Quiet down, old hoss. Ain't nothin' to worry about."

The voice came from beyond the roan and I remembered there'd been a good-sized rock there that a man could lean on or hide behind, whichever he preferred.

But then, just as I was about to wiggle out of there and try to get behind him, a second horse nickered also from beyond the roan. And that made sense; Charlie had staked his horse out away from mine so I wouldn't see him and wouldn't be likely to come across him by accident. And that give me an idea.

If I could get around to Charlie's horse without Charlie hearing me I could ride it back to town. If I could pull that off it would mean I wouldn't have to kill Charlie or risk being kilt by him. Of course it would mean leaving the roan but I didn't owe him nothing and it would also mean leaving my boots. But maybe I could come back for them if Charlie hadn't already spotted them. Otherwise, well, it was time for a new pair anyway.

Quietly as I could I inched backwards until I reached a small tree, then I stood up in its shadow and began making a wide circle around the little tree I'd tied the roan to. I'd made about a quarter of a circle when I came to the road. I crossed it and began walking alongside it, keeping a sharp eye out for Bailey's horse. Way I had it figured the horse was on my side of the road while Charlie himself was on the other side with my horse.

In back of me a late moon was finally beginning to rise, giving just enough light to silhouette trees and brush and rocks and—yep, there he was, Charlie's horse tied to a bush and grazing quietly. I moved farther off the trail so I could come up on it, at the same time being hidden by it from Charlie in case he happened to look my way. I was lucky. That was not a skittish horse. I moved up on it slow and gentlelike. It looked up without alarm when I came up to it. I patted it on the neck and on its muzzle, then I untied the reins, threw them back over his head, and climbed into the saddle with every intention of moving at a slow and quiet walk off toward town until we were well out of Charlie's hearing.

But then, without so much as a second thought and hardly even a first one, I swung him directly toward where I figured Charlie was waiting, dug my heels into his flanks, give a cowboy yell at the top of my lungs, yanked out my six-gun, and began shooting. Me and that horse went charging across the road right at where I figured Charlie had to be.

I heard him holler in total surprise and saw him scramble to his feet and throw himself behind the rock he'd been sitting against. He was so anxious to escape he never thought to reach for his gun. At the same time he was ducking away the roan tore loose from the little tree I'd tied him to and took off across the prairie with me right behind him. I herded him off to my left toward town and after about a quarter of a mile he slowed down and I reined Charlie's horse over close to him and reached down and grabbed his reins. Then the three of us trotted on to town.

At the livery stable I dismounted, unsaddled Charlie's horse and turned him into the corral. When I went to do the same for the roan I got a surprise. Charlie had found my boots and had hung them around the saddlehorn, figuring, I guess, that I wouldn't never have any more use for them. It wasn't the first mistake he'd made tonight.

CHAPTER 14

I WAS TOO TIRED and hurting too much to stop and put my boots on. Instead I slung them over my shoulder and walked—staggered was more like it—down to the Staghorn. It was after midnight and the barroom was empty except for a couple of stragglers. As usual Gil Dellah was behind the bar polishing it with a dirty dishrag.

I didn't say nothing to him, just made my way to the stairs and started up them. I made the first step and that was it. I just kind of sagged to my knees and then fell slowly forward with my head up the stairs. I wasn't out; I was just weak from loss of blood and exhausted from all that running and crawling and riding.

Dellah saw me collapse and came hurrying over. "You all right, boss?" he asked in concern, bending over me. By this time I was trying to struggle to my feet.

"I'm all right," I gasped. "Gimme a hand up."

He grasped me by my left arm and I let out a shout, partly of surprise but largely of agony. He let go of me in a hurry and I fell forward again on my face, bumping my forehead hard on the edge of a step. I swore then, loud and long, figuring Ma would understand, even if she wouldn't approve. Dellah stood there looking down at me, wondering what he had done wrong.

"What's wrong? What'd I do?" he asked anxiously when I'd quit cursing.

"Nothin'," I ground out through clenched teeth. "It wasn't yer fault. Take my other arm."

Just then Annie Laurie called from the top of the steps, "What is it? What's wrong? Is that you, Del?"

I looked up. She was standing there with a light robe wrapped around her and her black hair falling around her shoulders.

"It's me," I said. "I'm all right."

"No you're not," she said, advancing down the stairs. By now Dellah was pulling me to my feet by my right arm and Annie reached for my left one.

"Don't touch it. Leave it be," I growled. "It's hurtin'."

As I talked, Dellah threw my good arm over his shoulders and with his help I slowly made my way to the top of the steps. In the meantime Annie Laurie had rushed to her rooms and gotten a lamp. She opened the door to my apartment and held the light while Gil helped me into the bedroom, where I kind of fell on the bed. Gil picked up my feet, swung them onto the bed, and pulled off my moccasins.

"You can go now," Annie said. "I'll take care of him."

He started to argue but she gave him a look that stopped him dead.

"I'll be downstairs if ya need me," he grumbled and stomped out.

"Tell him to get hot water and clean cloths," I muttered. "I been shot."

She called Gil back. "Go put some water on to boil and go roust out Ed Alliso. Del's been shot."

"Yes'm," he said and left on the run.

"Where are you hit, Del?" she asked worriedly. "Who shot you?"

"Feller named Charlie," I grunted. "In the arm and back."

She help me turn over on my right side and gently pulled up my shirt which now she could see was caked with blood and was sticking to my back. I gasped in pain as she pulled it away from the wound and as she watched it started to bleed again. And I passed out.

When I come to she was bathing my forehead with cold water and somebody, who turned out to be Alliso, was tsk-tsking and working with surprisingly gentle fingers on the wound in my left arm. He'd already bandaged the wound in my back above my waist.

"There," he said, straightening up. "You ought to be as good as new in a few days. That bullet dug a furrow in your back and side and burned the underpart of your arm. It doesn't seem to have done much damage except for the blood you lost.

"I've put a powder on it that I make from some of the desert plants. It helps the healing and seems to prevent infection. An old Indian medicineman taught it to me. Strange old man. Looked like he could have been a hundred years old. Came from some strange tribe I never heard of, Mimbres or something like that. Too bad some drunken buffalo hunter had to go and shoot him.

"How'd you hurt your head? That's a nasty abrasion you have there."

"I fell," I said.

He reached into his kit and fetched out a tin that held some kind of salve. He dipped out a fingerful and smeared it on the abrasion. "Same as the powder," he explained. "Only I mix it with beef tallow to make a salve.

"I'll leave some of the powder with you for when you dress the wound. It makes a great tonic, too. Kind of funny tasting but it's a real blood builder."

He handed a little cloth bag to Annie Laurie. "Mix it in boiling water, about a teaspoon to a glass. I'll drop by tomorrow after the funeral and check on the patient."

He turned to go and I noticed he was still wearing his nightshirt that he'd tucked into his pants. When Annie Laurie had sent for him he'd come in a hurry.

"Thanks fer everything, Doc," I said. "Sorry to drag you out in the middle of the night."

"No problem," he said, waving a hand good-night.

I watched him go, wondering about him. He wasn't no doctor, or so he said, but he had gentle, competent hands and seemed to know about wounds and such. He wasn't no dentist either, but he was the only man in town who could pull a tooth. On top of this he was the town's undertaker and along with all of that was a pretty good barber. I wondered what he'd been before he came to Shalak Springs and what he'd done back where he came from and why was he here.

The West was full of men like Ed Alliso who'd been something back East or over in Europe, men who were educated, able men who for some reason had drifted out here, either because they were tired of civilization or because they were in trouble wherever it was they came from.

I wished I knew more about him, but I probably never would because in the West you didn't butt into another man's business or pry into his past. It was what you were out here that mattered, not who you had been or what you'd done back where you came from.

Oh well, there was other things to worry about without puzzling over Ed Alliso.

"What time's the funeral?" I asked Annie Laurie as he went out the door.

"One o'clock," she replied, "but you're to stay right here in bed."

"Can't," I said. "I can't swear to it, but I think there's gonna be trouble."

"Oh, no! Not at Nate's funeral," she protested.

"I hope not," I said. "But I wouldn't bet on it. You need to get Jack Sears over here first thing in the mornin' and Marshal Johns and send someone out to get Billy Jeff Linton and Hallie Hope here early. Don't say anything about any of this to Two Horse or Dellah. I don't know where they fit in. Also get Ferd Wislon over here first thing. I need to talk to him."

"Well," she said, "if you're going to be that busy you'd better get some sleep. If you need anything I'll be in the other room."

"Go to bed," I ordered.

"Good-night," she said and leaned over and kissed me on the cheek. Then she picked up the lamp and went out.

It was bright daylight when she awakened me. She'd fixed a tray with some ham and eggs and beans and toast and coffee. "First drink this," she said, helping me to sit up and fixing a pillow behind me.

The "this" was Ed Alliso's tonic. Surprisingly it didn't taste too bad and, even more surprisingly, in a minute I began to feel a surge of energy. Maybe it was this stuff that made that old Indian medicineman live so long.

The Mimbres? I'd heard vaguely of them. They'd been here before the tribes that were here now, the Utes and the Cheyenne, the Navajos and even the Hopis. According to Alliso, the old medicineman must have said the formula for the medicine was handed down from the Mimbres.

Whatever it was or wherever it came from it seemed to be helping and that was all that mattered. I pitched in and ate what Annie Laurie had brought and drank the coffee and then sent her to round up Sears and Wislon whilst I taken care of some personal things.

My arm and back were stiff and sore, especially my back, but I found I was able to get up and get dressed. Fortunately the wound in my back was above my waist and I could button my pants and tighten my belt. And I could use my left arm even though it hurt when I moved it.

By the time I was slinging my gunbelt on I heard steps on the stairs and in a moment Jack Sears came stomping into the room.

"What in tarnation is goin' on?" he demanded. "Annie said fer me to get over here pronto. Said somethin' about you bein' shot, too."

"Flesh wound," I grunted. "Look, Jack, I think somethin' is

125

goin' on but I don't exactly know what. All I know is that Cy Fierman and some of his men are camped outside of town. Why, I don't know. Ain't nothin' here in town for 'em; they've already robbed the bank. It just don't make sense, but they're out there."

"Well, let's go get 'em," Jack growled. "Ain't that why we're here? They're out there and that sure beats hell out of you and me chasin' 'em all over the mountains."

"It ain't that simple, Jack. There's at least five of 'em out there and I wouldn't swear to it but I think they got friends here in town. I had a hunch last night. I don't like the way Two Horse has been actin'. Him and Gil Dellah been havin' a lot of private talks and Dellah's been standin' up fer Fierman. Anyway, after I caught 'em talkin' the last time I figured somethin' was up so I moseyed on out to the chief's place and sure enough he had a meetin' there with Fierman."

"Ya shoulda taken me along," Jack growled.

"You'd a probably got us both kilt," I said. "As it was I almost got me kilt."

Before I could say anything more there was a knock on the door and Annie Laurie and Ferd Wislon came into the room, followed by Wayne Johns.

Without preamble Wislon said, "Annie says we've got problems. You want to tell me about 'em?"

"Yeah, tell us," Johns said.

"It's Cy Fierman," I said. "Him and his gang are camped outside of town. I don't know why but I thought maybe the city council might wanna put together a posse and try roundin' 'em up."

"You sure it's Fierman?" he said.

"We could ask Chief Two Horse," I said. "They stopped by his place last night."

"Oh, no!" Annie Laurie blurted out.

"Yep," I said.

"Never did trust that Injun," Wislon said. "Let's get him up here and see what kind of lies he tells us."

126

Annie said, "I'll get him," and left the room.

She was back in a minute. "He's not around," she said. "Neither is Gil Dellah."

"Don't surprise me none," I said. "I been wonderin' about both of 'em. I think they been in cahoots with Fierman all along. I think they was feedin' him information and actin' as his lookouts. Dellah comes from Carson City an' so does Fierman. I don't know what the chief's connection is."

"But why would they leave now?" Annie Laurie asked.

"After last night they must of figured I caught on to 'em. Thing that bothers me is neither one of 'em seems like the type would kill old Nate Hale in cold blood."

"We can stay here and talk all day if we want to," Jack Sears broke in. "But me, I'm tired of talk. Let's put a posse together and go take 'em. Fierman killed my wife and killed Nate Hale and all you want to do is stand around and talk."

He glared around the room, mad as all get-out.

Wislon looked at him calmly. "We can put a posse together without any trouble. This town has some good men in it but Two Horse and Dellah will have warned them by now and they will have either disappeared or be lying in ambush.

"And furthermore, I can tell you what they're doing out there. The thing you don't know is that the bank has more money in it today than it did when Nate Hale was alive. Gus Simpson has taken it over effective today and he has deposited $10,000 of his own money in it."

"But he can't do that," Annie Laurie protested. "That was Nate's bank and he—."

"Yes he can," Wislon said. "He owns the building. Nate rented it from him. He's notifying all the depositers and everyone who does business with the bank that from now on they'll do business with him. Him and Twain Sawyer. He's put Sawyer in charge. You and Tackett here should be hearing from one of them pretty quick."

"But he can't—" Annie Laurie started to say but Wislon interrupted her again. "But he has, Miss Burns. Possession is nine points of the law and more importantly, everyone who had money in the bank when it was robbed is being told their money is safe and is available to them in full. You would not get any public support if you were to protest."

Annie Laurie clamped her lips shut tight and turned away. I could see she was furious but that was no concern of mine now. The fact that there was $10,000 in the bank was. I knew now why Cy Fierman was lurking nearby.

All told, there were a couple of hundred people living in Shalak Springs, at least that many on the surrounding ranches, and a few more who came to town once in a while from some one- and two-man mines in the nearby mountains.

No more than twenty of these showed up for Nate's funeral. They included the remaining three councilmen and their wives, Gus Simpson and a lanky young woman with a sour expression who turned out to be his daughter, Twain Sawyer, Ed Alliso and his wife, a heavy blond woman who might have been pretty at one time, Hallie Hope and Billy Jeff Linton, me and Annie Laurie, and Jack Sears who was there because I asked him to come.

You might have thought more people would show up for the funeral of someone as prominent in town as Nate Hale but bankers aren't never real popular folk. They're needed but they're not liked. They have to say no to too many people.

Alliso had hired a couple of Mexicans—a man and his son—who lived on the outskirts of town to dig the grave and help bring over the coffin with Hale's body in it before the small crowd gathered.

Jack Sears stood on one side of the crowd next to Billy Jeff and Hallie Hope whilst Wayne Johns and I stood across the grave from them. The little cemetery—you couldn't hardly call it a Boot Hill because it was on a flat piece of land just outside of town—only had a dozen graves. The town hadn't been there long enough and wasn't wild enough to really fill it up.

It was a clear, hot day with just the hint of breeze to say that autumn might not be too far away. We didn't have no preacher so Ferd Wislon fetched his old family Bible and began to read over Nate Hale's closed coffin.

He'd hardly got started with what he said later was the 23rd Psalm, "The Lord is my shep—," when something poked me in the small of my back and Gil Dellah's voice said, "Just you stand quiet, Boss, and won't nobody get hurt."

I stood quiet as a statue. Looking across to Sears I saw him standing real still, too, and close behind him, half hidden, I caught a glimpse of Chief Two Horse.

"He maketh me to lie down—" Wislon was intoning when someone shot off a gun and everyone jumped. Behind me I heard the cloppity-clop of a trotting horse and off beyond Sears and the Lintons I saw another horse and rider. To my right was another and to the left still another. Thing I noticed was all of the riders had their six-shooters in their hands. No doubt about it, they were ready for trouble.

Behind me a voice said loudly, "Now everyone just stand hitched and ain't nobody gonna get hurt."

I wasn't about to move and a quick look told me nobody else was fixing to be brave either.

The man on the horse behind me dismounted and pushed his way to where Wislon was standing quiet, the Bible still open in his hands.

When he reached Hale's coffin he leaped lightly on top of it and turned so he was facing in my direction. He was something over six feet tall and lean of body and face. His face was lined and partly covered by a black handle-bar mustache. He wore two guns tied down and a black peaked hat. I hadn't never seen him before, but I knew who he was. He was Cy Fierman.

He gazed around with narrow, piercing blue eyes.

"Like I said," he announced in a voice loud enough so we could all hear, "if nobody moves nobody gets hurt. Fer those of you who don't know me my name is Cy Fierman. Thanks to the man in this coffin here I'm a bank robber. He foreclosed on my ranch a while back and didn't leave me no choice.

"But I'm here to tell you one thing. Cy Fierman ain't no sneak murderer. I'd have been glad to kill Nate Hale in a fair fight but I wouldn't stab a man in his bed.

"Now I know a lot of you won't believe this, but it's true. If it wasn't I wouldn't have risked comin' here to tell you this—I never killed Nate Hale. And none of my men did. You hear? The man who murdered Nate Hale is one of yours; not one of mine. You hear?

"That's what I come to tell you. That's all I come to tell you. I'm goin' now but in case any of you got any ideas about bein' a hero there's them four men out there and they're loaded fer bear. On top of that there's also a sharpshooter with a rifle out there somewhere. If anyone wants to find out where just make a wrong move."

He leaped off the coffin and had taken one step toward his horse when Sears' voice, filled with hatred, cut across the open grave. "Fierman!"

Fierman turned.

"Yer a yellow-bellied sonofabitch," Sears snarled. "Ya kilt my wife. Now I'm gonna kill you."

"I ain't never killed a woman," Fierman said, surprised.

"Ya run my Mary Lou down with a horse when ya robbed the Nora bank. Ya knocked her into a hitchin' post. Ya kilt her." Sears said. "Get this Injun's gun out of my back and I'll kill ya where ya stand."

Fierman shrugged and shook his head. "Some other time, maybe."

Deliberately, he turned his back and strode to his horse. Mounting, he drew his gun and called to Two Horse and Dellah, "You two get yer horses and get out of here. We'll keep ya covered."

"I'll follow ya to hell if I have to, Fierman," Sears yelled to him.

Fierman smiled sardonically. "I'll see ya there, Mr. What-ever-yer-name-is."

"Sears," Sears snarled. "Jack Sears. Remember it."

For the next five minutes whilst Two Horse and Dellah were beating their retreat nobody said anything. Then Fierman wheeled his bay gelding and trotted off. As soon as he was out of pistol range, Johns shouted, "Let's go after him."

Still holding his Bible Wislon said, "Don't be a damn fool, Marshal. You wanta get a bunch of us killed?"

He didn't wait for an answer but turned to the rest of us. "I suggest we get on with the services." He paused a moment and began at the beginning: "The Lord is my shepherd. I shall not want..."

CHAPTER 15

As THE TWO Mexicans began shoveling dirt on top of the coffin and the group of mourners was heading back toward town Annie Laurie turned to me and said, "I need to go back to Nate's house right away and I want you and Billy Jeff to come with me."

"What is it?" I asked.

"There's something not right about Gus Simpson taking over the bank. That isn't the way it was supposed to be. I'll tell you about it later. Right now it's important that we go to the house. And I think it's better that we don't take Mr. Wislon. He may get angry, but he's too close to Simpson."

"If yer worried, you go get Billy Jeff and Hallie Hope and I'll round up Sears and we'll head out there right away," I said.

I looked around for Sears and saw him striding toward the stable. The damn fool was going after Fierman and to hell with whether I went with him or not. I hollered at him, but if he heard me he ignored me. I wasn't in no shape to run after him but as I started to quicken my pace I felt a hand on my shoulder. It was Gus Simpson.

"Look, Sackett,—" he began.

"Tackett," I said. "It's Tackett."

"Call yourself whatever you want. You look like a gunfighter to me," Simpson said. "How much do you want to kill Fierman?"

"I told ya once I ain't a hired gun," I said. "And I ain't no killer."

I shrugged his hand off my shoulder and walked away, but he followed after me.

"Fierman killed Nate Hale and Nate was my friend and I want his killer dead. I'll pay yer price."

"You heard him. Fierman says he didn't do it."

"Of course he did. If not him, who? He's the only one who wanted Nate dead. Look, just name yer price. Whatever it is will be on top of the reward that's already been posted for him."

I turned and faced him. "For the last time the answer is no. As far as I'm concerned, Mr. Simpson, yer gonna have to shuck your own corn. Now get away from me."

I turned away and headed for the stable just in time to see Sears riding off in the direction Cy Fierman and his men had taken.

Wasn't anything I could do except watch him go. I went on to the stable and hollered at the kid to hitch Mouse to Annie's trap. Billy Jeff and Hallie Hope were already there and Billy Jeff had already hitched up his buckboard.

"I've gotta get Annie Laurie," I said. "You go on. We'll meet you at the house."

Annie Laurie came out of the Staghorn as I drove up, carrying a parasol in one hand and a small handbag in the other. I helped her in gingerly, taking care not to pull my wounds open, and we taken off after Billy Jeff. A couple of times I started to ask her why we were going out to Hale's place but it was plain she didn't want to talk, so we rode most of the way in silence. When we got there Billy Jeff and Hallie Hope were standing outside with worried looks on their faces.

"What is it?" Annie asked "What's wrong?"

Hallie Hope was nervously twisting a handkerchief in her hands and trying to keep from crying. "Oh, Miss Burns," she wailed, tears rolling down her round cheeks. "Some 'un done tore up the house."

"Damn," she swore, much to my embarrassment, even though I'd heard her before. I looked at the young Lintons and both of their faces had turned red. They might have been from the backwoods of Arkansas, but where they came from a lady—and they plainly viewed Annie Laurie as a lady—didn't swear. Not ever.

Annie Laurie never noticed their reaction or mine. She brushed past Hallie Hope and hurried up the porch steps and into the house, with me right behind.

The place was a mess. Furniture was turned over. Nate Hale's big rolltop desk had been jimmied open and its contents were scattered around. Pictures had been torn off the walls and all the throw rugs had been tossed into one corner.

"Whole place is like this," Billy Jeff said, coming in behind us.

Annie Laurie turned to him. "It's all right, Billy Jeff. They never got what they were looking for. You and Hallie Hope straighten up the rest of the house and leave Mr. Tackett and me alone for a bit."

They trooped out and Annie Laurie shut the door behind them.

She gestured at the heavy old rolltop desk. "Del, can you move that to the middle of the room?"

I taken hold of it and with her help pulled it into the middle of the room, trying to ignore the pain that shot through my back and my left arm. She saw me wince and was immediately contrite.

"I'm sorry, Del. I forgot about your wound. When we're through I'll have Billy Jeff put it back."

"I'm all right," I said, putting on a brave front even as I felt the blood begin to trickle down my back. What a dang fool I was, showing off how strong I was when I should of called Billy Jeff in. A man'll do some dumb things sometimes when a pretty woman's involved.

The walls of the big living room were random-width knotty pine planks, seasoned by age and smoke from the huge fireplace at the end of the room. It was easy to see the big desk hadn't been sitting where it was for very long because there was no change in the color of the planks behind where the desk had been.

Annie Laurie went over to one of the planks that was about a foot wide and pushed on what appeared to be just another knot in it. When she released the pressure the plank swung silently outward on well-oiled hinges. Behind it was a small safe set in a second wall about five feet off the floor.

Without hesitating Annie Laurie moved the combination dial back and forth, stopped, and pulled the safe door open. She reached in and took out a sheaf of papers. Then she closed the safe and swung the plank door shut. She went around to the front of the desk and began trying to push it back in place. I went over and leaned against it and between my 200 pounds and her efforts we were able to slide the desk back against the wall.

When the intruders had pried the desk open they had pushed up the rolltop and we had left it that way when we moved it. Now Annie Laurie took the sheaf of papers she had taken from the safe and spread them out on the surface of the desk.

"Del," she said, "I want you to see these things so you can testify as to their existence in case anything happens to them. We'll go over them carefully back at the Staghorn."

She picked up one. "This is a deed to the house we're in now and the land around it."

She poked at some others. "These are letters between Nate and his wife after she moved back East. You'll see that she hated him and was trying to turn his son against him. His daughter—her name was Naomi—died shortly after she left him. After she'd been East a while she moved and didn't leave a forwarding address and she never wrote him again. As a result he lost all track of them until two years ago."

There was a quaver in her voice as she talked about the letters and she stopped abruptly and turned away from me. After a moment she turned back and picked up what looked like some sort of legal document.

"This is his will," she said. "In it he leaves everything to his son, Shadrach, with the proviso that if Shadrach does not claim his inheritance within a year then the estate is to be divided equally between Shadrach's wife and any living offspring the couple may have."

She looked up at me and her eyes were brimming with tears. In a low voice she said, "I am Shadrach's wife. Or maybe his widow. He disappeared nearly three years ago and I haven't seen him since."

"Well, dang!" I said, because I didn't know what else to say.

I was pretty sure I knew what had happened to Shadrach but this didn't seem like the time for me to say so. Instead, I took a step toward her and suddenly she was in my arms, crying as if she'd never stop.

But she did. After a few minutes she stepped back and drew a deep breath. She dipped her hand into her bosom and brought out a teeny lace handkerchief and dabbed her eyes and blowed her nose.

She gave me a weak smile. "I'm all right now," she said. "Let's go back to town. I asked Wayne Johns if he would watch the Staghorn until we returned. He said he would. But I don't want to impose on him too much.

"You know, Del, he might make a pretty good bartender for us. We could pay him a little more than he's making and as you know, for all his size and bluster, he's not much of a marshal."

"He ain't very bright," I said.

"I know, but he's honest," she replied. "And besides, I think he could handle any trouble that came along."

Annie Laurie opened the door and called for Billy Jeff. He came in, looking straight at her with one eye and out the window with the other, making it hard to remember that when he had to he could focus on trouble with both eyes.

"We're going back to town now, Billy Jeff." Annie said. "You and Hallie Hope hold down the fort here. And don't worry, everything's going to be all right. Just get the place put back in order."

"Yes'm. Thank you ma'am," he said, turning to lead the way out of the house.

Of a sudden I had me a thought. "Billy Jeff, we're going to leave the trap here. You saddle us up a couple of horses. We're going back across country. We don't need somebody shootin' at us again."

Billy Jeff looked embarrassed. He looked at the ground and kind of scuffed his feet in the dirt. "Mr. Tackett, we ain't got a sidesaddle fer Miss Burns to use."

"Well, dang!" I said, but Annie Laurie said, "It's all right. I'll just be a moment," and she hurried back into the house.

I followed Billy Jeff to the barn and I saddled a big red gelding for me whilst Billy unhitched Mouse and threw a saddle on her. We had just finished when Annie Laurie reappeared wearing an old pair of black jeans faded by much washing to a dark gray, a man's plaid shirt, and a scuffed pair of riding boots.

Everything was twice too big for her except for the boots, which were small for a man, but she'd tucked the shirt into the jeans which she had cinched around her slim waist with a length of rawhide. "I'm ready to go," she said, smiling.

"What about them papers you came to get?" I asked.

She patted her shirt. "They're in here," she said.

Billy Jeff helped her as she mounted Mouse and then adjusted the stirrups for her. As soon as he was through we taken off, heading at an angle away both from Shalak Springs and from the road.

We took the horses along at a lively trot and swung wide around the clump of rocks where we'd been ambushed, was it only yesterday? To me it seemed like a year ago.

I thought for a second that we might ride over and take a look-see at where the rifleman had hidden out, but I'm no detective. Hoofprints all look pretty much alike to me unless there's something real unusual about them. Same way with rifle shells and cigarette butts and boot tracks. They just don't mean very much to me. I was going to have to catch the shooter in the act if I was ever going to know who shot at us.

So I kept heading on the big circle route toward town. But as I glanced over at the rocks I thought I caught a glint of light from the sun reflecting off of metal.

"Let's go," I yelled, reaching over and swatting Mouse on the flank, and we were off and running, with Annie Laurie hanging on to the horn of her saddle for dear life. The horses ran all out for about a quarter of a mile before I slowed up the red gelding and brought him to a stop. Annie Laurie followed suit.

"What did you do that for?" she demanded, not at all happy.

"Caught a glimpse of something over by the rocks," I explained. "Didn't know who or what it was but thought we oughta get out of there. Didn't want to get pinned down out there in the open. Sorry I scared ya."

"How could anyone know we were coming this way?" she asked.

"Didn't have to," I explained. "They coulda been waitin' for us to come down the road but spotted us comin' along in back of 'em. On the other hand, it might of been nothin' but my imagination, but I sure didn't want to take a chance.

"I have a hunch," I said. "Let's go see Twain Sawyer."

"Let's not," she said. "Your back is bleeding through the bandage and your shirt. We're going back to the Staghorn and put you to bed."

"Ya shouldn't of said that," I said. "I wasn't payin' no attention to it. Now I can feel it bleedin' and it's hurtin'. Arm hurts, too. Let's head for the Staghorn. We'll get to Sawyer later."

We walked the horses the rest of the way.

The Staghorn was crowded when we walked in and some of the men looked at Annie Laurie kind of funny; she wasn't dressed for no fashion show, that was for sure. But it was just as well since they didn't pay any mind to me and that was how I wanted it. I didn't want anyone thinking I was bad hurt. Down the line a lot might depend on some folks thinking I was in fighting trim.

Wayne Johns was behind the bar, wearing his marshal's badge and serving drinks like he knew what he was doing. He grinned and lifted a hand when he saw us. It was plain he liked the job.

"Our new bartender," Annie whispered as I limped up the stairs beside her.

At her door she stopped and said, "You go on in and get your shirt off. I'll be in in a minute to look at your wound and change the bandage. If I have to I'll send for Ed Alliso."

"I'll be all right," I grunted and turned toward my own door and went in. First thing I noticed was I was not alone.

There was a tough-looking blond man sitting on the big leather-covered couch in my front room. He was sucking on a bottle of beer and holding a lighted cigarette.

"Howdy, Del," he said, setting his beer on the floor and rising to greet me.

"Well I'll be danged," I said, surprised. "Lew Haight. What're you doin' here?"

He came over and shook my hand. "Miss Esmeralda sent me," he said. "She's come back from the East and when she heard you was up here in Shalak Springs she sent me to see when you was comin' home. Said if you wouldn't come I was to drag ya."

Home. It was a strange word to me. I hadn't had any place to call home since I'd left the little cabin Ma and I lived in up in the gold country of the High Sierras. That was near thirteen years ago when I was sixteen. Ma was dead now, died almost a year ago, and the cabin was abandoned. I missed her bad, even though I hadn't seen her since I left home. I'd been wandering over the West all those years, punching cows, driving stage or riding shotgun, working in the mines now and then, and once, even, I'd done a brief stint as a town marshal.

Lew told me what I'd already heard from Sears, that after she heard I'd been killed, Esme had gone East, saying she wanted nothing more to do with the West. But it wasn't long before she had changed her mind and come back. About the same time Obediah Shrifft had moved on from Shalak Springs to Nora, and Blackie Harrington, Lew's saddle pardner, had learned from him that I was running the Staghorn Saloon. Which wasn't quite true. I owned it; Annie Laurie ran it.

Regardless, when Blackie told Esme where I was she sent Lew to find me and if he had to, to drag me bodily back to the R Bar R.

Well, he wouldn't have to drag me, that was for sure, but he would have to wait awhile. I hadn't planned it this way but it turned out that I had me a mess of unfinished business here in Shalak Springs, business I dang sure intended to finish before I left.

CHAPTER 16

LEW HAD JUST finished talking when the door opened and Annie Laurie came hurrying in. She stopped when she saw the two of us.

"Oh, I'm sorry. I didn't mean to intrude," she said, looking embarrassed. Then she collected herself.

"Del, why aren't you in bed? We need to take care of your wound."

Lew's eyebrows had gone up when Annie Laurie came busting into the room.

Now, his voice cold, he said, "I seem to have interrupted somethin' here. Sorry. I'll be goin'."

He was reaching for his hat when I said, "Sit down, Lew. It ain't what I think yer thinkin'. Annie, this here is Lew Haight. We worked together on the R Bar R down near Nora. He came here a-huntin' me.

"Lew, this here is Annie Laurie Burns. Her and me are kind of pardners in the Staghorn. We're in business together and that's all."

Annie Laurie stared at the two of us. "I don't know whether to laugh or be angry," she said. "I think the best thing for me to do is ignore the both of you. I'm going to go find Ed Alliso and he can take care of your back, Del. As for you, Mr. Haight, I don't appreciate your insulting insinuations one little bit. When I come back I'll expect an apology."

She swept out before I could say anything.

Lew looked at me and shrugged. "Sorry about that," he said,

then asked, "Wound? What wound?"

"Got shot last night," I said. "Bullet got me in the back and arm, but not bad. Only thing is, the one in back started bleedin' again. Annie went for the doc just now. If you wasn't here she'd of probably changed the bandage herself."

"You and her in love?" he asked. "That'd break Miss Esme's heart."

"No. Her and me ain't in love," I said. "She's got a husband somewhere, but she don't know where. He's been missin' awhile. I think he's dead. I'll tell ya all about it after they fix me up."

"Whyn't you go lie down?" he said. "I'll come sit with ya until the doc gets here."

We went into the bedroom and Lew helped me take off my shirt, pulling it away carefully from the bloody bandages on both my back and my arm.

"I'll leave the bandages for the doc," he said as I sat down on the edge of the unmade bed and then carefully lay down on my good side. He pulled off my boots and then, seeing me begin to shiver, threw the blanket over me.

"You wanna talk or sleep?" he asked.

"Sleep," I mumbled and closed my eyes. But I hadn't hardly got them shut when Ed Alliso bustled in, followed by Annie Laurie. Alliso set down his little medical bag and came over to take a look at my bandages.

Leaning over me he was blocking my view, but I heard Lew say, "Mrs. Burns, I was out of line there a while ago. I sure didn't mean to be. I wanna apologize."

"Why, Mr. Haight, that's very thoughtful of you. Your apology is accepted," Annie Laurie said sweetly.

Anything else they might have said was interrupted by my shouted "Owww" as Alliso tried to unstick the bandage from the wound.

"Sorry," he said matter-of-factly. "I didn't mean to hurt you. I got it unstuck, though. Wound looks pretty good even if you have been doin' dumb things. No sign of infection. That old medicine man's powder is good stuff."

He went to work then and rebandaged my arm. As he turned to go, he said, "I forgot to mention it last night but I'll be sending you a bill."

"How 'bout I pay you off in likker?" I asked.

"The way I drink anymore it'd take twenty years to pay off the bill," he laughed and went out.

I struggled out of the bed and fetched out my other shirt, which was almost clean, and Annie Laurie, without even looking at Lew, came over and helped me put it on.

"I have some work to do, so I'll leave you two to talk," she said as I buttoned my shirt.

Lew watched her go and when she'd closed the door he said, "You may not be in love with her but sure as shootin' she's in love with you."

"Yer out of yer mind, Lew," I said. "I'm a one-woman man and that woman's down at the R Bar R."

He grinned. "You better be. Miss Esme'll scratch the eyes out of any gal tries to latch onto ya."

"Like I said, it ain't gonna be Annie Laurie. I ain't her kind of man. And besides, I tell ya, she's got a husband. Now let me tell you what's goin' on here. Then you can go back and tell Esme I'll be there as soon as I can make it."

"My orders are to stay with you 'til yer ready to come," he said.

We'd been talking a little while, mostly about what I'd been doing after I left the R Bar R, when there was a knock on the door and Annie Laurie came in with two huge mugs of steaming hot coffee.

"I'll fix some supper for you in a little while," she said. "That way you won't have to go out and it will be easier on your back."

When she'd gone Lew looked at me and grinned again. "See what I mean?"

145

I taken a sip of the coffee. It was hot and black and tasted good.

"Dang it, Lew," I said. "That don't mean nothin'. She's just bein' helpful. She made it real plain when we first met that she didn't want nothin' to do with me."

"Whatever you say," he said. "Whyn't you tell me about her and how she fits in here?"

So I told him about how I'd won the Staghorn off of Obie Shrifft.

"Heard about that from Obie," he interrupted.

Then I told him about the deal I made with her to run the Staghorn and about Cy Fierman robbing the bank and Nate Hale getting shot and then getting stabbed in his bed. And about finding the hidden valley and the skeletons of the horse and rider who'd been shot probably by a rifleman hidden on the cliff. And about the isolated stone cabin and the rooster whose crowing had led me to it.

"Tough old bird," I said. "Been out there by hisself for nigh on to two years. I hope he makes it."

"Who do you suppose lived there?" Lew asked.

"I think I know," I said. "But I ain't sure 'cause there's just too many loose ends around here."

All of sudden Lew asked, "Where's Jack Sears? Ain't he supposed to be around here somewhere? Ain't this where he come huntin' fer Fierman?"

"Dang fool has gone out by hisself to try to run him down," I said. "I was gonna go with him 'til I got shot. He shoulda waited fer me to heal up a bit. I ain't sure he can beat Fierman man to man and he dang sure can't take on the whole gang. If he don't come back in a day or two you and me'll have to go out and find him."

"In that case you better get some rest." Lew said. "I'm gonna go over to the hotel and get a room. I'll come back in a little while and have supper with ya."

146

He went out and I lay back and closed my eyes but it wasn't my day for sleeping. There was a tap on the door and Annie Laurie, who'd seen Lew leave, came in.

"You'll be leaving soon?" she asked, seating herself on the edge of the bed. "Is that why Mr. Haight came?"

"Yeah," I said. "And call him Lew. He's a R Bar R hand. Owner sent him to find me."

"Why do you have to go, Del? You own the saloon here and you have me to handle the business. You could stay, you know."

"Leave it be, Annie," I said. "I got to go as soon as I tie some loose ends together here. The Staghorn is yers when I leave. You've earned it."

"It's that woman at the R Bar R isn't is?" she asked softly. "Just like you said."

I felt my face turn red. "Yeah," I said, not looking at her.

"Well, then, you'd better go," she said in an emotionless voice. She started to stand up but I reached out, taken her hand, and pulled her back down.

"Annie," I said, "fer a lot of reasons including that yer a very special person in my life, I can't go yet, much as I'd like to."

"You don't owe me anything," she said, still with that flat tone of voice.

"Friends always owe friends or they ain't much as friends," I said.

She smiled suddenly. "You're right," she said. "You stay as long as you think you should and go when you think you should. We'll be friends, regardless. And, Del, I owe you a great deal."

"It don't matter," I said, and changed the subject. "I think you oughta tell me about you and Nate Hale and his boy—you say his name was Shadrach?"

"Is, not 'was,'" she said. "At least I pray it's not 'was.'"

"I think it's 'was,' Annie," I said gently.

She looked at me without saying anything, but there was a question on her face.

"Yer husband ever talk about a sunken valley or a hideout he might of had near the stone cabin?" I asked.

She shook her head. "Why do you ask?"

"I stumbled across one the other day," I said. "It's purty well hidden but men have been in there. I thought mebbe he was one of 'em. In fact one man or what's left of him is still there. I've a hunch it could be yer husband."

She gasped and put her hand to her mouth. "Oh, no, what makes you think so?"

"Only because he's been missin' for a couple of years and that skeleton of him and a horse don't seem to be much older than that."

"What happened to him?" she asked.

"Someone shot him. Him and his horse. Probably from the cliff above the valley."

"Was there anything to identify him?"

"Nothin' offhand. Might be you could see somethin', knowin' him like you do. But nothin' that meant anything to me."

"Could you tell the color of his horse?"

"Hard to tell. Bay, mebbe."

She nodded. "His horse was a bay. Could you take me there?"

"Sure," I said. "Soon's we get some of this other stuff straightened up."

"In a way I hope it's him," she said. "Then at least I can put that part of my life behind me. It's better than not knowing."

"I think ya purty much knew when you decided to leave the cabin and come to Shalak Springs," I said.

"I was pretty sure by then," she said. "If Shad was alive he'd have come back or at least found a way to send word. And when he didn't I decided the only thing to do was leave. The question was, where to go?"

"And then?"

"I had never been to Shalak Springs—Shad wouldn't let me

come until he was certain his father would accept the both of us—so I just packed up, hitched Mouse to the trap, loaded up Maxwelton, he was our mule, and came on to town. It was easy enough to say I'd come from Denver because I was in Denver when I met and married Shadrach.

"We'd only been married a little while when he disappeared. He'd come from Connecticut not too long before we met. His mother had died and he was trying to locate his father whom he hadn't seen since he was a little boy.

"When he found out that he was here Shad decided to move here and meet his father and at an appropriate time tell him who he was. Shad's mother had left him a little money so he didn't have to find work right away. Actually, he had hoped eventually to go into banking with his father. But before he had a chance to tell Nate who he was he disappeared."

"Well, what were ya doin' out there in that stone cabin? That's a ways from town," I said.

She got kind of a puzzled look on her face. "I don't know," she said. "Shad said he stumbled across it one day when he was out scouting as we were on our way to Shalak Springs. He said it would be a good place for us to stay since it wasn't more than 10 or 15 miles from town. But I always had a feeling that he'd been there before.

"There was something else funny, too. That rooster was already there. Whoever had lived there before evidently had a few chickens but when they left the weasels and coyotes probably got the rest of them."

She stopped talking and just sat there for a few minutes. Then she said, "You look tired, Del. Why don't you take a nap and I'll bring you some supper in a little while."

She stood up and leaned over and kissed me on the cheek, turned, and went out. And I went to sleep.

When I awoke it was dark and I lay there just thinking. Esme, the only woman I would ever love, had come back and if I was halfway smart I would pack up and leave tomorrow for the R Bar R. But I couldn't. I hadn't been here very long but in just a little while I'd gotten all tangled up in the town and its problems and especially with Annie Laurie Burns. I wasn't in love with her, I knew that, but still, we'd become special friends, and I wanted to stay and see that she wasn't cheated out of her inheritance.

Tomorrow, we'd go find Ferd Wislon, who I still thought was an honest man even if he was friends of Simpson, and lay out the situation to him and take him with us to see Simpson and Twain Sawyer. I was convinced they were trying to steal the bank out from under her and I was going to stop it if I could.

My musings were interrupted by a tap on the door and Annie Laurie came in carrying a trayful of food and a steaming cup of coffee. I sat up and the first thing she did was give me a glass of the tonic made from Ed Alliso's secret powder. I drank it down and then dived into the beef and beans and corn tortillas she'd brought up. It was a meal to put hair on a man's chest, which I didn't need because I already had it.

After I'd wiped up the last of the beans with the last of the tortillas and had swallowed the last of the coffee I heaved a sigh of contentment and leaned back against the headboard of the bed, being careful to sit so as not to put pressure on my wound.

Annie Laurie set the tray on the floor and came and sat on the edge of the bed.

"I'm glad you told me about the dead man in the valley," she said. "If it is Shad I won't cry. He's been gone too long and as I look back I think more and more it was a marriage based pretty much on loneliness, not on love. We were both lonely and alone. It just seemed natural to get married."

We sat quiet for a minute, and then she said, "So many things seemed odd out there at the cabin. I still don't understand it. Why he insisted on being out there alone instead of in town. Why he stocked provisions to last a long while. I was glad he did, though, especially when he never came back. That's how I got by. That and shooting a deer now and then. Once a stray steer wandered by and I shot and butchered it, too."

I looked at her quizzically. "I thought you said you was from Denver."

"I grew up on a ranch in Wyoming," she said. "Then I went to school in the East. But my father was getting along in years—mother died when I was a youngster—so he sold the ranch and moved to Denver. Daddy died shortly after I came home so I did what I had to do; I went out and got a job. It was a job in an accounting firm and I found that accounting and business came easy to me, which is why, my dear friend, I am a better business-man than you or Obie Shrifft will ever be."

She went on, "Sometimes I think I should never have gotten married, other times I think about going back to Denver. But I won't. I've found a home here and this is where I'm going to stay."

"Del," she said, suddenly grim. "You wait. I'm going to own this town. I may not be good enough to be a town councilman but when I'm through the town council will answer to me."

She laughed a smug little laugh but I didn't resent it because I knew what she said was true. She was good, she was tough, and at the same time she was a lady. She would make it here or any-where. I never had no doubts about that.

And she'd get married again. I knew that, too. And she'd make some man not only a good wife but a good partner, some-one to walk alongside him and not behind him. I looked at her closely—a handsome woman indeed—and she looked right back at me.

"What is it, Del?" she asked.

"I was just thinkin'," I said, "that I'm lucky to have you for a friend."

"That goes both ways, Del," she said, I thought a bit sadly. "Good night. I'll see you in the morning."

After she'd gone I lay there thinking, and suddenly it hit me.

By her own admission Shadrach had disappeared before he could ever tell Nate Hale who he was, and that meant Hale didn't know who she was either, so why would he have left everything to her?

Unless, of course, she had told him about her and Shadrach and offered him some sort of proof that Shadrach was his son and her husband. That might have been what happened. Or maybe, in spite of what she said and what I wanted to believe, they were more than just friends.

I was still trying to figure it all out when I drifted off to sleep.

CHAPTER 17

Most always I'm up with the daylight, but I was tired and still weak from losing all that blood and I slept until midmorning. I got dressed and went down to the kitchen to get me some hot water to wash my face and shave.

There were three of them sitting around the table—Annie Laurie, Lew Haight, and Wayne Johns—drinking coffee. When I came in Annie quick went to the stove and poured me a mugful. It was strong and hot and tasted good.

Water was boiling on the stove so I took a dipperful and went outside where I added a little cold water and washed and shaved without nicking myself.

Back inside Annie Laurie gave me the news: Johns had resigned as marshal and would go to work full-time as the Staghorn's chief bartender, replacing Gil Dellah who had gone off with Cy Fierman. We still needed a swamper and a general handyman to replace Chief Two Horse who, as far as we could tell, had also joined the Fierman gang, if he hadn't been a part of it all along.

"What are we goin' to do?" I asked Annie Laurie.

"We'll find someone before the day's out," she said. "I'll put out the word. There's kids and old folks around who could use a job.

"Right now, Del, if you're feeling up to it, you and I need to go see Gus Simpson and Twain Sawyer. Wayne tells me he saw Mr. Simpson riding into town when he was coming over here.

"Wayne, I guess it's time you opened for business."

"Yes'm," he said, getting up and heading for the barroom.

I said, "I'm fine. Let's go."

Lew said, "I'll just wander along with you two. I'll wait outside and keep an eye on things."

"Where's Wislon?" I asked.

"He was by earlier. He said he'll meet us there," Annie said.

We walked through the empty barroom where Wayne Johns was standing behind the bar, still wearing his badge, polishing glasses. He looked right at home.

We stepped outside into the bright sunlight and stopped a moment to accustom our eyes to the light. Down at the end of town two horsemen were walking their horses slowly down the road toward us. One of them was swaying drunkenly in the saddle.

I took a longer look and suddenly swore. "Dang," I said. "That there is Jack Sears and he looks hurt. And dang! He's ridin' Old Dobbin."

"And that's Gil Dellah," Annie said excitedly. "I wonder what's happened?"

I turned back to the saloon. "Wayne," I hollered. "Git out here! Quick!"

We waited impatiently as the two horsemen came up the road and finally stopped in front of the Staghorn. Jack Sears sat there holding on to the saddlehorn with both hands, a glazed look in his eyes, his shirt bloody.

"He's hurt bad," Dellah said. "You better get him some help."

Big Wayne Johns went over to Sears' horse and lifted Jack gently from the saddle. Cradling him in his arms he carried him through the bat wing doors and headed for the stairs with Annie and Lew right behind him.

I looked at Gil Dellah and he stared defiantly back at me. "We better talk," he said after a moment and climbed down from his horse, tied him to the hitching rail, and headed for the barroom.

Inside he went directly to the bar where he fished out two beers, opened them, and brought them over to the table where I was waiting. He wiped off the lips of the bottles with his sleeve, handed one to me, and taken a big swig out of his. "Thirsty," he said. "Been a long, slow ride."

Lew came down the steps from the upstairs two at a time, saw me, and called over his shoulder without stopping, "Goin' after the doc."

I turned back to Dellah. "Ya wanna tell me what this is all about?"

"Boss," Dellah said, looking me straight in the eyes, "I ain't a part of Fierman's gang. I owed him. He helped me out of a tight spot once in Carson City and I paid him back, is all."

"Who shot Jack?" I asked.

"Fierman," he said. "It was a fair fight. But Jack didn't have no chance. Cy shot him twice afore Jack could even draw his gun. Cy's the fastest gun I ever saw. And I was tendin' bar in Luke Short's White Elephant saloon in Fort Worth when Short gunned down Jim Courtright. That was just afore I come up here. And Cy's faster'n either one of 'em."

"How'd it happen?"

"One of the gang spotted Sears followin' us and he wasn't very smart about it. We laid in the weeds for him and when he come ridin' by Cy stepped out and asked him if he wanted anything. Sears went fer his gun and Cy shot him out of the saddle. Hurt him bad.

"Cy told me to bring him back to town, see if Ed Alliso could save him. Cy's a hard man but fair and he ain't no killer. He only fights when he has to. I wasn't gonna go with him, anyway—I ain't cut out fer that kind of life—so I brought him on in."

"Why's he ridin' Old Dobbin?"

"One of the gang was ridin' him but Fierman said to take him back to you. Said he didn't want you thinkin' he was no horse thief."

Dellah made a noise halfway between a chuckle and a snort. "He robs banks but he don't want no one thinkin' he's a horse thief."

"I guess I owe him one," I said. "Me and Old Dobbin been together a long time."

"What happened to the chief?" I asked.

"He dropped off when we passed his shack. Said somethin' about headin' for 'Frisco. He wasn't mixed up in no robberies either. Cy was payin' him to keep an eye on things around Sha-lak Springs is all."

I didn't answer him but I was sure there was more to Chief Two Horse than that. I couldn't get the picture of him out of my mind when he found me at the stone cabin. He wasn't nobody's swamper or handyman then.

While we were talking Ed Alliso had come in and hurried upstairs, as usual carrying his little medical bag. Gil and I got to our feet and also headed up the stairs.

Wayne Johns had carried Sears in and laid him on my bed. Alliso was bending over him, seeing what he could do for him. He'd run out Johns and Lew Haight, but had kept Annie Laurie in with him to help.

We stood around not saying much for ten minutes or so until Alliso came out. His face was somber.

"He's not gonna make it, Tackett. But he's conscious so you might want to go in for a minute."

"Lew," I said, "he'll wanna see you, too."

I went in, with Lew right behind me. Jack was lying there white as a ghost, with Annie Laurie sitting beside him, holding his hand. She was almost as white.

I went over and looked down at him. He looked up at me with a kind of lopsided grin. "It was a fair fight," he said. "Don't tangle with him, Del, he's too fast."

He closed his eyes and for a moment I thought he was gone. But he opened them again and said in a strong voice, "Don't look like I'm gonna get that chance to whup yer tail after all."

"Yer gonna make it," was all I could say.

"But as I looked at him I saw his eyes begin to glaze over. "I'm comin', Mary Lou," he said in a loud, clear voice. "I'm comin'."

He shuddered then, and sank back all relaxed and limp, dropping Annie Laurie's hand, which he'd been clutching tightly.

I felt the tears well up and I brushed them away roughly with the back of my hand. Jack Sears and me had started out as enemies. He'd come to kill me once and I had taken him by surprise and knocked him down and stomped him and thrown him in a watering trough. Twice after that he'd had chances to kill me or let me be killed but he wouldn't do it unless it was a fair fight. And before that could happen we'd become close friends.

I'd been a lonesome and a lonely wanderer the most of my life and not wanting nor expecting much more. But back there on the R Bar R I'd not only met the woman I loved, but I'd also found good friends in Jack Sears and Lew Haight and Blackie Harrington. And there was a dog back there, too, that I loved. A big black dog named Beauty and I was aching to see her almost as much a I wanted to see the others. To my way of thinking nothing beats the love of a good woman, but the love of a faithful dog comes in a mighty close second.

Now Jack Sears was dead, killed in a fair fight with Cy Fierman and I was still a long way from being able to head for the R Bar R. There was still the job of making sure Annie Laurie got what was coming to her and I knew also that I'd never rest until I met Fierman face to face.

He might have killed Jack in a fair fight but him and his gang had robbed the Shalak Springs bank and shot old Nate Hale and they was responsible in one way or another for his death and the death of Sears' wife, Mary Lou. And I had to try to find out who'd stabbed Hale to death and who'd taken those shots at Annie and me. It was beginning to look like it might be a long time before I got back to the R Bar R.

"Looks like we got another buryin' to do," I said as Lew reached down and pulled the cover over Sears' face. "Annie, you get ahold of Alliso and see if we can do it first thing in the mornin'. Then you and me'll go see Simpson and Sawyer. If there's gonna be a bank in this town yer gonna run it. That is, if you want to."

Alliso was waiting in the next room. "I thought I ought to stay around and see what you want to do," he explained. "I can have a coffin built today if you think he won't last."

"He died whilst we was in there," I said. "I'd like to have the buryin' tomorrow, say around nine o'clock."

Alliso reached out and taken my hand. "I'm sorry about that," he said. "I know he was your friend. I tried but there was nothing I could do. He'd lost too much blood."

"I think we all need a cup of coffee," Annie said. "There's some on the stove. We'll have that and then we'll go to the bank."

Wislon was waiting in the barroom when we went down and he joined us in the kitchen.

Whilst Annie Laurie was pouring the coffee Johns said, "Now that Dellah's back maybe I'd better take the marshal's job again."

"Sounds like a good idea," Wislon said. "This was a pretty peaceful place 'til Tackett come along and it'll probably be a pretty peaceful place after he's gone."

He laughed and said, "When are you leavin', Tackett?"

"I hope never," Annie said.

"Real soon, I hope," I said. "Soon's I get a couple of things cleared up. With yer help mebbe we can start today."

Wislon shook his head doubtfully. "Miss Burns showed me the papers she got from Nate's personal safe and they look valid. But like I said before, possession is nine points of the law. And even more importantly Simpson has put money in there to make sure the bank is solvent. I don't think you'll find much support here if you and Miss Burns attempt to take over."

"What about you, Mr. Wislon?" I asked. "Where'll you stand?"

He shrugged. "I'd like to stand with Miss Burns," he said. "But Gus Simpson's a mighty hard man to stand against. This wouldn't be much of town without him."

"It ain't much of a town period. Not if the people who run the town let Gus Simpson take what ain't rightly his," I said hotly.

"Cool down, boy," Wislon said. "It's not quite like it looks. There was a time when this town didn't have a bank. Then Gus Simpson built the bank and brought Nate Hale in to run it and after it was doing pretty good he sold it to Hale. I don't know whether or not Hale paid him off. He may have some kind of legal claim to it."

"I think we should go talk to Mr. Simpson," Annie Laurie said. "Let's find out what his plans are. Will you gentlemen go with me?"

The four of us got up and headed for the door.

The bank was open as it had been every weekday since Nate Hale had been shot, but today Twain Sawyer was not in the teller's cage. Instead a matronly looking woman was there, a woman with a round pleasant face, gray hair, and a ready smile.

"Is Mr. Simpson here?" Annie Laurie asked her.

"He's in the office there with Mr. Sawyer. I'm sure it will be all right for you to go on back. Just knock."

With Annie Laurie leading the way we trooped on back to the office that had been Nate Hale's. At her knock Simpson's voice impatiently said, "We're busy. Come back later."

Annie pushed the door open and went in with Wislon and me on her heels, whilst Lew stayed outside in the hallway.

"This can't wait," she said, facing the two men in the office. Simpson was sitting behind the desk that had belonged to Hale and Twain Sawyer was sitting in a straight-backed chair half facing the desk and half facing the door.

"I said we're busy," Simpson snapped. "Now get out. All three of you."

"Ain't no way to talk to a lady, Mr. Simpson," I said pleasantly.

"Well," he said, "if it isn't the gunman, butting in where he doesn't belong. Miss Burns, you and Wislon here take this two-bit gunslinger and get out."

"Seems to me yer the wrong person to be tellin' anyone to be gettin' out," I said. "Miss Burns here, not you, is the rightful owner of this bank."

Twain Sawyer snickered. "Just because Nate was keeping her doesn't mean he meant to leave her the bank."

I heard Annie Laurie gasp even as I took three quick steps across the office and picked Twain Sawyer up by the front of his shirt.

"Don't hit me," he squealed as I drew back my fist.

"Drop him, Tackett," I heard Simpson say and the tone of his voice made me look around. He had a Colt .45 six-shooter in his hand and it was pointed at my head.

I let go of Sawyer's shirt and he sank back into his chair.

"I'll make you eat that gun one day, Simpson," I said.

"Don't be in a hurry," he said. "I wasn't always a fatcat rancher."

Annie Laurie said, "Mr. Sawyer, as soon as I have established my ownership of this bank you will be fired. Furthermore, if you ever speak to me or of me again like that I will take a horsewhip to you."

"Gus," Wislon said, trying to get things back on track, "Miss Burns has some papers that indicate that Nate left all his possessions to her, including his property and the Shalak Springs bank."

"Ferd," Simpson said, settling back in his chair and chewing on his dead cigar, "let me tell you something. Any papers Miss Burns has aren't worth the powder to blow 'em to hell. I own this building. Nate rented it from me. It was cheaper than buildin' his own. Nate tried to pass off that the bank robbers only got a thousand or so dollars. He lied. They cleaned him out of every dollar he had. The only assets he had here were a few small mortgage notes. And they're not enough to cover what he owed his depositors.

"Now if Miss Burns wants the bank she can have it, but when I leave I'm takin' my money with me—the $10,000 I have deposited in order to keep the bank solvent—and I will expect Miss Burns to pay the rent when it comes due. Now, if you all will excuse us Mr. Sawyer and I have business to discuss."

CHAPTER 18

WELL, WE WENT out of that bank kind of like whipped dogs, our tails between our legs, me wishing all the time that I really was one of them gunslinging Sacketts. If I was I'd send the word out to my kinfolk and we'd run Gus Simpson out of town and out of the country and then we'd track down Cy Fierman and I would go up against him one on one.

Trouble was, I wasn't one of them Sacketts and would never be. I was just a big old boy from a mining camp deep in the High Sierras of California and there wasn't one person in the world that I could call kin.

I felt like cussing real good, but knew that Ma, looking down from whatever heaven she was in, would be frowning at the thought, so I contented myself with a couple of good "dangs." And then I really began to get mad, mad at Fierman for robbing Nate Hale's bank, mad at whoever it was killed him, mad at Gus Simpson, and mostly, mad at myself for not being of more help to Annie Laurie.

We stomped through the bat wing doors of the saloon and tramped back to the kitchen where Annie Laurie put on a big pot of coffee and the rest of us slouched around the big eating table.

After a minute Ferd Wislon said, "Well, I guess that's that. Simpson has the bank and there doesn't seem to be anything you can do about it. And maybe it's just as well; runnin' a bank is a man's job anyway. And, Annie, you've still got the Staghorn and as far as I know Nate's house and property are yours, too."

"What're ya tryin' to say, Wislon?" I asked. "That ya ain't gonna help Annie get what's hers?"

"You could say that," Wislon said calmly. "There's serious doubt in my mind that the bank is hers. And even if that wasn't the case, I'm not going up against Gus Simpson. He could break me in my business and he could kill you or have you killed if you interfere in his. And I don't think he'd hesitate to do either one if it suited his purpose. That there is a mean man."

"I understand," Annie Laurie said resignedly. "If I were in your shoes I wouldn't buck Gus Simpson either. Thanks for going with us today."

There was an awkward silence for a moment, then Wislon stood up and put on his hat. "I'll be going," he said. "Luck, Annie."

After he'd gone I looked at Lew. "You wanna go back to the R Bar R or you wanna stay here and fight?"

"I'll stay," he said. "I went home now Miss Esme'd run me off for desertin' ya."

"I guess we'd better figure what we do next," I said. "I got me a couple of ideas, but we better talk 'em over."

"You two go ahead and talk," Annie Laurie said. "I'm going over to the bank and close out my account and the Staghorn's. I could deal with Gus Simpson if I had to, but I'll not do business with that little weasel, Twain Sawyer.

"Furthermore, I going to tell Gil not to serve him if he comes into the Staghorn."

"What're ya gonna do with our money?" I asked.

"I don't know," she said. "Put it in a tin can for now or hide it under the mattress. Maybe I'll start a bank of my own."

She stalked out.

"That there is some woman," Lew said as she disappeared into the barroom. "Too bad she's in love with you. I'd make a play for her otherwise."

"Go right ahead," I said. "The only woman in my life is down on the R Bar R and I'm gettin' in a hurry to get there."

We spent the next half hour going over the things we needed to do. I figured we had four, maybe five men we could count on, me and Lou, Gil Dellah, Billy Jeff Linton, and maybe Wayne Johns.

We were still talking when Dellah poked his head in.

"Annie Laurie come chargin' in a minute ago, went upstairs, and come right back down carryin' a horsewhip. What's happenin'?"

"Well dang," I said. "Look's like someone's gonna get a whuppin'. Let's go watch."

We reached the street just in time to see Twain Sawyer running out of the bank with Annie Laurie behind him lashing at his back with a horsewhip she'd got from somewhere. Sawyer stepped in a rut in the road and stumbled and fell flat. Annie stood over him and whipped him until he curled up and began hollering like a baby.

By the time I got to Annie Laurie it was plain he'd had enough so I reached out as she was raising the whip one more time and stopped her swing by grabbing her wrist.

"That's enough, Annie," I said. "You'll kill him."

"That sonofabitch," she swore gasping for breath, her face still contorted with anger. "I intend to. No man talks to me like he did and gets away with it."

"What'd he say?" I asked.

"He told me if I hadn't withdrawn our money he was going to cancel our account. He said he didn't do business with sluts and whores."

There was a crowd of about a dozen people standing around us by now and one woman, young and flashily dressed, said, "Funny. He does business with me."

A couple of men in the crowd snickered and Annie turned to me and burst into tears. I taken her in my arms and patted her on the back, then I kind of shifted her over to Lew who was standing next to me. And whilst he comforted her I reached down and hoisted Sawyer to his feet by the back of his coat collar. There was dirt all over the front of him and his face was tear-streaked. There were some mean welts on his right cheek where the whip had caught him as he was trying to escape.

"Sawyer," I said, "you done tore it good. Don't you ever let me hear of you talkin' to or about Miss Annie Laurie. Don't you never go near her, neither. You see her comin' you cross to the other side of the road, you hear me? Because if you don't, if I hear or see anything at all of you sayin' or doing anything to hurt her I won't kill ya, but I'll make ya wish I had, you hear me?"

I shoved him away and he went stumbling off toward the bank.

Just then Wayne Johns came striding up important-like. "What goes on here?" he demanded.

"You the marshal again?" I asked.

"Oops," he said. "I ain't been rehired yet. That was a unofficial question."

Lew who was still holding Annie Laurie close to him looked over her shoulder at Johns. "You missed a first-class horsewhippin'," he said. "Annie here made a real Christian out of Twain Sawyer, or at least she tried to."

Annie Laurie pulled herself free from Lew and turned to face us, dabbing at her eyes with one of those dainty hankies she kept in her bosom. "I guess I lost my temper," she said. "I'm sorry but he shouldn't have talked to me like that."

A matronly looking woman, one of the last of the dwindling crowd, called to her, "You done good, Miss Burns. That there is a mean little man."

Annie didn't answer but gave her a grateful smile.

We were standing there undecided as to what to do next when Ed Alliso came walking toward us.

"I've got a man making a coffin," he said. "Should be done in another hour. In the meantime I'd like to send my two Mexes to get Sears' body, I'll put him in the back room of my shop until the coffin is finished. You still want the funeral tomorrow at nine?"

His question shamed me. There'd been so much going on I'd forgotten all about Jack Sears lying cold and dead in my bed up above the Staghorn barroom. Jack Sears, my friend and a man who'd saved my life and I'd forgotten all about him. I felt myself flushing with embarrassment.

"Tell the Mexes to go get him," I said. "But treat him gentle. He was my friend. Let's have the funeral early whilst it's still cool. Nine o'clock all right with everyone?"

Annie Laurie and Lew nodded and Alliso headed back toward his shop.

It was getting toward midafternoon and all of a sudden I realized I was hungry. We hadn't had nothing to eat since breakfast and I was not only hungry but I was feeling weak and trembly all of a sudden.

It had only been two days since I was shot and I was a long ways from getting my strength back.

"I need food," I said. "If it ain't too late leave us go get some food over at the cafe. You-uns have to be hungry, too."

"Hold up a minute. Here comes trouble," Lew said.

I looked where he was facing and saw big, gangly Gus Simpson striding toward us from the bank.

Simpson had a scowl on his face as he came up to us and without stopping or any warning he just walked up and slugged me alongside the jaw. I went down like I'd been poleaxed. I was lying there in the dust, flat on my face so I didn't see the kick Simpson aimed at me. I didn't see it miss, either, as Annie Laurie was all over him, clawing and scratching and biting. Or so Lew told me later.

Through the haze, though, I heard him hollering, "Get offa me. Goddamn it, get her offa me."

Then I heard Lew shout, "Get offa him, Annie, so I can slug the sonofabitch."

And through all the shouting came Wayne Johns' voice: "This is the law. Everyone stand where you are. Haight, you put up your gun. Now don't nobody move. That includes you, Simpson."

A second later Annie Laurie was kneeling by my side. "Are you all right, Del? Are you all right?" she asked frantically.

I struggled over on my good side and pushed myself into a sitting position.

"I'm all right," I said, rubbing my jaw. "He sucker-punched me."

"You get up, Tackett, and I'll knock you down again," Simpson snarled. His face was bloody from where Annie Laurie had scratched him and there were toothmarks on his neck where she'd bitten him.

I grinned at him. It hurt but I grinned at him. "I ain't gettin' up now," I said. "But when I get well I'll hunt ya up and we'll see who knocks who down. Or maybe I'll just sic Annie Laurie on ya again."

"That hellcat comes near me again and I'll forget she's a woman," he growled. "And the next time I see ya it won't do ya any good to hide behind her skirts or pretend yer hurt."

He stomped off and I climbed slowly to my feet.

"Dang it, Annie," I complained. "You horsewhip Twain Sawyer and Simpson comes out and slugs me. That ain't hardly fair."

All of sudden she laughed. "You went down like you'd been hit by lightning," she giggled. "But I protected you after that. I kept him from kicking you."

"She sure did," Lew grinned. "He's lucky Johns come along or she'd of scratched his eyes out."

"Johns," I said, "you still ain't the law. What're you doin' messin' into things?"

"Old habits die hard," he said with a wink and a smile as he began walking away.

We walked down to the little cafe which was empty except for us and the waitress who was busy mopping the floor.

"You're either late or early," she said. "Cook won't have much this time of day."

"Coffee will be fine," Annie Laurie said, and Lew said, "Make it two."

I rubbed my jaw and kind of moved it around. It wasn't busted but it hurt to move it much. "You got any aigs?" I asked.

The waitress nodded. "A few."

"Scramble me up five or six and bring along a plateful of beans," I said. I didn't order a steak even though I wanted one. Someone else would of had to do the chewing for me.

We were drinking coffee, waiting for my food, when Wislon walked in.

"Been lookin' for ya," he said. "Been talking to Simpson. Says he damn near broke his hand on your jaw."

"Yeah," I said. "Well you tell him he dang near broke my jaw on his hand."

"I'll tell him but he's not gonna laugh. Fact is, he says if you're not out of town by sundown tomorrow he's gonna run you out."

"I don't run very easy," I said. "But I ain't lookin' for trouble with him either. Leastwise not 'til I'm feelin' better. What's his beef, anyway?"

"Says you put Annie up to tryin' to steal the bank from him and says you put her up to horsewhippin' Sawyer."

"Them ain't very good reasons," I said. "There's something else behind all a this."

"I'm just the messenger," Wislon said. "But I think you ought to know, if Simpson goes to run you out of town nobody here will stick up for you."

"I will," Annie Laurie said indignantly.

"I wouldn't if I was you," Wislon said. "You can't stand against Simpson by yourself. If he has to he'll bring thirty men into town

169

to do whatever he wants done. Includin' burn down your saloon or run you out of town. It wouldn't bother him a bit you being a lady and all. Furthermore, if I was Tackett I'd leave while I still had a whole hide."

"I'll think on it," I said.

After he'd left, I said, "You know, it's funny. Just yesterday Simpson was still tryin' to hire me to go after Cy Fierman. Wanted him dead, he said, on account of him killin' Hale. Leastwise that's what he said. Now he's tryin' to run me out of town. And you, too, Annie, if he thinks he can get away with it. What do you two make of it?"

"I think he's wanted to get rid of you all along," Annie Laurie said. "He probably thought that if you went after Fierman he'd kill you and that wouldn't be too bad either."

"That makes sense, except for one thing," I said. "He didn't know we was gonna try and steal the bank from him until this mornin'."

She looked at me strangely. "We weren't trying to steal the bank. It's mine. Nate left it to me or, rather, to my husband."

"I know that," I said. "I was teasin'."

"You know," I said, changing the subject, "I think I'll do what Simpson wants. I think I'll leave town tomorrow. Matter of fact, Annie, maybe you'd like to go with me."

CHAPTER 19

COME DAYBREAK I was already up, but when I went down to the kitchen Annie Laurie had beaten me there and the coffee pot was hot.

She was frying bacon with one hand and flipping flapjacks with the other, so being the thoughtful gent I am, I poured my own coffee. It was black as sin and tasted even better.

Whilst I was drinking it Lew Haight came in, looking hungry. He sat down just as Annie Laurie set a big platterful of pancakes and bacon on the table.

She had butter and wild honey to put on the pancakes and I and Lew wolfed down all but a couple of them along with about a dozen slices of bacon. When we were through there wasn't much left for her but when I went to apologize she swore she never ate much for breakfast anyway.

I'd had me a big meal the night before and that, along with Ed Alliso's special tea, had me feeling almost back to normal, except for my sore jaw. I pushed my chair back and stood up. "I got some things to do before we go," I said. "So I better get to gettin'."

The night before Annie'd said to me, "If you're taking me along that must mean you're planning on coming back."

"That's right," I said.

"But I thought Gus Simpson told you to leave town for good."

"He'll cool off," I said. "Or mebbe after I get clear well I'll try and cool him off. In the meantime there's a couple of things I wanna look at and maybe a thing or two you outta see."

She didn't say anything more, but went off to bed. And she didn't bring the subject up again at breakfast or even act like she had it on her mind.

So, whilst she was cleaning up the kitchen I moseyed on down to the stable and hitched Mouse to the trap. Then I saddled Old Dobbin and tied him behind it. Man never knows when he'll need a horse and besides it was good to have that big old bay back with me.

I rubbed his nose and fed him a lump of sugar and told him I'd missed him. And I got to thinking that there were only three critters, now that Ma was gone, that I really loved—Esme Rankin, although you couldn't rightly call either her or Ma a critter, Esme's big black dog, Beauty, and Old Dobbin. If I had them three there wasn't nothing else I really wanted.

I drove the trap on down to the Staghorn and in a moment Annie Laurie came out carrying a wicker basket.

"Lunch," she said in answer to my unspoken question.

"You forgot somethin'," I said.

She looked at me questioningly.

"Jack Sears. We got to bury him," I said.

"I know," she said. "I didn't forget."

She fetched her little locket watch from her bosom. "It's about time," she said.

I flicked Mouse with the whip and we headed off to the little burying ground. The Mexicans had already dug the hole and the coffin was sitting alongside of it. Ed Alliso had already arrived as had Lew and Gil Dellah. And there wasn't anyone else; just the five of us.

We men took off our hats and I said, "Lord, he was a good friend. Take care of him please. Amen."

Alliso turned to me and said, "If you got things to do we'll get him in the ground."

I helped Annie back in the trap and we taken off at a brisk

trot, heading out of town toward the shack of Chief Two Horse. Behind us and off to one side, trying not to be seen, was a lone rider. Annie didn't see him and I didn't say nothing although I knew who it was. It was Lew Haight. A man never could tell when an extra hand or an extra gun might come in handy.

For a while Annie didn't say anything but her curiosity finally got the better of her. "Where are we going?" she asked.

"Two or three places," I said. "Thought we'd start out by visitin' Chief Two Horse. See if he's home and if he is see how he's makin' out."

She looked surprised. "I thought he'd taken up with Cy Fierman?"

I shrugged. "Dellah says not. Says Fierman paid him to keep an eye on things in town, but says the chief was never part of the gang."

"But why would he—?"

"I guess he needed the money. He told me he was tryin' to save enough to get to 'Frisco or one of them big cities where he could sell his paintings."

"I never saw any of them except the one he gave me," she said. "Have you?"

"Was at his place once. Saw a bunch of 'em. Most of 'em were pictures of the mountains although he had one picture of an old Injun medicine man. I thought they was pretty good but I sure ain't no expert on picture paintin'."

We came to the turn-off to the chief's place but I noticed that the signboard pointing the way had been taken down. When we came up to his shack it appeared to be deserted.

"I think he's gone," I said. "I'll go see."

I handed the reins to Annie Laurie and climbed down from the trap and went and tried the door. It was unlocked, which I might of expected since the only way to lock it was to put down the bar on the inside.

The chief was gone, apparently for good. All the pictures

were gone from the walls and from where they'd been stacked against them. There was a lot of empty frames lying around and that was all. Apparently he'd taken the pictures off their frames so he could roll the canvasses up and pack them on the back of a horse or mule, or maybe lie them flat in a wagon.

I went back out. "He's taken off," I said. "He's taken his pictures and everything he owned 'cept the furniture."

I climbed back into the trap and headed back to the main trail. When we reached it I headed away from town and in the direction of the stream that led to the hidden valley or, if you crossed it, toward the stone cabin.

"Where to now?" Annie Laurie asked

"Well, I thought we might go see if that old red rooster is all right," I said, "but first there's another place I wanna show ya."

We'd been riding along for a ways when Annie said, "There's been a wagon along here in the last day or two. See the tracks?"

"Dang," I said. "I never noticed 'em."

She laughed. "I don't know how you've gotten along out here all these years without seeing things like that. You probably wouldn't see an Indian war party until you were on top of one."

"Aw, I ain't that bad," I said, not looking at her. "It's just when I'm with a good-lookin' woman I don't notice much of anything else."

She laughed. "Del, you've hardly noticed me since you been here, except as someone you're in business with."

"That ain't so," I protested.

"Yes it is. You've got a girlfriend down in Nora and you don't even look at other women."

Well, when she said that, I didn't say anything because I was too busy feeling guilty remembering a woman named Ada Venn and the night she and I had spent together after I'd left Nora. I hadn't planned it but it had happened and I still wasn't sure whether or not I wished it hadn't.

When we came to the stream I surprised her again by turning

off the trail and headed upstream toward the mesa.

"You're following that wagon," she said.

I hadn't been paying much attention being all wrapped up in what she'd said earlier. "Danged if I'm not," I said, suddenly alert. "Where in the heck to you suppose he's goin'?"

"Where are we going?" she asked.

"You'll see," I said noncommittally.

The sun was high in the sky now and she changed the subject by asking if I was getting hungry. "We'll eat up where the stream comes out of the base of the mesa," I said. "It won't be long."

"Are you going to call Lou in to join us?" she asked impishly.

"Well I'll be danged," I said. "I didn't think you'd see him. Yeah. I'll call him in."

She laughed. "Fortunately only one of us on this ride is blind."

"That ain't true," I protested again. "But dang it, pretty girls sure enough distract me."

I taken off my hat and waved it at Lew who was still riding to the back and one side of us and he came cantering over.

"Miss Burns here is wishful that you would join us for lunch," I said. "We was going to eat up ahead where the stream comes out of the base of the mesa. But there's wagon tracks here that Miss Eagle Eye has spotted so I'm gonna go on ahead and see what the situation is. You two wait here."

I climbed down from the trap and mounted Old Dobbin and we taken off at a fast trot, paralleling the stream but riding well away from it. As we got close to the mesa I slowed him down to a walk and when we were about a hundred yards off I dismounted and tied him to a small tree. Then taking a roundabout way and doing my best to keep trees and rocks between me and anyone who might be camped or waiting at the stream, I headed for the spot where it flowed from the mesa.

When I got closer I was surprised to see a horse and wagon standing in a little open place near the base of the mesa. A closer look told me the horse was Old Dan and he was tied to a tree. There was no sign of Chief Two Horse or anyone else, for that matter, but not wanting to take a chance, I moved as quietly as I could toward the clearing, being careful to keep what cover there was between me and the wagon.

Finally I dropped down on my belly and crawled the remaining few yards to the last tree between me and the clearing. Old Dan sensed my presence and looked in my direction and whinnied. Carefully I scanned the area and finally on the far side of the wagon I saw something that might have been a body.

I stood up and, staying among the trees and brush, worked my way around to the other side of the wagon. Sure enough, it was a body. Taking a chance that whoever had shot him had left I drew my gun and stepped out into the clearing, bracing myself for the feel of a bullet or the sound of a voice ordering me to drop my gun.

Nothing.

Relaxing a little but still holding my gun, I went over to the body. It was Chief Two Horse Hyde, the last of the Mohicans. Dang, I thought, too bad he wasn't a Sioux or a Ute. There's still a bunch of them around. I pushed the thought aside and bent over to see where he'd been shot and the first thing I noticed was that he was still breathing.

I squatted down and turned him over. He'd been shot in the chest twice, both times from the front. His gun was lying close by. I picked it up and taken a quick look. One shot had been fired which meant he'd had his chance, but lost. The blood around his wounds had dried which made me think it had been some time since he was shot. It seemed a miracle to me that he was still alive.

I didn't have nothing to get water with so I taken off my bandanna and went to the stream and soaked it good. Then I went back to Two Horse, raised his head up, and squeezed water from the bandanna between his dry and feverish lips. After a moment he groaned, opened his eyes, and gazed at me uncomprehendingly.

"Howdy, Chief. It's me, Tackett," I said.

He blinked his eyes a couple of times and managed to focus in on me. "How, Paleface," he whispered, "Injun in heap big trouble."

"Who done this to ya, Chief?" I asked. "Who shot ya?"

"I didn't want to double-cross you," he said, his voice so low I had to strain to hear him. "I needed money to get to 'Frisco so I could sell—my—paintings."

He closed his eyes and his head kind of sank back in my hand and I thought for a second he was gone. But he opened his eyes again and again I asked, "Who shot ya?"

"Don't know," he whispered. "Someone was hiding inside the mesa."

"Where the stream comes out?" I asked.

He didn't answer. Instead he muttered, "The money's in there somewhere. I have to find it."

He didn't say anything more, just looked at me. But even though his eyes were open his stare was the stare of a dead man.

I laid his head gently back on the ground. Then I went and unhitched Old Dan and led him to the stream where I let him have a good drink, but not too much, and then retied him to the tree.

I was sorry the chief was dead. Yeah, he'd gone over to the other side but he was one of a kind—an educated Indian, a real artist who'd come West to paint the land and seek his roots. Now he was dead, gone to the Happy Hunting Ground of his fathers. "Dang," I said aloud. "The last of the Mohicans. I'm gonna miss him."

I picked him up and carried him to the wagon and laid him gently on top of the layers of canvas that he had packed carefully in the wagon bed. I untied Old Dan, hitched him back to the wagon, throwed the reins over his head, and started to climb aboard when a sound by the creek made me turn.

There, standing in the middle of the stream right where it emerged from the mesa, was Twain Sawyer, and he had a .30-caliber Winchester rifle pointed squarely at my belly. The red marks were plain on his face where Annie had slashed him with her whip.

"Well, if it isn't Mr. Tackett," he said nastily in his high nasal twang. "What brings you out here?"

"Same thing as brought you out," I said. "I wanted to take another look around that little hidey-hole back in there."

"It wouldn't have done you any good," he said. "If Shad Hale hid it there he hid it pretty well. Neither the chief nor I have been able to find it."

"What's in there?" I asked.

"What's in there?" he repeated. "Money, you fool! Money. Four thousand dollars in gold. Hale got it in a train robbery. I've seen the wanted poster. He came here to hide out."

Four thousand dollars! That meant Shad Hale had been using the sunken valley as a hiding place. No wonder he had holed up at the stone cabin with his new wife—to be near his money. But that meant Shad Hale was a wanted man. Did Annie Laurie know that? And was he really Nate Hale's son? How would Nate have known anyway? He hadn't seen his son since he was little.

Dang! Every time I found an answer to what was going on it seemed like two more questions arose.

"Them Shad Hale's bones in there?" I asked, trying to distract him.

"Them's Shad Hale's bones," he mimicked. "I don't know why I'm talking to you. I might as well kill you now and get it over with."

He began to raise the rifle and I said in a hurry, "Hang on a minute. If you wanna kill me there's nothin' I can do about it. But it wouldn't hurt ya to tell me a couple of things first."

I was stalling for time and he knew it, but he wanted to brag some, too, and show me how smart he was.

"Make it quick," he said.

"Why'd ya kill Chief Two Horse here? He wasn't hurtin' nothin'."

"You don't know anything," he said. "Everyone around here thought he was an oddball, an educated Indian and an artist who cleaned saloons for a living. Well, let me tell you, he was looking for Shad Hale, too. He knew about the money and he found where Shad had it hidden. I followed him one day and after he left I went in. I barely got out before Hale came along. That's when I put two and two together.

"And let me tell you something else about Two Horse. Five years back I was working in a Bank in Dodge and he was in a gunfight there and I've never seen a faster gun. I remembered that today but almost too late. Even though I was holding the rifle on him he got one shot off before I killed him. I had to kill him, you know. Otherwise he'd of killed me."

"I'll be danged," I said in wonderment. "A Injun gunfighter. Never heard of one. He told me he come from the East. Said he was half Mohican."

"He did come from the East but it was a long time ago."

Sawyer quit talking and raised his rifle and I steeled myself for the bite of a bullet. "I'm tired of all this talk," Twain Sawyer said, and a shot rang out.

But I didn't feel anything and my first thought was, he missed.

But then I saw him drop the rifle and crumble to the ground, his head and shoulders lying on the bank of the stream and the lower half of his body in the water.

"You all right, boss?" It was Lew Haight's voice.

I turned in its direction, my knees trembling a bit and my voice shaky. "I'm all right," I said, "thanks to you."

Lew came out from the brush on the other side of the creek and the two of us walked over to Twain Sawyer.

He was still alive and moaning. "Help me," he groaned, pressing his right hand against a wound in his left shoulder, while blood oozed through his spread fingers. "I'm dying. Don't let me die."

He saw me standing over him. "I talk too much," he said. "I should have known better."

"Yer bad hurt, Sawyer," I said, leaning over him. "I don't think yer gonna make it. I need to know something afore ya cash in yer chips."

He looked up at me. "Why, not," he gasped. "Shoot."

"I already done that," Lew said drily.

Me and Sawyer ignored him. "Who killed Nate Hale?" I asked. "Was it you?"

He nodded his head. "It was my chance to take over the bank."

"Was it you or the chief killed Shad Hale?"

"I shot him from the top of the cliff," he said. "I tried for you, too, the other day but missed. I wouldn't have this time."

"Help me get this miserable son of a bi—gun on his feet," I said to Lew, knowing Ma would have been proud of me. "He ain't hurt all that bad. We get some of Alliso's medicine on him and he'll live to hang."

We lifted him to his feet none too gently, which is probably why he hollered, and half carried, half dragged him to Chief Two Horse's wagon.

"In ya go with the chief," I said and we tumbled him into the wagon next to the dead body of the Mohican. We found Sawyer's horse tethered nearby in a clump of trees, with his boots tied together and draped around the saddle horn. We threw the boots and saddle in the wagon and turned his horse loose, figuring he'd eventually wander back to Shalak Springs.

"I guess we better get back to Annie Laurie," I said. "She all right?"

"Was when I left her," he said.

I drove the wagon and Lew followed behind to keep an eye on Sawyer, even though he wasn't likely to give us any trouble seeing as how he had passed out when we put him in the wagon. I didn't know why he'd fainted, whether it was pain or loss of blood or the idea of riding next to a dead Indian. Could have been all three.

CHAPTER 20

ON THE WAY back to where we'd left Annie Laurie we stopped for Old Dobbin and tied him to the rear of the wagon. As we neared the place where Annie was waiting I smelled dust. I pulled up the wagon and beckoned Lew alongside.

"I think we got company," I said. "Why don't you ride wide and see if you can stay out of sight?"

He nodded agreement and taken off at a trot. I flicked Old Dan lightly with the end of a rein and we headed on downstream. We rounded a bend of the stream and there ahead of me were six riders facing Annie Laurie who was sitting in the trap watching them calmly. As I drew closer I saw one of them was Gus Simpson.

I reined up within easy talking distance of them and set the brake. "Howdy," I said. "You fellers want somethin'?"

"We want what you've got in that wagon," Simpson said roughly.

"You're welcome to 'em," I said.

"What do ya mean, `them'?" Simpson demanded. He turned to one of his riders.

"Darman, go see what's in the wagon."

A blond rider with a scarred and pockmarked face and a mean look reined over to the side of the wagon and leaned in and a gun went off in his face, blowing him out of the saddle.

I didn't stop to think. I dived off the wagon seat, hit the ground rolling, and scrambled behind a rock, dragging my gun from its holster as I went.

A hailstorm of bullets raked the front and side of the wagon as Simpson and his remaining riders unlimbered their guns. And more began ricocheting off the rock I was crouched behind. At the same time I heard Annie Laurie scream and Mouse, startled out of her wits, taken off at a gallop. I caught just a glimpse of her as she went by with the reins flying loose. Off to the other side Old Dan whinnied and reared but didn't go nowhere because it was a heavy wagon and I had set the brake. Old Dobbin who'd been through a war or two shifted nervously but made no effort to break loose.

From the wagon itself came a frantic call: "Don't shoot. I surrender," and a six-shooter Sawyer must have been hiding under his shirt came flying over the side of the wagon and landed near what was left of Darman's skull.

"Yeah, fellers," I hollered. "Quit yer shootin'. Somebody go after Annie Laurie afore she gets hurt."

"Throw yer gun out, Tackett," Simpson called. "Now, if ya wanna live."

I wanted to live so I tossed my gun out and stood up holding my hands shoulder high.

"That damn fool! That damn fool, Sawyer," I said bitterly. "You ought to of kilt him."

"You, Addison, drag out whoever's in that wagon," Simpson ordered. An older rider, gray and balding, with the beginnings of a paunch, spat tobacco juice and rode over to the wagon. Holding on to the saddlehorn with one hand he leaned over and looked in.

Then he straightened up. "Two of 'em here. A dead Injun—that Two Horse feller—and Twain Sawyer. He's been shot. You want him outta there?"

"Get him out," Simpson said.

Addison leaned over again and hauled a hollering, squirming Twain Sawyer out of the wagon by the front of his shirt and dropped him on the ground where he landed in a heap, moaning in pain.

Simpson walked his horse over to where Sawyer lay looking up at him. "Ya killed Darman," he said. "I'm gonna hang ya fer that."

Sawyer who'd begun to try to sit up, recoiled back down to the ground.

"It was an accident," he yammered. "I didn't mean to. I thought he was Tackett."

"I think he's tellin' the truth, Simpson," I said. "And ya shouldn't hang a man for makin' a honest mistake. On the other hand I'd bet a dollar he's stolen all yer money from the bank and ya might wanna hang him fer that."

Simpson glared down on him. "You miserable weasel. Is he tellin' the truth?"

"I didn't steal it," Sawyer said, frantically. "She did."

"Who?" Simpson asked. "Who?" I echoed.

"Annie Laurie," he said. "Annie Laurie Burns."

"Speakin' of Annie," I said, "are ya gonna send someone after her?"

"No need to," one of the cowboys said. "Here comes the trap now with her and some fella in it."

"Forget her for now. Just make sure she don't get away," Simpson said. "Now let's back up here. Just what are you sayin', Twain?"

"Help me," Sawyer pleaded pitifully. "I'm bleeding to death."

"You'll be dead of rope burns on yer neck if ya don't start talkin'," Simpson said.

"Annie Laurie," Sawyer said. "She had a key to the bank. Hale must have given it to her. And she knew the combination to the safe. I couldn't sleep last night and I was out walking when I saw her sneak into the bank. She came out in a few minutes with a couple of heavy sacks. She carried them around to the back of the bank where she had her horse waiting.

"I caught up with her there and offered to keep still in return for half the money, but she just laughed at me—said no one would believe me—and rode off. That's all I know."

"No it ain't," I said. "Tell these fellers how come you kilt Chief Two Horse and what yer doin' out in this neck of the woods."

"I didn't kill the chief," he lied. "He was dead when I ..."

Before he could say any more he passed out again.

"Somebody gimme a hand here. She's hurt." It was Lew's voice.

I been so interested in what Sawyer had to say I hadn't heard the approach of the trap. I turned and saw Lew lift Annie Laurie off the seat and lay her gently on a laprobe he'd taken from the back of the trap. She was unconscious.

"Bullet hit her in the thigh," he said. "She's still bleedin' and I don't know." He looked up embarrassed.

Simpson climbed down off his horse and went over to where Annie Laurie was lying. He looked at Lew with contempt. "Ain't you never seen a female leg before?" he asked.

He kneeled down and pulled up the side of her riding skirt. The bullet had gone into and on through her thigh and from the way her leg was torn up it looked like a ricochet.

Without saying anything Simpson took hold of her petticoat and tore out a big chunk which he tore in two pieces. He folded each one into a square and placed one on each of her wounds. Then he turned to Addison.

"Get me Darman's belt. He don't need it anymore."

When Addison brought the belt he cinched it tight around Annie's thigh and pulled her skirt down over it.

"Addison," he said, "you climb on your horse and hightail it into town and get Ed Alliso out to the ranch pronto. We'll take her and Sawyer along and meet you there. Couple of you fellers put the two of 'em in the wagon."

Addison mounted his horse and taken off at a gallop. Two of the cowboys started to lift Sawyer into the wagon.

"There's that dead Injun in the wagon. What do ya want to do with him?" one of them asked.

"Throw him out," Simpson said callously.

"Hold on," I said. "You leave him there. There's room."

"Throw him out, I said," Simpson repeated.

"Hold on," I said again. "That there was a man, like you and me. An' he was my friend. Furthermore he was the last of the Mohicans. And you ain't gonna treat him like no animal."

I moved over toward the wagon and Simpson followed me. "I said, throw him out," he snarled and reached to pull me away.

Instead of backing up I moved in toward him, brushed his right hand away with my left, and sunk my right fist into his belly up to the wrist. Oh, it felt good. One sucker punch deserves another, I thought, and as he bent over gasping for air I drawed my right fist back and clouted him alongside the jaw. He fell like he'd been hit by lightning.

I stepped back, rubbing my bruised knuckle and looked into three drawn six-guns.

"Boss'll be wantin' to hang ya when he comes to. Right alongside of Twain Sawyer," one of the cowboys said grimly.

Off to one side, standing by the trap, Lew Haight said, "If you all don't drop yer guns you ain't gonna have a boss."

He had snaked my Winchester from its boot on the trap and was aiming it at Simpson's head. As he spoke he moved up closer and placed the rifle muzzle against Simpson's skull. "Drop 'em, fellers," he said.

The guns thudded to the ground and I picked them up one at a time and unloaded them and tossed them into the wagon. Then I went and picked up my own gun from the spot where I had thrown it. I thought I remembered seeing a shovel in the back of the wagon and I went and got it out and handed it to a cowboy.

"We'll bury the chief here," I said. "He can have his own Injun burial ground. You fellers can take turns diggin'."

Grumbling, he went to work. Another said, "You can't just let the boss lie there. Let me help him."

He went to the stream and got a hatful of water and dumped it on Simpson, who sat up suddenly, shaking his head and rubbing his jaw. When he'd got his bearings he glared up at me. "I'll kill you for that," he said.

"Mr. Simpson," I said, "if I thought ya meant that I'd shoot ya right now. Yer just sore because I sucker-punched ya. Same thing you did to me the other day. I figure we're square now and I really don't want nothin' more to do with ya. But if you insist on fightin' me, you name the time and the place and I'll fight ya with guns or knives or fists, whatever you want."

He stood up and said, "Oh, hell, I don't wanna fight ya. We got enough other problems."

He started to turn away but then, almost as if he'd had a second thought, he turned and threw a long, looping roundhouse left at my jaw. But he was still shaky and slow from being knocked out and I was half looking for him to do something like that anyway. I blocked the punch easily and started to throw my own left, but I had a second thought and pulled it back at the last instant.

"Let's wait'll we're both feelin' better," I said.

He grinned suddenly. "Hell of good idea. I'll get to you later."

He stood silent for a moment, then he said, not so much to me as to himself, "Gotta lot of loose ends to tie up here. We're gonna have to squeeze the truth out of both Twain and Annie. We'll take 'em out to the ranch and talk to 'em after Alliso fixes 'em up."

The cowboys finished digging the grave and we lay the chief in it and filled it up with dirt. "I think someone ought to read over him," I said. "Anyone here know any Bible verse?"

"Won't do any good. Injuns are heathen," Simpson said.

Lew spoke up. "I'll say somethin'." We gathered around the grave, all of us, even Simpson, taken off our hats, and Lew said, "Ashes to ashes, dust to dust. The Lord giveth and the Lord taketh away. Blessed be the name of the Lord. Amen."

"And happy huntin' in the Happy Huntin' Ground," I added. We put our hats back on and headed for our horses.

Simpson had said they would bury Darmen in a little boothill they had at the ranch, so they draped him over his saddle and tied one arm to one leg under the horse's belly so he wouldn't slide off. One of the cowboys drove the wagon and I drove the trap, with Old Dobbin tied to the back.

We headed on down the stream to the main trail where we turned toward the mountains and Simpson's ranch. It lay on the far side of a low pass that led into a good-sized valley where white-faced cattle grazed, where pasture was cross-fenced, where there were acres of apple and peach orchards and hay fields and where there were barns and stock pens and silos and outbuildings of all sorts. The main ranch house was a big, sprawling one-storied building and off to one side were four small houses where, I figured, men with families lived, and a good-sized building that turned out to be the bunk house. Everything that could be painted had been painted.

Simpson might have been a mean and difficult and head-strong man but there was no doubt about it; he was a good rancher and a good farmer, too. He'd seen when he first came into the country that there would be a need for more than just beef and he set out to meet it.

It was near dark when we finally got there and both our wounded were in bad shape, moaning and drifting in and out of consciousness. Simpson and one of his men had ridden on ahead and as we drove into the ranchyard there were hands to meet us with makeshift stretchers. They loaded Annie on one and Sawyer on the other and carried them on into the main house. Simpson who had supervised the task turned to me and Lew.

"You might as well come on in," he said ungraciously. "There's supper for ya in the kitchen and after that we'd better talk. Too much goin' on that doesn't make sense and we need to figure it out."

He stomped off toward the house with me and Lew following behind. The kitchen was big and roomy with a long eating table in the middle of it. There was a Chinese cook wearing the loose clothes of his native land and sporting an honest-to-gosh pigtail. He was being assisted by his wife who also was Chinese.

Main thing is, he was a good cook. The beef he fed us was tender and there were potatoes and carrots and green beans from a kitchen garden. And there was an apple pie, made with fresh apples, that me and Lew finished off all by ourselves. And that pleased the cook.

"You likee Chinese cooking?" he said with a big grin, all the time holding his hands together and bowing up and down.

"Me likee yer cookin'," I said, "and so does he." I gestured at Lew.

Simpson, who had gone to check on the wounded whilst me and Lew ate, came back in about then.

"Good cook, ain't he?" he said, gesturing at the Chinaman. "I brought him in from 'Frisco. Peggy—that's my daughter—Peggy said she wouldn't stay on the ranch unless I found us a decent cook. She's all I got since her ma died and I don't want her to leave. I told her if she gets married I'll give her half the ranch for a weddin' present if she'll stay around. So far, though, she ain't showed much interest in men.

"You'll meet her if yer around tomorrow."

"How's Annie doin?" I asked.

"We gave both of 'em a couple of slugs of whiskey when we came in. That eased the pain some and they're both asleep right now. Neither one of 'em's in very good shape, though. Alliso better get here pretty quick."

A cowboy stuck his head in the room with an answer to his wish. "Alliso's here," he said. "Who do ya want him to see first?"

"Speak of the devil," Simpson said, going out the door.

He came back in a little while looking haggard. "Alliso's workin' on Annie Laurie," he said. "Says she'll be all right. Twain Sawyer's dead, though."

"Well, dang," I said. "That bullet in his shoulder shouldn't of kilt him. What'd he do? Bleed to death?"

He nodded. "Yeah, but not from the shoulder wound. A bullet went through the side of the wagon and caught him low down. We didn't notice it because it lodged in him and all the bleedin' was inside."

"He say anything afore he died?"

"Nope."

CHAPTER 21

So THERE I was, sitting in Gus Simpson's big kitchen with a lot of unanswered questions and me not having hardly any idea of where to turn for answers.

Nate Hale was dead and it was the robbery of his bank, followed by his murder, that had resulted in this mess and had landed me right in the muddle of it.

Without that I'd have been on the R Bar R by now and maybe me and Esme would be making plans for our wedding. And maybe not, too. Since I'd left there I had learned to read and write, but I was still nothing but an ignorant, footloose cowboy, hardly good enough for any woman, much less a high-class lady like Esmeralda Rankin.

I shook that thought away and came back to the present. Twain Sawyer had had some answers I wanted, I knew, and so had Chief Two Horse. Between them I might have found out more about Shadrach Hale, if that was really his name, and how he and Nate Hale and Annie Laurie and even Gus Simpson and Cy Fierman fit into the puzzle or, rather, puzzles that were worrying me.

But now neither one of them was ever going to be of any help. That seemed to leave only Annie Laurie for sure and possibly Gus Simpson and maybe Cy Fierman, and in his case I didn't see much chance of him dropping by for a chat.

The three of us, me and Lew and Simpson, sat there sipping our coffee and not saying anything.

Finally Lew said, "I'm goin' out and get me some fresh air."

He got up and left. No sooner had he walked out than Ed Alliso came in. His sleeves were rolled up and there was blood on his forearms and on his shirt. He looked tired.

"That daughter of yours is a good woman, a good nurse," he said to Simpson. "Pitched right in. Never got sick or anything. You can be proud of her."

Simpson nodded. "Thanks. Peggy'll be glad to hear someone appreciates her. She thinks nobody here does."

I interrupted. "How's Annie, Ed? She's gonna make it, ain't she?"

"That's a bad wound," he said. "Chopped up her leg pretty good. She'd of bled to death if Gus hadn't strapped that bandage on her. Trouble is, I don't know what else to do for her. She needs a better doctor than me, that's for sure, but as far as I know there ain't one much closer than Denver. I don't even want to think about me having to cut her leg off."

"Ed," I said, "you got to save it. You just got to. Won't that old Injun medicine do the trick?"

"I'm praying it will," he said. "I've sure sprinkled enough of it on. Look, you go in and see her. She's conscious and is asking for you."

"Take the door on the other side of the living room and go down the hall. She's in the first room on the right," Simpson said.

I found my way to the room and tiptoed in. Annie Laurie was lying in a big bed. Her face was as white as the sheet she was lying on and her eyes were closed. I went over and taken her hand.

She opened her eyes and tried to smile at me. "I'm glad you came," she said in a voice so low and weak I could hardly hear her.

"Like I told ya before, Annie, yer a very special lady," I said. "I'll stay with ya as long as you want. I'll be here whenever ya need me."

She gave my hand a weak squeeze and a tear rolled down her cheek. "I don't deserve your friendship, Del," she said. "I've lied to you and deceived you and would have cheated you out of the Staghorn."

I knew I wasn't hearing her right. "Yer not thinkin' clear, Annie," I said. "You get some sleep now and we'll talk when yer feelin' better and when ya know what yer sayin'."

Before she could answer I leaned over and kissed her gently on the lips. Then, releasing her hand, I backed slowly out of the room.

Simpson and Alliso were still sitting in the kitchen drinking coffee and smoking a couple of good-smelling cigars when I walked in. Simpson saw my look of envy.

"Want one?" he asked.

"One would surely taste good," I said.

"Mao, go get a cigar for Tackett here," he said to the Chinese cook.

Mao disappeared into the living room and in a second was back with a long, black cigar. He clipped the end off with a kitchen knife and handed it to me. I smelled it appreciatively, licked it gently to paste any loose leaves back to the body of the cigar, stuck it in my mouth, and let Mao light it for me. I taken a deep drag on it and it tasted as good as it smelled.

Now I ain't much of a smoker, but nothing beats a good cigar after a good meal or when a man needs to relax and meditate. And that was a good cigar.

"Order 'em direct from Havana," Simpson said proudly. "They come by boat to New Orleans, then up the Missouri to Kansas City and overland to me by train and stage."

"You got good taste," I said.

"Annie awake?" Alliso asked.

"Yeah, but she ain't makin' much sense. I think she's hurtin' real bad," I said.

"Say anything?" Simpson asked.

"Nothin' that made any sense."

"Been a long, mean day," Simpson said, standing and stretching and yawning. "Think I'll turn in. Ed, you take the bedroom next to Annie Laurie in case she needs help during the night. Peggy'll be in the bedroom across the hall in case you need her. Tackett, you and your pard can find a couple of empty bunks in the bunkhouse. We'll talk tomorrow."

I got up and walked through the living room and out the front door. There was a kind of a veranda running across the front of the house and off to one side of the door I saw a couple of figures sitting in a swing. As I stood there puffing on my cigar one of them got up and headed toward me.

"That you, Del?" Lew asked.

"Yep. Simpson says there's empty bunks in the bunkhouse. We can sleep there."

"Wait a minute," he said. "Lemme say goodnight to Peggy— Miss Simpson."

He walked back to the swing, spoke low for a minute to Peggy Simpson, and then joined me as we headed for the bunkhouse. It was a big barracks-like room with the bunks scattered around the edges and two wood stoves about fifteen feet apart down the middle.

It wasn't all that late and the coal oil lanterns were still burning. There was twenty or so men sitting or lying around in various stages of dress and undress. There were more, I knew. A few of the married ones lived in the houses around the ranchhouse and the rest were scattered around out on the range or in line shacks. This was a big outfit.

A poker game was going on under one lantern, a couple of cowboys were mending gear, and a few had already gone to sleep.

Baker Addison, the cowboy who'd fetched Alliso, was sitting in a chair he'd tilted back against the wall and was idly picking his nose. He looked up when we came in.

"Howdy, Ad," I said. "You gold minin' or grave diggin'?"

"Well, if it ain't the two-bit gunman who tries to pass hisself off as a Sackett," he sneered.

I strolled over to where he was sitting and looked down at him. "What's eatin' you, cowboy?" I asked.

He didn't answer, just looked down at my feet and without warning spat a great gob of tobacco juice on the toe of my boot. Clearly he was looking for a fight, so I gave it to him.

I handed the butt of my cigar to Lew, then turned back and hooked a foot under the front leg of Addison's chair and upended it. Addison went sprawling on the floor. Whilst he was scrambling to his feet I reached down and yanked off the boot he'd spit on and as he stood up I hit him across the face with it. The edge of the boot heel caught him on the cheek and cut a long gash in it. As he staggered back I dropped the boot and caught him with a left hook alongside the jaw. He stumbled backward against the poker table, knocking it over and scattering cards and chips all over the floor.

He regained his balance and stood shaking his head to get rid of the cobwebs. I waited to see what he was going to do. Suddenly his right hand stabbed toward his hip where his gun should have been. But it wasn't there. It had come out of its holster when he had sprawled on the floor after I pulled the chair out from under him. He stood there with an empty hand and a blank look on his face and I busted out laughing. In a second the rest of the men in the room were laughing, too.

I picked up my boot and put it on. Then I went over to where his gun was lying, picked it up, shook out the bullets, and handed it to him. He taken it and shoved it in his holster.

"There'll be another time," he growled, so I hit him again, this time with a solid right hand. He went down and even though he was conscious he stayed there.

I looked down at him. "There ain't gonna be another time, you hear?"

Just then another voice spoke up. "That's right, there ain't gonna be another time. Ad, you start any more fights around here and you're gone. You got that straight? I don't care if you are one of Gus's pet gunmen."

Pet gunman he said? Well, that opened my eyes

I looked around. A slim, gray-haired man with a gray mustache and piercing gray eyes was standing there. "Name is Scott Randolph," he said, sticking out his hand. "I'm the foreman here. Wasn't no excuse for what he done."

I taken his hand and shook it. "I wasn't lookin' to cause trouble," I said. "Maybe my pard and me better find another place to sleep."

"Yer welcome to bunk here," he said. "There ain't gonna be no more trouble."

"Thanks," I said. "But there's no sense in lookin' for it. Me and Lew'll bed down in the barn tonight if it's all right by you."

He shrugged and turned away. "Suit yerselves," he said.

"Come on, Lew," I said. "Let's go."

We stepped out of the bunkhouse and stood for a moment adjusting our eyes to the dark. As I looked around, a movement by the corner of the ranchhouse caught my eye. "You go on to the barn," I told Lew. "There's someone sneakin' around over by the house. I'm gonna take me a look-see."

I headed for the corner where I'd glimpsed the movement. There wasn't anyone there. I moved quietly along the side of the house until I came to the back corner. I peered around cautiously and saw the tall figure of a man in a peaked hat tapping at the back bedroom window. In a moment the window went up and Simpson's voice said, "What in the hell do you want, Cy?"

Cy Fierman's voice replied. "Wanna talk to you, Gus. About money among other things."

"Dammit, I've gone to bed. Can't it wait?" Simpson demanded in a low growl.

"Now!" Fierman said. "I'll be waitin' by the wellhouse."

The wellhouse was about fifty feet from the kitchen door and Fierman strolled over to it, squatted down, and casually lighted a cigarette.

Dang! He was too far away for me to hear what he wanted to say to Simpson. I had to get closer without them knowing it. I darted back alongside the house, walked quickly across the front-yard, and kept going until I was on the far side of the barn.

I cut around it until I could see the yard between the back door and the side of the wellhouse. There was no one there. Simpson had either already come out or was yet to come. I taken a chance and sprinted from the barn to the rear of an outhouse, peeked around it and still didn't see anyone, so I dashed the short distance from the outhouse to the back of the wellhouse.

I eased along the side of it that was away from the kitchen door and got to the front corner just in time to hear Simpson say, "All right, cousin. What in the hell do you want at this hour of the night?"

A man can learn a lot by just listening. And that's what I did for the next little while. I sat down with my back against the wall of the wellhouse and homed in on the conversation between the rancher, Gus Simpson, and the man he had called cousin, the outlaw Cy Fierman.

Cousin! That kind of knocked me for a loop. Simpson and Fierman cousins. But there was no reason why they shouldn't be. And come to think of it they looked enough alike to be brothers. Both of them were the tall, gangly type, with big-boned hands and wrists and those long stringy muscles that can pack a wallop as I'd found out a day or two back. They both had gaunt faces with big noses and prominent brows and chins.

Yeah, I figured, they could easy be cousins.

Listening to them I discovered that they were more than cousins; they were also partners of a sort. And right now they were partners who were having a falling out.

"I checked with the Denver bank," I heard Fierman say. "They said there hadn't been any deposits for a while and in fact that you drew out $10,000. And you done it without sayin' a word to me. What've you done with it? Where is it? You stealin' from me, cousin?"

I could hear the sneer in his voice when he said "cousin."

"Look, Cy, you'll get yers back. Just hold yer horses. And don't you go callin' me a thief. Look, I didn't complain when you robbed Nate Hale's bank even though I had some money in it, 'cause I knew I'd get half of whatever you got. And besides, I knew that Nate kept enough of a reserve hidden away so that his bank wouldn't go bust if someone did come along and rob it.

"But the trouble is, whoever stabbed Nate—and it looks now like it was Twain Sawyer—stole his reserve money too. Sawyer's dead, by the way. Him and that Injun, Chief Two Horse, both."

"I knowed about Two Horse," Fierman interrupted. "I was watchin' when Sawyer shot him. If he hadn't, I would of. He knew too much. Knowed where the hideout is. Figured him pullin' out that way meant he might be wantin' to collect the reward on me. Now what about Twain Sawyer?"

"It looks like old Twain not only killed Hale but cleaned out his safe, too," Simpson said. "That meant that if I wanted to keep that bank goin', and for a lot of reasons I did, it meant that I'd have to put in some cash of my own. Which I didn't have. So I got the $10,000 from the Denver bank. I was gonna tell ya as soon as I saw ya."

"I'd hate to think you wasn't, cousin," Fierman said. "Fer both our sakes. I sure wouldn't want to think you was stealin' from me. You don't never wanna forget you wasn't nuthin' but a strugglin' two-bit rancher 'til we got together. Now yer sittin' here livin' the good life, a respected citizen, while I'm on the run. One of these days, though, I'm gonna wanna retire so you'd better begin thinkin' about how we split everything up fifty-fifty, includin' this place.

"In the meantime you keep yer hands off the money in that Denver bank, you hear?"

"Damn it, Cy, you take it easy. I'll be puttin' it back pretty quick."

Fierman gave a low chuckle. "You don't and I'll come and get it," he said. "I've made withdrawals at that bank before, ya know. I'll be going now, but I'll be seein' ya around."

A moment later I heard the kitchen door slam which told me Simpson had gone inside. I got to my feet and peered around the corner of the wellhouse, but Fierman had disappeared in the darkness. Which was fine by me. I wasn't in no mood to go after him anyway.

CHAPTER 22

KEEPING AS MUCH as possible to the shadows I made my way back to the barn. There was a light inside which meant Lew had gotten a lantern from somewhere. He'd spread some loose hay on the dirt floor and unrolled our bedrolls on top of it. He was sitting on a feed sack smoking a cigarette when I entered.

"Saved the butt of yer cigar for ya," he said and tossed it at me. I caught it and stuck it in my mouth. That Cuban tobacco made it a good chewing cigar and instead of lighting it I settled for chomping on it.

"Find anything?" Lew asked.

"Learned a few things," I said. "I know now why Simpson was after me to kill Cy Fierman. They're cousins and partners. Fierman owns half of this spread. If I was to kill him Simpson would get it all. That's easy worth five hundred or a thousand to him.

"Lew, I got me a idea. You kill Fierman and then you marry Peggy and eventually you get it all."

Lew chuckled. "Only two things wrong with that. I ain't no killer and I ain't the marryin' kind."

"I was funnin' ya," I said. "And this really ain't no laughin' matter. Lew, we got a couple of bad fellers here and I ain't sure I know what to do about it. I wish Annie Laurie hadn't been shot. She might of had a idea or two."

I pulled off my boots and crawled into my bedroll after setting my cigar butt on the brim of my hat to keep it clean. I'd stick it in my shirt pocket in the morning and save it for after my next good meal.

Lew put out the lantern and crawled into his bedroll with the admonition, "Let's sleep on it. Can't hurt."

We climbed out of bed as soon as morning light began seeping into the barn. I fetched my razor from a saddlebag and went in search of some water and a mirror, both of which I found outside the bunkhouse door. There was a chill in the air and the water which I poured from a bucket into a tin basin was not far from ice. Fall was well on its way and it was time I was heading south for the R Bar R.

I was in the middle of shaving when Baker Addison stumbled sleepily out of the bunkhouse. He saw me and glared but I waved the razor casual-like at him and said, "Mornin', Ad."

He didn't reply but stomped out toward one of those little houses with the half-moon in the door. It surprised me. I thought I'd kicked it all out of him the night before.

After I finished shaving, Lew and me headed for the ranch-house kitchen. The hands didn't eat there; they had their own mess hall off the bunkhouse, but I figured me and Lew were guests and we'd go eat with the important folks. Besides I wanted to see how Annie Laurie was. The things she'd said to me last night were bothering me and I wanted to talk to her again if she was feeling better.

There was smoke rising from the kitchen chimney as we walked around to the kitchen door and went in. Mao, the Chinese cook, and his wife were busy preparing breakfast. "Got any coffee?" I asked. He nodded and bowed and picked up a big tin pot whilst his wife scurried to get out a pair of mugs.

The coffee was hot and black and tasted about as good as any coffee I'd ever drunk. One thing about Simpson, he was living well off the profits of his ranch and his share of Cy Fierman's loot.

Me and Lew were sitting there sipping our coffee when Simpson walked in. He looked at us with surprise mingled with disapproval showing on his bony face.

"Thought you boys would be eatin' with the hands," he said.

"Food's better here," I said. "Old Mao there makes the best coffee I ever drank. It'll go good with this here cigar."

I pulled out the stub of the Havana. It wasn't smelling quite so good this morning.

Simpson wrinkled his nose. "Throw that away. I'll give you another one."

"I'll save this for outside," I said. "Is Alliso up yet?"

"Yeah. He's lookin at Annie Laurie now. He'll be in in a little bit."

"Ya know she was married to Hale's son?" I asked casually.

"What arc you talkin' about?" he asked, and his surprise seemed real.

"Her and Hale's boy was married. She done told me herself."

"Hale didn't have a son. Died right after his wife took him East."

"That ain't what Annie says."

"I don't give a damn what she says. Nate was only married once and both his kids are dead. Anybody who says different is lyin'. Look, I've known—knew—Nate Hale ever since he came into this country and I know folks who knew him back in Carson City."

"Meanin' yer cousin?"

He kind of gaped at me. His jaw dropped and his face turned white. Then he got control of himself.

"What d'ya mean by that?"

"Yer cousin. Cy Fierman."

"That cigar must of addled yer brain, boy."

"I was takin' a walk last night to cool off. Came up behind the wellhouse. Heard a couple of fellers talkin'."

Simpson looked at me for maybe a minute without saying a word. Then he said grimly, "Mao, get their guns."

I looked around. Mao was right behind me. He had a wicked-looking meat cleaver in his hand and was holding it about an inch from my neck. One move on my part and he'd take my head off.

"Please to put guns on table," Mao said, gesturing slightly with the cleaver.

Me and Lew tossed our guns on the table. Simpson reached over and picked them up.

"Outside, you two," he said. "Mao, when Alliso comes in tell him I'll be back in a minute."

He followed us outside and herded us around to the bunkhouse. "Inside," he said.

We went in. There was still four or five men inside including my friend, Baker Addison. A look showed me they were the same men who'd been with Simpson yesterday. Now that I looked at them carefully, it was plain that they were a tough, hard bunch who hadn't hired on just to punch cows.

"Yer just the man I wanted," Simpson said to Addison. "You and Algore take these two to the wellhouse and tie 'em tight. Come dark we'll get rid of 'em."

"Perow, as long as the Mexes are diggin' graves for Sawyer and Darman have 'em dig a couple more. We're gonna need 'em.

"Rest of you fellers stay close. I'll be goin' to town in a little while with Ed Alliso and I'll be wantin' some of you along."

He turned and headed for the house. Baker Addison smiled at me as he left and it wasn't a nice smile.

"Move, you two," he said and jammed his gun roughly into my side. As I turned to go out the door he gave me a shove that sent me stumbling into Lew who tripped and fell with me on top of him. He and Algore laughed as we sprawled on the ground.

"All right, get up," Addison said and kicked me in the ribs viciously. I stifled my rage and climbed to my feet and helped Lew to his. My turn would come, that was one thing I knew for sure.

They marched us to the wellhouse and pushed us inside. It

was damp and cool in there, for which I was grateful; it was going to be a long day.

Algore fetched a rope and whilst Addison watched he tied us both separately with our hands behind our backs and our feet tight together at the ankles after he taken our boots off. We weren't going anywhere, that was for sure, but I was grateful he didn't hogtie or gag us. That wouldn't have been no way to spend the day.

When Algore was finished Baker came over and tested the ropes. Then, straightening up, he gave us each another kick.

"That'll hold ya 'til tonight," he said. "Then I think I'm gonna ask the boss to let me cut on you a little before he kills ya."

He spat a wad of tobacco juice at me as he went out the door but his aim was a little off and it hit me in the shoulder instead of the face.

They locked the door behind them and Lew and me were left alone in semidarkness, with the only light coming through a small, dirty window high on one side of the wellhouse.

I lay there quietly until I was sure they had gone then I spoke low to Lew.

"They missed my hideout knife," I said, "the one I strap to my calf. If we can get at it maybe we'll be the ones what do the cuttin'."

I scooched around so that he could reach the knots on the rope around my legs with his fingers. But after an hour of trying he gave up.

"They're too tight and I can't get a grip on the rope," he finally said in disgust.

"I wish I hadn't drank so much coffee this mornin'," I replied.

We lay there a few minutes thinking, and finally I said reluctantly, "Well, there might be a way."

"How's that?" he asked.

"If you could unbuckle my belt maybe you could pull my

jeans down and get at it that way. I got my long johns cut off so they don't cover the knife."

"I don't know, Del," he said slowly. "I really wouldn't be comfortable pullin' yer pants down."

"Ya got to do it," I said. "They mean to hang us, boy."

"What if someone comes in when yer pants are down?"

"I been caught with 'em down before. Come on, Lew. You got to do it."

Well, we scooched around again until he was lying across my legs with his back to my belly. I wiggled around and he fished around and finally got hold of the end of my belt. After a lot of trying he managed to push it through the loop and pull the belt loose from the little pointed thing that fits into the holes in the belt. He pulled the end of the belt free of the buckle and then just lay across my lap exhausted.

"Don't quit yet, Lew," I said. "You got to take my pants down."

He turned back on his side and fumbled around and found the top button to my jeans which he managed to unbutton. Then he got hold of the fly and yanked it open.

"Dang," I said. "I hope ya didn't pop any buttons."

"Now what?" he asked.

"First you roll off a me," I said. "Then we're gonna lie back to back and yer gonna grab the top of my jeans and hold on to 'em tight whilst I try to wiggle out of 'em."

We managed to get in the back-to-back position and he got a good grip on the top of my jeans. I wiggled and squirmed and squirmed and wiggled until we finally got them dragged down to my knees.

"They won't go no farther, Del," Lew gasped. "And I can't hold on no longer. My fingers are all cramped up."

"Get a hold of 'em with your teeth," I ordered.

"I'll try my hands again," he said.

"Tell ya what," I said. "I can spread my knees a little. You see if you can get your feet in between 'em and maybe we can pull 'em down that way."

"I don't want to hurt ya, Del," he said.

"You got to do it, Lew," I said. "Just be mighty careful."

I bent my knees and spread them as wide as my jeans would let me and Lew hooked his heels into the top of them and he pulled in one direction and me in the other. All of a sudden there was a ripping sound and Lew's legs came free.

"Gol dang it," I swore. "There go my jeans. If we can't get that knife now I may be the first feller you ever knew to die with his boots on but his pants off."

"It could of been worse," he said. "I could of been wearing my boots and spurs."

"I'll count my blessings later," I replied.

It turned out that Lew had ripped the crotch right out of that old pair of jeans but in doing so he had also loosened them up so that he was able to drag them down nearly to my ankles.

After that it was easy. He managed to get the knife out of its scabbard and we scooched around until we were back to back again and he commenced to saw at the ropes binding my hands.

That knife was fine steel and I kept it honed to razor sharpness. Fact is, I'd shaved with it more than once. Careful as he was he nicked my hands a couple of times and once even stuck me in the back but five minutes after he began I was free. I rubbed my wrists to get some circulation going, then quickly cut the ropes that bound Lew's hands. "Leave us untie our legs," I said. "We may need some rope."

In a minute we were up and moving around the wellhouse. I had buckled my belt so my jeans were staying up but I had nothing to fasten the great rip in the crotch. It didn't really matter, I figured. I had no plans to go a-courtin'.

I removed my knife scabbard from around my leg and hooked it into my belt so it would be handy when Simpson and his men came for us. I knew the two of us didn't have a chance against that bunch of armed men, but I was going to get that knife into one of them, Baker Addison preferably, before they killed us.

Over the hours our eyes had grown accustomed to the dimness and we began looking around the room for anything that might do for a weapon. There was a couple of cured hams hanging from the ceiling and a few odds and ends lying around but nothing that looked like anything we could use.

But then my eye lit on the pump handle. If I could just get it loose. Which I did. It was fastened to the pump with a pin that was held in place by a cotter pin. Using the back of my knife I was able to straighten out the ends of the cotter pin and work it through the hole in the bigger pin that held the handle in place. I pushed it out and pulled the handle free. It was a two-foot long piece of cast iron. I handed it to Lew.

"Well," he said, hefting the handle. "Between the two of us we ought to be able to do some damage."

"What we gotta do," I said, "is find a way out of here without them doin' any damage to us."

I went over and looked at the window. It was big enough so a man might squeeze through it, once he broke the window out, but it was higher than my head and I couldn't see what it looked out on.

"Hoist me up," I said to Lew, and he made a sling out of his hands that I stepped in and then I was high enough to see out.

"Dang," I said as he let me down. "It faces the bunkhouse. Ain't no way we can get out of here through that window in the daylight."

"Too late anyway," Lew whispered as we heard someone fiddling with the latch on the outside of the door. I stepped over and crouched beside the door, my knife in my hand. Lew stood on the other side of the door holding the pump handle in both his hands like one of them bats they'd used in that baseball game I saw in Kansas City.

The door opened and Mao came shuffling in in his slippers, blinking to accustom his eyes to the dimness. I stepped behind him and wrapped my left hand around him whilst I jabbed him gently in the neck with the point of my knife.

"Make a noise and yer one dead Chinaboy," I hissed.

He froze. Lew swung the door shut then stepped in front of him and showed him the pump handle. I took my arm from around him and stepped back.

"What're you doin' here?" I demanded.

"I come to get ham for suppah," he said. "Mistuh Simpson's favolite suppah."

"Where's Simpson now?" I asked.

"Go to town. He come back in time for suppah."

"Let's tie him up," I said. "We sure can't turn him loose."

We tied him and gagged him with cloth we tore from the loose shirt he was wearing. Then I opened the door a ways and peered out. There was nobody in sight.

"Lew," I said, "I'm gonna make a run for the kitchen. Give me a few minutes to find a gun then you come, too."

I took another look and sprinted for the kitchen. It was empty, with no sign of Mao's woman. A quick look showed me the living room was empty, too. I went in and off to one side was a gun case. It held two shotguns and three rifles. One of the shotguns was an old four-shot revolving Colt. There was a drawer under the case and it was filled with ammunition including shells for the Colt. I loaded it quickly and looked around for the doorway to the hall that led to the bedrooms.

I tiptoed down it until I came to the room where Annie Laurie was lying. I peeked in. Annie was sleeping and Simpson's daughter, Peggy, was sitting beside the bed, obviously dozing. She'd had a hard night.

I stepped past the doorway and tiptoed on down to the end bedroom which I knew from the night before was Simpson's.

There was a gun belt with a Colt .45 six-shooter stuffed in the holster hanging on a peg in the wall. I figured it was Simpson's spare. I quickly buckled it on and headed for the door. Then I stopped and went back and started going through Simpson's things until I finally found what I was looking for—a pair of jeans.

They were a little long in the legs so I rolled them up and a little tight in the waist so I sucked in my belly. Main thing was, the crotch was in good shape. I buckled the gunbelt on again and headed back down the hall. Peggy Simpson was still dozing but Annie Laurie had her eyes open and looked right at me. I quick put a finger to my lips and went on. I knew she was smart enough not to say anything.

I went back to the kitchen, opened the door, and waved. In a second Lew came sprinting across the yard and joined me in the kitchen.

"What now?" he asked as he entered.

"Danged if I know," I replied.

CHAPTER 23

"WHYN'T WE HAVE a cup of coffee while we think on it?" Lew said.

He went over to the cupboard and found a couple of mugs and poured them full from a pot that was staying hot on the big stove's warming burner.

"What'll we do if that Chinese woman comes in?" he asked as we sat down at the kitchen table.

"Danged if I know," I said. "Maybe put her out with her husband. What'll we do if that Simpson girl comes in?"

"Damned if I know," he said. "Man comes in, though, and we'll shoot him."

"What's this about shooting someone?" Ed Alliso asked, coming through the kitchen door. He didn't wait for an answer, but yawned and stretched and asked, "You got any more of that coffee?"

"Thought you'd gone back to Shalak Springs," I said, dropping my half-drawn gun back into its holster.

"That's a pretty sick woman in there so I thought I'd stay over a day and see if there was anything else I could do," he said, accepting a mug of coffee from Lew.

"Ed," I said, "I don't think this is any place for a law-abidin' citizen like you. I think you oughta get out of here while the gettin' is good."

He looked at me quizzically. "I ain't got any idea of what you mean," he said. "Gus Simpson is the biggest man in these parts. Without him Shalak Springs wouldn't be more'n a wide spot in the road."

"It ain't now," I said. "But that don't make no difference. Just so as you know, Gus Simpson and Cy Fierman are cousins. More'n that, they're pardners. Fierman's been robbin' banks to pay for building up the ranch here."

Alliso shook his head. "I don't believe it."

"Ed," I said, "I wouldn't want to think you was callin' me a liar."

He blanched a bit. "No, no. Of course not. But Gus Simpson and Cy Fierman, pardners?"

"They have been, but I don't know if they still are. They had a fallin' out last night. And I got me a sneakin' hunch there's gonna be a war between the two of 'em before much longer."

"Maybe I better stay," he said. "If there's a fight they'll be needin' some doctorin'."

"Suit yerself," I said. "But if you stay you got to keep those two women from raisin' a fuss. And by the way, the Chinese cook is tied up out in the wellhouse. In case somethin' happens to me I wouldn't want him just left there.

"You got any idea when Simpson's comin' back?"

"He said he'd be back by dark. He said he had a chore to take care of."

"Me and Lew are the chore. He was gonna kill us and bury us alongside Sawyer and that cowboy of his that Sawyer kilt."

"He said you'd already gone back to town," Alliso said. "Now I know why."

The sound of hoofs in front of the house interrupted our conversation. I got up in a hurry and went to the living room window and peered out. There were half a dozen horsemen there, one of whom was Cy Fierman. As I watched, two men straggled out from the bunkhouse and came toward them.

When they got close Fierman hollered, "Put up yer hands and you won't get hurt."

I hurried back into the kitchen. "Cy Fierman's out there and it looks like he's gonna try to take over the ranch. Ed, you got a choice. You can be on his side or ours."

214

He didn't hesitate. "What do you want me to do?"

"Tell him we hung around 'til a little while ago, then headed back to town. Lew, you and me better make ourselves scarce. And thanks, Ed."

I picked up the Colt shotgun and Lew grabbed up the Winchester he'd gotten from the gun rack and we went out the back door. We raced across the yard until we had the wellhouse between us and both the bunkhouse and the main house.

Beyond the wellhouse there wasn't much of anything besides flat land and some scrub brush and a few rocks scattered around about a hundred yards out. I looked around. There wasn't a tree, there wasn't a hole.

"Lew," I said, "you head for that scrub brush out there and I'll cover you. I'll come as soon as you get there."

He took off running and had covered about half the distance when he stumbled and went down on his face. I waited for the sound of shot but there wasn't one. In a minute he got up and began hobbling toward the brush. As he disappeared behind it I started to take off when suddenly I heard two voices.

"There's someone out there. I caught a glimpse of him out of the corner of my eye."

"Aw, yer seein' things."

"No, I ain't. There's someone out there."

"Well, you go get him. I ain't a goin' to."

"I know there's someone there. You watch me. I'll flush him out."

"What ya gonna do?"

"I'm gonna ride wide around him. He ain't got no place to run or hide."

Dang, I thought, he rides out there and Lew'll potshoot him sure, but he can't fight all of 'em. And if I shoot him I'm a sittin' duck.

I eased around to the side of the wellhouse that was away from the yard and the bunkhouse and lay down flat in the shadow, right at the corner where I could watch what was goin' on, but knowing I'd be hard to spot unless someone was looking for me.

If worst came to worst and they went after Lew I'd get a few of them before they got me but I'd have to do it at short range. That revolving shotgun was a great weapon up close, but it wasn't no long distance gun, that was for sure.

In a minute the rider came in sight, riding a pinto horse. He was headed out wide around the clump of brush where Lew was hiding. He rode until he was directly behind the brush and then he turned and headed right for it. Funny, he apparently didn't see any sign of Lew.

When he got close to the brush he suddenly pulled up, dismounted, and walked, it looked like, right into the middle of the patch. Then he disappeared. As he dismounted he'd ground-hitched his horse which stood there and began nibbling at some of the tender leaves.

Another horseman, the second man who'd been talking, started out also riding wide around the brush patch. As I watched he fell out of his saddle and at the same time the sound of a shot echoed from where Lew was hidden. The shot scared the pinto which took off running while the second rider's horse, a bay, ran a few yards and stopped.

Dang, I thought, that evens the odds a little, at least until Simpson gets back. I was lying there waiting to see what happened next when a voice behind me said, "All right, you. On yer feet and keep yer hands where I can see 'em."

I lay there for a moment, mentally kicking myself. I'd been so interested in watching what was in front of me that I forgot to pay attention to what might be behind me. It seemed to me that the same thing had happened to me before, not too long ago.

I got slowly and carefully to my feet and turned around holding my hands well away from my side. The man pointing a pistol at me was Cy Fierman.

"Well, dang," I said. "If it ain't the old bull of the woods, hisself."

He smiled, but I didn't see no smile in his eyes. "In person," he said. "Now call yer friend in so as I don't have to kill ya."

"Call him in yerself," I said.

"Turn around," he ordered, "and step out where he can see ya."

I did as he told me. He stood directly behind me, prodding me in the back with his gun. "You out there," he hollered. "Come on out or yer friend is dead."

"Stay where ya are, Lew," I shouted, at which point my head exploded.

The next thing I knew, I heard someone groaning and when I opened my eyes and thought about it I discovered it was me. My head was pounding like it was being kicked by a galloping horse. I tried to reach up to hold it but couldn't. It turned out that my hands were tied behind my back. Again.

"You awake, Del?" Lew's voice asked.

"Yeah," I said, "But I wish I wasn't. What happened?"

"You hollered at me to stay where I was and he slugged you with the barrel of his gun. I was gonna shoot him but he ducked down behind ya so I come on in."

"Ya shouldn't of," I said. "If Fierman don't kill us Simpson will."

"I didn't have no horse, Del," he reminded me. "They'd of shot me down out there. Way it is we're both alive so we still got a chance."

I didn't say anything. He was right and I knew it. I raised my head and looked around. We were in the bunkhouse. I was on the floor, tied tight, hand and foot. My boots were off again and this time I couldn't feel the knife pressing into my leg. Then I remembered, after we got loose in the wellhouse I'd tucked it into its scabbard which I'd hooked behind my belt with the scabbard and knife both tucked inside my jeans.

Another look showed me Lew Haight tied to a chair. One eye was swollen shut and turning color and there was blood on his upper lip and chin, the result of someone bloodying his nose.

"You been in a fight?" I asked.

He shook his head. "They didn't take to me shootin' one of their men."

Two other men, the ones I'd seen come out of the bunkhouse when Fierman and his gang had ridden up, were lying in bunks, also tied tight. Even as I looked, the bunkhouse door opened and two more men, hands overhead, came in, followed by two men with drawn guns.

One held his gun on them while the other tied them, kidding them as he worked.

"You boys just sit tight 'til we're through, then maybe we'll turn ya loose. Then again, the boss lets me, I might just set fire to the place. Have me some roast cowboy."

As he turned to go Lew caught his eye and he walked over and looked down at him. "Ya shot my pard," he said. "If you don't burn I'll talk the boss into letting me hang ya."

He reached down and twisted Lew's battered nose viciously. In spite of himself Lew yelped in pain. His tormentor let go of his nose and patted him none too gently on the cheek.

"That's just the beginning, sonny," he said as he went out.

In the next hour Fierman's men brought in and tied six more of Simpson's hands, including his foreman. That made ten.

When the foreman saw me and Lew a look of surprise crossed his face.

"I thought you two were long gone," he said.

"Yer boss thought different," I said. "He ever tell you him and Fierman were in cahoots?"

"Yer kiddin'," he said in disbelief.

"No I ain't," I said and took a few minutes and told him what I'd heard the night before.

"I never knew," he said. "But that sure explains some funny things that have gone on around here. We've always run this ranch on the up and up, but Simpson usually has five or six men around him who go with him and run errands but never punch no cows. But all of 'em look like they know how to use a gun. Addison's the worst of 'em but all of 'em are tough."

By now it was late afternoon, time, I thought, for Simpson to be returning. And when he came he'd be riding smack into the middle of an ambush. Unless someone warned him, but who? I was sure Fierman would have Alliso and Peggy Simpson under guard and that left the Chinese woman and I figured there was no way she'd be of any help.

Well, I was wrong. I learned later that Fierman's men had thought the way I did. She'd been told to stay in the kitchen to cook and after that they didn't pay much attention to her.

In midafternoon she went to the wellhouse to get the same ham Mao had planned to cook for Simpson's dinner. There she found her husband and turned him loose. He sneaked back in the house and got a six-gun he had hidden in the pantry. He stayed there until his wife, who he'd instructed to keep a lookout for Simpson and his men, saw them coming in the distance.

Then he went to the kitchen window and fired three warning shots. Before he could get a fourth one off, Fierman who'd been taking it easy in the living room, came into the kitchen and shot him dead.

In the bunkhouse we heard the shots.

"Well, there goes the surprise," the foreman, Scott Randolph, said with satisfaction. "Let's see what happens now." During the next few minutes there were a few desultory shots but after that it was quiet.

It was beginning to get dark in the bunkhouse, which meant it was about sundown outside, when the door opened and Fierman came in.

He came over and looked down on me. "Who's side ya on, Sackett?" he asked.

I started to correct him but stopped before I'd hardly got my mouth open. I might live longer if he thought I was one of the gunfighting Sacketts from Mora, with tough kinfolk all over the West.

"Nobody's," I said. "But yers, if I gotta choose. Simpson gets his hands on me and Lew we're dead meat. Otherwise, as far as I'm concerned the fight's between you and Simpson. All me and Lew want is out."

"Well," he said, "Simpson's back and he knows I'm here. And he's got us outnumbered so we're cuttin' out. I prob'ly oughta leave ya here but I ain't goin' to. You ain't done nothin' to me so I'm gonna turn ya loose."

He took out a claspknife, opened it, and cut the ropes binding my hands.

"Rest is up to you," he said and walked out. My hands were numb from being tied and it seemed to take me forever to untie my feet. Just as I freed myself I remembered my knife. I staggered to my feet and nearly fell when a spell of dizziness hit me. But I managed to shuffle over to Lew and cut him loose. Looking around I spotted my boots and pulled them on. Then I headed for the door with Lew right behind me.

"What about us?" Curtis called.

"Simpson'll have to turn ya loose. Yer on his side, not mine," I said.

I opened the door cautiously and peered out. Fierman and his men were just mounting up. The last man to swing onto his horse was Cy Fierman.

As he settled in the saddle, the front door of the house opened and the Chinese woman stepped out. In the growing dusk it was hard to tell what she was carrying in her hands, but it was either a rifle or a shotgun. As she came out on the porch she pointed it at Fierman and blasted away.

It was a shotgun and it blew Fierman out of the saddle. She threw the gun down and turned and walked back in the house.

One of the horsemen hollered, "He's dead. Let's get out of here."

And the batch of them taken off at a gallop with Fierman's horse following behind, empty stirrups flapping.

Behind them the man on the ground tried to struggle to his feet but fell back. Lew and I headed for him at a run.

"Alliso's in the house. Get him," I shouted.

Fierman was lying on his face in the dirt. I turned him over and one look showed me there wasn't much chance. The Chinese woman had gutshot him. He looked up at me.

"My own fault," he said. "I shot her husband after he warned Gus and I should of had her tied up. I never figured she knowed what a gun was for. I always figured I'd get it in a gun fight, but not from no Chink woman."

Ed Alliso came hurrying down the steps. "Move over, Tackett, let me take a look."

"Yer wastin' yer time, Doc," Fierman grunted. "I've done robbed my last bank." He groaned once and then was still.

I stood and turned to Lew. "It's time we was gettin'," I said. "You can bet Simpson'll be ridin' in in a few minutes."

"Take care of Annie Laurie, Ed," I said. "We'll be in touch."

CHAPTER 24

LEW AND ME headed for the barn at a fast walk, hoping that our horses were where we'd left them the night before. But I stopped before we went inside.

"Lew," I said, "if we run now we're gonna have to keep runnin' 'til we're out of the country 'cause sure as shootin' Simpson'll come lookin' for us in Shalak Springs. He's not safe as long as we're around, 'specially if he thinks we might head fer the county seat and talk to the sheriff or wire fer a United States marshal."

"Yer right," he said. "So let's stay and fight. Two of us oughta be able to take on fifteen or twenty of them."

"I got a better idea," I said and quick outlined it to him.

As we turned back toward the house I spotted a woman's figure walking up to the bunkhouse door. It went inside and I instinctively knew it was Peggy Simpson who'd gone to cut loose the men Fierman had captured.

"Let's go," I said, and we sprinted for the back of the ranch house. There was a light in the kitchen but we ducked under its window and went on to the window that opened from Simpson's bedroom. It went up easy and in a moment we were both inside.

And right then I changed my mind again. I'd planned to wait for Simpson to come into the bedroom and take him captive, but the more I thought about it the more I knew that wouldn't work. We'd have to turn him loose sometime and when we did we'd be no better off than we would be if we up and ran.

For sure, I had no intention of trying to take him the fifty or sixty miles to the county seat and I figured the jail in Shalak Springs wouldn't hold him ten minutes if his men decided to turn him loose.

"Lew," I said, "I changed my mind. We're gonna do it different. When Simpson gets here I'm gonna brace him. It's the only way I know. Otherwise we'll always be on the run from him. What I want is for you to cover me from the front window. Holler loud so everyone knows not to pull any funny stuff. But first you got to go into the kitchen and tie up that Chinese woman. We don't wanna make the same mistake Fierman did. I'll take care of Alliso and the Simpson girl."

We went down the hall and as I stepped into the bedroom where Annie Laurie was Lew went past it and on to the kitchen.

Annie Laurie was lying in a big bed awake but looking mighty pale. Alliso was sitting in a chair beside the bed.

Peggy Simpson, who'd already come back from the bunkhouse, was saying, "One of the men went after Daddy. He should be here soon."

She'd no sooner finished speaking when she saw me. "Don't nobody do anything dumb and there won't be any trouble," I said. "Ed, I'm sorry, 'cause I almost trust ya, but I'm gonna have to tie the two of ya up fer now. When this is all over someone'll turn ya loose."

"When what is all over?" Peggy Simpson demanded. "What are you doing here?"

"I got business with yer pa, miss," I said, "and I can't have you buttin' in. Ed, you tear some strips off a one of them sheets and tie her hands behind her."

As soon as he was done I herded the two of them into the kitchen where Lew had finished tying up the Chinese woman. Using strips of toweling we tied the three of them to chairs.

"You keep an eye out at the front and let me know when they're comin'," I said. "I gotta go talk to Annie."

She was lying with her head propped up on pillows and she managed a wan smile when I came in. "I'm so sorry, Del," she said. "A lot of this is my fault."

"Ain't no way," I said.

"No. I mean it. I haven't been honest with you. There's a lot I have to tell you."

Just then Lew came into the room and said, "They're comin'."

"Whatever you got to say can wait," I said. "And when this is over it prob'ly won't matter." I went over and kissed her on her forehead and went out and into the living room.

Lew was standing by the raised window with a rifle in his hands and a shotgun leaning against the wall. We'd found our six-guns in the bunkhouse and we both had them belted on. We waited silently as Simpson and four of his men rode up. Randolph, the foreman, was waiting for him at the foot of the steps.

"Now," I said and stepped out of the door.

"All right, don't nobody move. There's three rifles aimed at ya," Lew said loud enough for them to hear.

Baker Addison, the rider next to Simpson, cursed and went for his gun. Lew never hesitated. His first shot caught Addison in the right shoulder. He sent his second shot deliberately over their heads.

"No need for nobody to get kilt," I said as men streamed out of the bunkhouse. "Tell 'em Simpson. Tell 'em yer a dead man if they interfere."

"Back off, boys," Simpson said. "All right, Tackett, what do you want?"

"Somebody help me," Addison said. "I'm hurt."

"Try that again and yer dead," Lew said from the window.

"I said, 'What do you want'," Simpson repeated.

"You," I said. "You. Yer a crook and the cousin of a crook and I'm sick of you tryin' to push me around. And I think you and

225

me had better settle this right now. You can have yer choice: guns or knives or fists."

Simpson glared at me for a moment then he sort of sagged in his saddle. "I won't fight ya," he said, looking away.

Algore, Addison's sidekick, said, "You got to, boss. You got to."

All of sudden I was filled with a mixture of anger and contempt. Here was the old bull of the woods who had built his own ranching and farming empire, who dominated the town of Shalak Springs, who owned the bank, and who'd done it all with crooked money. And now he wouldn't fight for what he had. He'd sucker-punched me once after I'd been shot and he'd tried to sneak-punch me again. And he was brave as hell with his men around to protect him. But under it all he was yellow.

"He'll fight me all right," I snarled, going down the steps after him. He tried to rein his horse away but I was too quick for him. I grabbed him by the leg and dragged him out of the saddle. He sprawled on the ground and tried to skittle away from me as he got to his feet.

Just then a voice from the window said, "It's all right, boss. I've got this feller here."

Lew shouted, "Watch yer back, Del. He snuck up on me from behind."

At the sound of the voices Simpson suddenly turned and went for his gun, shouting, "Get him, men," as he drew.

I threw myself to one side, drawing as I dived to the ground. Dimly I heard shots behind me but I concentrated on the man in front of me.

An old time gunfighter had told me once, "Take your time. Make yer first shot count. You might not get in another one."

I shot once, rolled over and shot again and again. Simpson was surprisingly fast. He drew and shot twice whilst I was still leveling my gun, but one shot went where I'd been standing and the next one kicked the dust where I'd hit the ground.

He never got off a third round. Because I was still rolling my first shot only grazed him, but the second and third ones caught him dead center. They kind of lifted him off the ground, then he stumbled backward a couple of steps and crumpled to the ground. I stayed down, looking to see who else might be looking for a fight, but Lew's voice came again, "Don't nobody move. I got 'em covered, Del."

I climbed slowly to my feet. "Who's next?" I asked of no one in particular.

"It's all over," Mac Curtis said, straightening up from where he'd been leaning over Gus Simpson. "He's dead. I don't think nobody here wants to fight anymore."

"Del," Lew said from the window, "send someone in to untie Ed Alliso. Annie's in here on the floor and she needs some help."

One of the men from the bunkhouse hurried inside to turn Alliso and Peggy Simpson loose.

In a moment Peggy Simpson walked out the front door and over to where her father lay. She looked down at him and then she looked over at me.

"I suppose I should be sorry," she said, "but I'm not. He was cruel to my mother and he...he wasn't very nice to me. He always said he wanted me to get married but he drove off every boy who came around. He...he wanted me to himself."

Mac Curtis came up. "Miss Simpson," he said, "I guess yer the boss now. You got any orders?"

She straightened her shoulders. "Yes," she said crisply. "Have the men put my father's body in the tackroom. We'll bury him tomorrow. Tomorrow you fire Addison and Algore and those other men he had hanging around. Then you and I will sit down and go over what needs to be done here."

She turned to me. "When Miss Burns is well I'm going to ask

her to run the bank. She's a smart woman and that would be better than running a saloon, I'm sure you'll agree."

"Whatever she wants to do," I said. "Lew and me'll be hittin' the trail in the next day or two. If she don't want to run the saloon, maybe she can find someone to buy it. Heck, maybe Gil Dellah could run it."

Me and Lew Haight rode wearily into Shalak Springs, dismounted, and tied our horses and walked into the Staghorn. I needed a drink and so did he. After we'd had a couple he was going to head for the hotel and I was going upstairs and hit the sack. It had been a rough, mean two days and Lew and me both had blood on our hands, blood that neither one of us wanted.

The only real satisfaction I had was knowing that I'd found the answers to most of the things that had puzzled me and that Gus Simpson wouldn't be bothering anyone again, not me, not Annie Laurie, and, I guess most important, not his daughter.

But Annie Laurie was another matter. In a way she'd had me fooled, seeming to be an honest, caring woman. And maybe I was half right. I still think she was a caring woman.

Oh, she set out to cheat old Nate Hale out of his bank and me out of the Staghorn. And she used both of us, no doubt about that, and she'd used Chief Two Horse, too. But at the same time she'd given a lot of comfort to Hale and she'd been there to bandage my wounds and to comfort Jack Sears when he was dying. And when you came right down to it, in the end she'd probably saved my life.

Whilst I was out challenging Simpson, one of his men had sneaked through the back door and gotten the drop on Lew. But he hadn't seen Annie Laurie who had crawled out of bed and dragged herself into the living room. Somewhere she'd gotten hold of a six-gun and when the cowboy pulled his gun on Lew she hadn't hesitated. She'd shot him dead.

Because of that there was no way I could hate her and I knew I'd always remember her. She was a tough woman and a smart woman in a land where a lone woman had to be both tough and smart if she was to survive.

Me and Lew had left her out at Gus Simpson's ranch to recover from her bullet wound. After she got well I didn't know what she'd do. Peggy Simpson had said she could run the bank and she owned the Staghorn, because I wasn't going to renege on that deal, mainly because I wasn't no saloon keeper. So it didn't look like she'd be hurting for money.   And Nate Hale had left her his place and she had Billy Jeff and Hallie Hope to watch over it for her.

I'd talked to her the morning after the shootout. Peggy and the Chinese woman had gotten her back into bed and Ed Alliso's powder seemed to be helping her wound. At least it showed no sign of infection, he said.

She was sitting up when I went in and there was some color in her cheeks.

"How you feelin'?" I asked

She smiled. "Ed's tonic is working wonders. I feel almost human today."

Then she took on a sober look. "Del, there are things I must tell you."

"There's nothin' I need to know, Annie Laurie. Me and Lew'll be headin' for the R Bar R in a day or two. We made our deal on the Staghorn and I'll live up to that.

"I just come in to thank ya for what ya did last night—that taken a lot of courage—and to say good by."

She reached her hand out for mine. "Not yet, Del. Don't go yet.

"When we started out the other day, were you taking me to the stone cottage?"

"There and to the little sunken valley the stream runs through. I thought you'd like to see 'em both again."

She looked puzzled. "What valley?'

"Ya mean ya don't know about the valley? There's bones in

there that I think are yer husband's. I figured you and him used it for a hideout."

"So he is dead," she whispered. "I thought so but I didn't know. And I don't know anything about a hidden valley. But my husband is one of the things I wanted to talk to you about. When we were married he passed himself off as Nate Hale's son from the East and said we would go to Shalak Springs where he would go into business with his father's help. I still don't know what his real last name was. He was my husband and I don't know what my last name is."

For a moment I didn't think she could continue, but she taken a deep breath and went on.

"Instead of taking me to Shalak Springs he took me to the stone cottage where he said we would live until he convinced Nate he was his son. I think what he was really doing was trying to ingratiate himself with Nate so he could set up some kind of a swindle. But I never knew that until later when I found out Nate's children were dead.

"Then it turned out that Shadrach was also a robber, trains and banks, both. I didn't know that until one time he came back after being gone for nearly a month.

"He had a wound in his side and finally admitted he'd been shot during a bank robbery down in New Mexico. He never said so, but I think he was with Cy Fierman's gang. The next time he went away he never came back. I don't know how he got into that valley you talk about."

"I think I do," I said. "I think he'd been in this part of the country before. He probably stumbled across it then and figured it would make a great hideout. Trouble is, he got careless and Twain Sawyer was able to follow him there. Sawyer then went up on top of the mesa and shot him from there. He figured that's where yer husband hid his money."

"I don't know if he had any or where he hid it if he did," she said in a tired voice. "Maybe someday we can go back and look."

"You go," I said. "I ain't lost nothin' there."

She went on: "Like I told you I waited for him for a long time, then left and went to Shalak Springs. I was just sorry I couldn't take that old rooster with me. He and Mouse and Maxwelton were the only company I had all that time.

"In Shalak Springs I got that job with Obie Shrifft and after that I made friends with Nate Hale, intending to tell him I was his lost son's wife, but before I could do anything that stupid I learned his children were dead.

"I've told you how I feel about being a woman alone in a man's world. Well, I decided I wasn't going to wind up depending on charity or having to marry the first man who came along, so I set out to swindle Obie out of the Staghorn.

"At the same time I decided I was going to marry Nate, if I had to seduce him to do it. He offered real security. The trouble is he insisted on treating me like a daughter instead of a potential wife. More than that, we became good friends and one day he told me he was going to make me executrix of his estate."

She saw my look. "The person who makes sure a person's wishes are carried out after he dies."

"Them big words still throw me," I said.

"I liked that," she continued. "It meant it would be easier for me to steal what I needed if I was patient enough to wait until he died. I didn't know he was going to leave me most of his estate. I guess he really did look on me as a daughter."

She paused, tired. Then after a moment she went on. "You're too trusting, Del. That paper you signed isn't what I told you it was. It makes the Staghorn mine." She looked away. "We'll tear it up when we get back."

"The Staghorn's yers, Annie," I said. "Ya saved my life and ya held Jack Sears' hand when he was dyin'. Ya earned it. Besides, I ain't no saloon keeper, nohow."

And that was the truth. I wasn't a businessman and on top of that I'd had nothing but trouble since I won it off of Obie Shrifft.

Besides, I wasn't going to wait any longer. Lew and me were going to head for Nora and the R Bar R as soon as I could get back to Shalak Springs and pack up. I hadn't had no real home since I left Lodestone and Ma when I was sixteen but the place that felt the most like home was the R Bar R.

Esme Rankin, the woman I loved, was there and so was Beauty, the big black dog that once had saved my life.

As me and Lew walked into the Staghorn a couple of fellers at the bar spotted us in the mirror and turned to look at us.

"Howdy, amigos," Blackie Harrington said.

Lew and me stopped dead in our tracks. "Thought you was down in Nora," I said casual-like. "What're you doin' up here?"

"Lookin' to buy the two of ya a drink," he grinned.

Lew and me walked up the bar and each of us shaken Blackie's hand. He was Lew's saddle pardner and I'd hired them on to the R Bar R nearly a year ago when I was ramrodding the spread for Esme Rankin and we were having big trouble with rustlers.

After we'd greeted each other Blackie turned to the man with him. He was a man about my age, tall and broad shouldered with dark curly hair, brown eyes, and a wide Irish smile.

Blackie said, "This here is Mo Hegan, he's a cousin of Miss Esme's who came back from Virginny with her and decided to stay on a while."

Hegan smiled and shaken Lew's and my hands. "Nice to meet you fellows," he said. "Esme and Blackie have told me a lot about you. Let me introduce myself formally. I'm a cousin of Esme's on her father's side. My name is Maurice Hegan the Third, but folks called my grandfather 'Mo' and my father 'Mo,' too. And now they call me 'Mo.' But I'm going to put an end to that nonsense. If I ever have a son I'll name him George or Charlie. I'm determined to be the last of the Mo Hegans."

He chuckled. "Get it—the last of the Mohicans."

"I got it," I said, "but it ain't funny. I just buried the last of the Mohicans."

He looked at me skeptically. "Surely you jest."

"I ain't in a jestin' mood," I said.

He immediately sobered up. "I'm sorry, Mr. Tackett. I was just funnin' you. I meant no offense."

"None taken," I said.

Blackie interrupted us. "Miss Esme's wantin' to see ya. She's at the hotel. Her and Beauty."

I looked at myself in the bar mirror. Even in the dim light I could see how I looked—dirty and uncurried, needing a bath and a shave and some clean clothes. Three days on the road and rolling around in the dirt from time to time hadn't helped any.

"Gimme a hour," I said. "I ought to get cleaned up a mite."

Suddenly I was filled with excitement and the tiredness that had me yearning for nothing more than a soft bed and a long sleep vanished.

"Gil," I said, "get some hot water goin'. I got to take me a bath do some cleanin' up."

I ran up the stairs and got out my razor and my other pair of underwear and socks that the Mexican woman who did some work for Annie Laurie had washed.

In less than an hour I was walking down the boardwalk toward the Shalak Springs Hotel. Before I could get there this big black dog came bounding out of the hotel door and raced up to me. As I leaned down to pet her she jumped up and put her front paws on my chest and began licking my face.

I felt myself choking up. "Beauty," I whispered. "Beauty."

She dropped down on all fours and I straightened up and looked toward the hotel. Esme Rankin was standing there on the porch, looking at me, not saying anything but with a wonderful smile on her face.

I started toward her.

Don't Miss
Any of the
Tackett Trilogy

TACKETT
TACKETT
1
TRILOGY

TACKETT
TACKETT
2
TRILOGY

AND THE TEACHER

TACKETT
TACKETT
3
TRILOGY

AND THE SALOON KEEPER

X